THE PRINTED

CAMERON FITZGERALD

THE NOBLE
INITIATIVE

CONTENTS

ONE

THE ROOM WAS clean and quiet except for the heavy breathing and stench of cold sweat from the man strapped to the chair in the center of the room. A red light flashed, and the man shuddered at its implications. He strained at his bonds, begging for mercy. But his pleas fell on deaf ears. His hands were wrestled down as a machine slid beneath them. The switch was flipped, and with a flash of light, the convicted trembled and seized at the electronic pulse. He was condemned and convicted, and there was no way out.

JASPER PLACED his hand on the scanner at the back of the van. It turned green and opened a door, revealing a fairly large box that had his name on it. He picked up the box, struggling for a second to balance it, and marched away from the van as a neighbor arrived to do the same. A young lady walked in front of him as he strained to keep the box from spilling over. He had never been accused of being strong. The young man faked doing the task with ease, avoiding the woman's eyes. Once he had left her line of sight, he let out frustrated breath and rested the box on his knee to get a better grip.

He opened his apartment with the scanner on the door and entered, kicking the door closed behind him. After setting the box on a counter by the door, he opened the tab to reveal an assortment of cans, bags, and bottles, which he distributed around the kitchen in the drawers and in the fridge. His face took on a grimace when he pulled out a can of soup labeled with the number 6.

Once he'd finished his work, the young man approached the couch that sat in the middle of the small space, and turned on the wall-mounted screen. Images of fire and smoke washed the screen with news headers reading, "Curfew confirmed after another deadly attack."

Jasper gave a quick sigh of annoyance at the confirmation that they would be under a curfew for who 'knew how long. Something bothered him about the video, however. His eyes focused on the repetitive stream of State buildings on fire and chaos surrounding them. In the repetition came frames that didn't match with the rest. One bit of footage playing behind the voice of a commentator would show an angry mob, then the next would show the dark of night suddenly illuminated by a fiery explosion. Though the footage wasn't high quality, he could tell that it was old and definitely not of the recent domestic terrorist attacks.

Why would the networks use old footage? Jasper wondered as he lay back into the couch. He thought for a moment and settled with the idea that whatever attacks had resulted in this curfew must have been so dangerous that the network camera workers wouldn't even want to get close. Though he had settled with his assumption, something in his mind didn't allow him to be at peace with it. Ever since he had graduated from the academy and been thrown into the workforce, his attention had been drawn to stark differences between what he witnessed at the State security offices and what he saw displayed on the networks.

Deciding to waste no more time on the topic, he returned to a pile of pictures strewn out on his floor. He picked up a photo of a man's face, pulled the cap off the pen, and put the pen to his lips. He stared at the picture, which was a still of old security-camera footage that showed a crowd of backpack-laden high schoolers in the hallway of their school. Jasper scanned the picture briefly, but his demeanor changed when he noticed something.

Jasper circled the youth and drew arrows pointing to different areas of the boy's face. He labeled the lines: "CONTEMPT." "ANGER." Flipping the card over, Jasper looked at the lettering on the back.

"2024 - Skyler Mason - Green Jacket - Killed 14 with firearm in school hallway."

Jasper turned the card face up again and confirmed he had circled the correct individual. The art of expression reading was new, but ever since he could remember, Jasper could read people's emotive responses, even if they were intentionally hidden. His gift had propelled him through the State's security academies and provided him with a prime job: Facial Confirmation Officer.

DURING THE WORKDAY Jasper Wood sat behind one-way glass, looking for a wrinkle, a dilation, a twinge on the face of the person sitting at a metal table, looking to see if the individual posed a threat to the State. If the young confirmation officer detected a threat, the person would be permanently labeled using the recently developed printing procedure, as required by law.

Day after day, Jasper watched the facial expressions of those claiming to be set up, extorted, or misguided, promising that they valued the State and believed in what it stands for. Fear, fear, fear, relief. One by one, people showed fear as they came in, then relief when he pushed the button indicating that the person's face proved the words to be correct. Sitting behind one-way glass, he did the same thing every day:

FEAR, CONTEMPT, ANGER

Red
Fear, Relief
Green
Anger, Anxiety, Contempt
Red
Surprise, Relief
Green

JASPER WAS THINKING it had already been a long day when a man entered the room and was told to sit at the table with anger and disgust plastering his face. The young analyst pushed the red button, indicating there was dangerous intent in the individual. The red light flashed in the room, and the man's face turned to intense anger, further condemning him to the fate he was assigned. Being restrained by the guard in the room, he had his right hand placed on the machine, which removed his print and installed a new one.

Watching this happen from the window, Jasper muted the sound from the printing room. Listening to screams all day was even less pleasing than listening to the computer technician who sat next to him, breathing through his mouth while eating a sandwich. The sound almost brought him to unmute the condemned man who was making up swear words. When the man was knocked out by an electric pulse at the end of the process, the guards came in to take him to the rehab room. This was the room where interrogated individuals were released back into the world—or where they would consent to the rehab procedure in order to regain State benefits.

"Four reds today. One more and it'll be a record," Jasper said to the noisily eating technician who nodded his mutual surprise at the influx of convictions for the day.

While there was no more sound coming from the room, he quickly put on some music before the technician could resume his nauseating feast.

Four weeks of this had flashed by since Jasper had graduated from the State Investigative Academy. For as long as Jasper could remember, he'd had a gift. He was young and talented, but the job was less gratifying than he had anticipated. The repetition of pressing red and green buttons as determined by the motives of the accused became tedious. Working for the State meant security and rare opportunities at every turn. What else could he want from a starting job?

But he could feel the work beginning to take a toll on him. Considering he had always thought of himself as an empathetic person, he found it alarming that he felt a rush of excitement every time he pushed the red button. When he had started, he'd felt only pity. But one emotion that caught him off guard from the first to the last person he had judged was confusion. *What is the motivation that compels people to test the law? The State has provided everything they needed, and it's not like the laws were unreasonable,* Jasper thought.

Switching from the thought that had consistently nagged at him, Jasper turned back to the technician. "How many more do we have today?"

The technician stopped eating to look at the data pad.

"Two more. It's getting close to curfew, so I assume they won't bring up any more from the waiting rooms."

The ten-hour shifts left them little time to get home before lights out. The curfew was imposed after the recent assaults on State ministers of justice. It required people to be in their homes by eleven, which was closing in tightly on Jasper.

As if the guard read his mind and was feeling the onset of the curfew as well, he rushed in the next accused. He was a shorter, heavyset man with dark skin and a beard that covered most of his face. Beards made it difficult to read certain expressions because they covered vital muscle points for several emotions. Jasper studied the man's face, and the technician sent the okay on the data pad for the questioning to begin.

Colonel Bernard Stockton sat at the table in front of the man.

Ready, waiting, formulating his approach to discover if this man was a danger to the State. This wasn't Jasper's first day working with the infamous Col. Stockton.

Japer had been taken aback when he first met Stockton. He had imagined him as a large, stoic man, with a thick deep voice. None of this was true, however. When the young analyst met him, he was shocked to find that he was a tall, scrawny man with a receding gray hairline. His disposition was also a disappointment. He was energetic, eccentric even. He would laugh louder than anyone else at anything that could be considered a joke and had a politeness about him that seemed forced. It wasn't, his face showed no sign whatsoever of it being a lie. In fact, his face didn't give away much of the normal expressions at all.

With a smile on his face, Stockton motioned for the bearded man to sit in the chair in front of him.

"How do you feel about our great country, friend?"

"It's home!" FEAR "I am grateful for the opportunities it has given me and my family. To be honest, I don't know why I am here."

"Good, I think we are just about done here"—Stockton looked at the guard—"Quickest one of the day."

Relief flooded the man's face, and he began to rise from his seat. The investigator looked at the tablet in his hand and stopped him.

"Just out of curiosity, where are you planning on moving to?"

"Huh?" The man looked surprised, and Stockton turned to face him.

"Moving! You are moving, aren't you? I mean, these emigration forms indicate you are. You also requested to clean your funds from the bank. So where is it? Africa? South America? Canada? Middle East?"

As Stockton named off options, Jasper saw the bearded man's face change from relief to fear once he heard "Middle East." Jasper flashed the green light in the room indicating the correct answer.

Noting the green light, the investigator brought his attention back to the seated man.

"Middle East! Interesting choice. What is it? Is it too cold here in the Northwest? Looking for something warmer? Are you bored in the peaceful utopia that this country's leaders have provided for you? Do you have a need for some political unrest?"

None of these options got a reaction. No indication on the man's face. Jasper sent no lights.

"Are you trying to get away from your wife? Because there's other ways of doing that."

Still no sign.

"Doesn't matter really. What interests me the most is the fact that you didn't go through the emigration office. You went through a private company. Why?"

The man sat in silence, trying to control his facial expressions.

"Was it because you still owe this great nation that invested in your education? Ahh, yes. Two additional years you are supposed to work for our great State. You would be turned away from the emigration office because you haven't fulfilled your civic duty. Sounds like someone who wants to cheat the nation he said he loves."

The man reacted slightly, but it seemed unnecessary at this point for him to confirm the emotion as Stockton had already begun his final push. Stockton nodded at the guard to seize him. As the guard put his hands on him, the man broke his silence. *"Hasbunallah wa nimalwakil!"* the man yelled as his hands were wrestled down with restraints and pressed against the printer.

"Ahh, religion! That's it! Why didn't you just say so, old boy? You wouldn't have had to hear me ramble on trying to guess," Stockton said as his face became laced with an eerie satisfaction.

Fear, anger, and contempt filled the face of the man as he was printed.

Questions flooded Jasper's mind. *The Middle East? How could he risk so much to go there? Here we have security and peace. Now that he is printed, he won't have access to State amenities. What of his family? This makes no sense.* He'd heard something in secondary school about religions having pilgrimages to areas thought to be holy, but they stopped teaching about religion a long time ago in the school system, so Jasper couldn't remember why. *If that was the case, why wouldn't he bring his family?* Jasper thought.

Answers to the questions teachers asked in school came easily. If you provided what they wanted to hear, then you were good as gold. Outside school, in the real world, many of the answers lapsed into subjectivity. Something Jasper had never had a good relationship with.

The printing commenced, and Jasper muted the sound in the room again.

Jasper stepped out into the hallway to get some fresher air. *One more,* he thought. *I can get through one more, then I can read the expressions of my own eyelids.*

A tall and broad-shouldered dark-haired man in his late twenties escorted by a guard walked down the hallway toward the interrogation room. His hands, cuffed in front of his body, indicated he was under more suspicion than normal. The man glanced at Jasper, meeting his eyes briefly as he passed.

Happiness

This prompted a double take from Jasper. Seeing anyone handcuffed and escorted show genuine happiness startled him.

The guard put his hand on the door's scanner, and it opened, letting them in, and that meant Jasper's hallway time was over.

Stockton, who sat in front of the printer, had had a transformation of his demeanor since the bearded man had been taken out. His attitude was chivalrous, innocent, even silly at times in the previous questioning. Now he sat with back straight, shoulders back, and face attentive to the man in cuffs.

Stockton's gaze lingered, not on the cuffed man's smiling face but on Jasper, though he couldn't see through the glass. He flashed his own glare to the analyst in an effort to communicate the direction he wanted the proceedings to go. CONTEMPT covered his face as he looked at the glass.

This look made it evident that the meeting wouldn't finish with everyone shaking hands. Then the colonel shelved his contempt effortlessly and replaced it with the happy-go-lucky attitude of a child beginning to play with its favorite toy.

"Forty-five minutes until curfew," Jasper said to the technician, who responded with a sorrowful shake of his head. It seemed he doubted they would be out of there in time.

The man sat down in front of Stockton and provided a sincere, "Hi, how are you?" HAPPINESS remained on his face, and to Jasper's shock, it still had all the signs of being genuine.

The interrogator rotated his head toward the glass as if, by that one question, the young man could be convicted. After seeing no response from the light bar, he turned back to the data pad where his information was displayed.

"Mr. Emmett Walsh, I speak for all of us here when I say that it's been a long day and we are anxious to be rested for the next. So please answer these questions honestly and quickly so that we can get on with this."

Emmett offered a nod in response.

"We will need vocal answers for these questions, friend."

Stockton said the word *friend* quietly, but his face was struggling to hold back the disgust that was behind it. *What is it about this man that affects Stockton so much?* Jasper wondered.

"You are Emmett Walsh?"

"Yes."

"You identify as a straight male?"

"Yes."

"Your housing is in Richland, Washington?"

"Yes."

"You were born in Boise, Idaho?"

"Yes."

"You work as an educator?"

"Yes."

"When is he going to start the real questioning?" The technician asked him, food still in his mouth. Something wasn't right about this.

The man in the chair was calm and unoffending and showed no signs of stress. Bernie was putting on a show unlike anything Jasper had seen to this point. Every muscle in his face was tense. Though Stockton's expression showed him to be in a pleasant mood to the eyes of most, Jasper could see the individual muscle patterns behind the face and knew something was wrong.

Disgust, anger, resentment—all swam around in his facial expressions like sharks awaiting feeding at the zoo.

"Ahh, you are a teacher? That takes a lot of patience, courage, and insight. I imagine that you are well respected in your field by the look of the awards you have retained." Emmett looked back flatly in reply. Stockton continued to scan through his file. "And you coach sports! What an asset you are, Mr. Walsh!"

"Am I here to receive an award, friend?" Emmett asked. His use of *friend* held no hint of contempt, but it was received with a silent rage by the investigator who sat in front of him.

However, Stockton quickly covered with a nervous laugh and continued. "Our students, as you well know, are growing up in unprecedented times, where their well-being physically and mentally is imperative to keep up with the chaos and injustice this world has to offer. Therefore, our curriculum is specifically designed in the education system to prepare our next generation to build on what we have learned and put into place. This requires everyone working within the system to join together with common cause, for the good of mankind. Correct?" Stockton looked at the man across from him, indicating he wasn't going to continue until he had some sort of confirmation that the man was following.

"Yes, the curriculum is designed to build on what has been put in place," Walsh replied carefully.

"I think you are missing the point." Stockton's irritation grew, and his friendly guise started to melt like a wax figure in the heat of the day. He stood and paced around Walsh. "We must all do our jobs. Yours is to teach; mine is to protect. My job isn't as brutal or heroic as that of a general in the field, but it is important, and you could even say I like it. I protect not from foreign powers, guns, bombs, or drones. I protect our State from tyranny, resentment, insurrection, and indoctrination. My shield is words; my enemy is corruption." Stockton looked up at the light to see if Jasper had found anything in the young man's face that would lead to a conviction. His pacing grew faster as he continued his lecture.

Jasper was confused by the turn the interview had taken. Stockton typically kept his cards close to his chest, fanning friendship and then pouncing like a cat on a mouse. But here, Stockton was off balance. His tempo of speech. The way he moved around the table. It was all wrong.

No light was lit, and the older man showed ANNOYANCE for a moment. Stockton walked behind Walsh to the guard at the door, who quietly gave him a leather-bound book. Opening it he glanced at a bookmarked page. "'I praise you, for I am fearfully and wonderfully made. Wonderful are your works; my soul knows it very well. Psalms 139:14.' How sweet, you have written in the margins, 'Lord, bless Everette with the understanding of who he is. That he is more than a broken human who can't do right. Don't let him get swept by the ways of the world away from who he is in You.'" Stockton walked around the table again.

"He stood directly behind Walsh, took a slow deep breath, and whispered, "What a waste." He placed the leather-bound book in front of the seated man, whose face slipped into SADNESS, leaving Jasper bemused. People in Walsh's position typically broke into fear, contempt, anger, or disgust. Not sadness.

Stockton tossed the book on the table in front of Walsh. "Corruption at its finest. The book that injected so much hate and hypocrisy into the world."

The book almost slid off the table, but Walsh made the first movement he had in minutes to catch it before it fell off. No fear registered on his face. Jasper was wrong again with his anticipated response to Stockton's methods. No fear. None, and it 'didn't take a trained face reader to see the man's expression and find it lacking signs of anxiety, anger, or frustration.

Stockton looked to the lights to see if he needed to continue but found none as Jasper had nothing to confirm.

Emmett looked down at the old leather-bound Bible, then opened it to find a note that was written on the inside of the cover as if it were for the last time.

Stockton needed no response. He looked at Emmett calmly reading, and something clicked inside him. He gestured to the guard and nodded to him. "Restraints!"

Jasper was frozen in his seat. No light had flashed, no confirmation from himself or the technician, and still Stockton had convicted. Jasper watched as the guard unclasped Walsh's hands and opened the container for the printing process. Stockton whispered something Jasper couldn't make out in Emmett's ear, pushed the preprogrammed selection on the printer, and left the room swiftly.

Emmett didn't yell; he didn't scream. There were short jerks of his head as he reacted to the pain, but nothing compared to the anger that most expelled. It didn't take long, and after a few seconds of stillness, he was taken out of the room. Stunned, but not fully unconscious he slouched in the wheelchair they put him in.

His hands were red from the procedure, yet he still tried to grab the leather-bound book on the way out. It slipped and was kicked across the floor by the guard as he led Emmett to the recovery rooms. Stunned by the erratic behavior of the interrogator, the technician and Jasper looked at each other for answers to what just happened. After a brief second the technician got up to leave. Jasper remained seated, frozen in confusion.

Why? he wondered. After spending day after day witnessing and diagnosing every kind of malevolent emotion of those convicted of beliefs contradictory to the State, he was astonished to see anything different. Anything that resembled peace. And for what? A book? One that had been outlawed because of hate speech? Many people had been printed for social injustice, but they all had one thing in common. They always turned to anger and contempt to fuel their defiance. What drove this man?

Trained to think analytically about the motivations of people to decipher intent, Jasper racked his brain, trying to figure out what propels this man. The interrogation room door shut, leaving Jasper alone with the most dangerous emotion he had encountered in ages. Curiosity.

TWO

WHEN HE REACHED the door of the recovery room, Jasper stopped. He realized that he couldn't remember walking down the three flights of stairs and crossing the complex's whole length. The recognition that he stood before the recovery room with his hand outstretched to the scanner to open it frightened him. For a couple of moments, he stood, attempting to remember why he was standing there. Curfew had been initiated, and Facial Confirmation Officers were not allowed to interact with the accused. The fact that his hand was outstretched to the scanner disturbed him. It was as if he was initiating a handshake with the end of his career. Before sanity could grip him again, his hand touched the scanner, and the door unlocked. Automatic lights turned on, illuminating the man lying down on a recovery cot.

The Printed rarely stayed overnight, but curfew had already begun, leaving the interior doors locked to those without clearance. The room's lights were bright compared to the after-hours hall lamps, and Jasper squinted as his eyes adjusted. He saw Emmett half rise from the cot he was in. Reacting groggily in the new light, the man attempted to grab the bed to pull himself upright but quickly fell back in pain. His hands still red from the printer, he obviously wasn't prepared for the pain of grasping something right after the procedure. Jasper continued to walk toward him, slowly realizing that every step took him closer to the side of the cot, although he had no reason for being there, no words to say, and no questions to ask.

"What am I doing here?" Jasper murmured under his breath.

"That's a funny question," the man said, startling Jasper, who hadn't realized he had spoken out loud. The prone man was still weak after the electronic pulse his body had undergone barely an hour earlier.

Jasper studied him for a quick second. Confusion tugged at Walsh's features, his right brow raised in subtle question, yet the same calm Jasper had seen before was apparent in his posture. His untucked dress shirt was stained from sweat. His hands were red and swollen from the reconfiguration, causing the typical M wrinkle shape on the palm to disappear.

"Does the swelling go down?" the man asked. Then, after an uncomfortably long silence, he said, "I suppose you might not know the answer to that."

Embarrassed, Jasper realized he was acting as if he was still behind the one-way glass he had grown accustomed to. "Did you find a satisfactory answer?" Emmett asked. It took Jasper more than a second to remember what the other man was referring to.

"No," he replied.

Emmett gave a half smile and looked up at the younger man. "Sometimes the questions we ask ourselves are the ones that we can never answer." Emmett continued, with no response from Jasper, who had just sat in the chair six feet from the side of the cot. "Are you an analyst or a technician?"

Jasper was surprised by the accuracy of his inquiry. Then he remembered they had seen each other in the hall outside the printing room. The idea that the door next to it was a staff lounge wasn't very believable. "Analyst it is." Jasper didn't know if the man had come to that conclusion through logic or by a guess, but for some reason, Jasper's mind couldn't process the situation at all.

Emmett sat back, instinctively careful not to lean on his hands. Jasper looked worriedly at the man. The young man's level of ease seemed to find a new low as he put together that, with the answer to that question, the man would know that he played a part in him being printed. *Did I confirm any facial expressions that lead to his conviction?* he thought, while preserving a well-planted posture, just in case the convict lashed out in retaliation. The bigger man noticed this, once again seeming to read his mind.

"With all your training, I would expect that you would be better at concealing your emotions. I am no threat to you," he said with a genuine smile. Jasper let his body relax, while trying not to make the adjustment evident on his face.

Words! Words! Just say something! Jasper's mind screamed as it tried to utter his consternation into existence.

"So why are you here? I'm guessing you have clearance to go home during curfew." The man continued.

Words! Still no words! Jasper's mind was spinning. Sentences, letters, and fragments were reeling as if his mind were a snow globe. The words danced faster and faster, as if a demented juggler was tossing them in his pattern of confusion. He thought of the question that had overwhelmed him with curiosity. How this man showed no signs of fear or contempt in the room and yet was shown to be guilty enough to be printed.

The question was carried in the winds of his mind. Every time he attempted to pick a word, it was swept away, leaving him more and more frustrated. With his eyes closed, Jasper grasped his head, hoping that maybe by pressing as hard as he could, order would be restored in his mind.

"No more!" Jasper screamed, not knowing if the words were contained in his mind or if they had escaped through his mouth. Only chaos remained. Time to get out. With a brief impulse of concrete thought, Jasper began to rise to flee the room, hands still pressed firmly against his temples. Before he could take a step, he was calmly pressed back into his chair. His mind reacted to the touch with instinctual fear, filling his body with panic.

But in a moment, everything changed. A wave of peace hit his body like the ocean meeting the coast. Jasper could feel himself breathing hard. His eyes opened to find that he was covered with sweat, his hands were still gripping his head, and a red and swollen hand was placed firmly on his shoulder.

Emmett Walsh's head was bowed with his eyes closed, and he was muttering something. Unable to make out what he was saying, Jasper sat, unmoving. Emmett raised his head with a smile and took his hand off the younger man's shoulder. Realizing how hard he still held his head, Jasper let his hands fall to the chair. His mind was clear.

His thoughts were succinct. However, that didn't mean he understood what had just taken place. He looked back at the man who had gone back to sit on the cot in front of him. His face was calm, unoffending, and laced with a quiet sense of contentment.

"What happened?" Jasper said, his voice now clear and sure.

"I don't really know," Walsh said, his smile lengthened in wonder. His eyes were bright with anticipation. Jasper knew what he was waiting for. Jasper now could verbalize the question he had inadvertently asked himself on the way in.

"I wanted to talk to you. Your face didn't match... It wasn't the practice that we hold to. No confirmation, and apparently none needed... And..." While the young analyst was verbally processing, his eyes passed from Walsh's to the corner of the room. A solitary black fixture was there. Coming out of the ceiling was a black circle. A dome of cameras, undoubtedly accompanied by a microphone that captured everything that happened in the room.

Jasper froze midsentence. Analysts were never allowed in the recovery room to avoid retribution from convicts who resented their confirmations, as well as the danger of leaking confidential information inside the State building. He would be printed or worse. His career, his home, his whole life was forfeit because of what he had just done. He scrambled to think of ways he could get out of it, explain it away. Every different road to redemption went through one man—Bernard Stockton. Jasper tried thinking of other ways to escape this mess, only to find Stockton's angular-eyed face interrupt its feasibility in very unsavory practices.

Emmett remained sitting, calm and confident, as Jasper's mind raced through scenarios. Sitting, waiting, and watching to see what Jasper's conclusion would be. After what felt like hours, the man's question, mundane though it was, snapped Jasper out of his daze. The guards would be back to release the man before dawn. The AI computers would alert the surveillance staff, and they would find that he had been there. The prosecution of his lonesome self would be led by the great Bernard Stockton.

"We need to go."

The man didn't say anything but got up and quietly left the room closely behind the young analyst. There were five guards in the facility, and Jasper was not aware of their patrol schedule after hours. They walked quickly down the halls, with Jasper walking ahead, as if he was just leaving the facility. Once Jasper had made sure the halls were clear, he motioned for the man to follow. After several tense minutes of hurried walking, they approached the door to the staff parking garage. Jasper placed his hand on the scanner so it would let him out the door. He looked back at the man, who, at that moment, took another look at his hands. The door clicked, and he followed the young analyst out after flashing him a brief thankful smile.

They stepped out into the brisk northwestern night and proceeded down some steps to the covered parking area. There was a chill in the air, but Jasper didn't notice it. His mind was racing. He must have been crazy. Why was he helping this man? Was he even helping him? His best chance was to go through the re-education process. Wasn't it? What had possessed him? He didn't know anything about this man. He couldn't even remember his name! An image of his mother calm in the face of his father's rage flashed before his eyes. Jasper suddenly pulled the man into a corner where he knew no mic or camera could reach him.

"What is your name?" he said, holding the man by the collar.

Startled, the man only stared at him. Jasper released him and asked again. "What is your name?"

"Emmett," the man replied, "Emmett Walsh."

They approached a white, electric sports car, and Emmett whistled in admiration.

"You must be doing well with the ladies," he said before sliding into the passenger seat.

"You would think so. It's why I got it. Once they find out what I do for work, they usually tell me they're married or aren't interested in guys," Jasper responded before starting the car.

"I'm trying to think of what would hurt me more," Emmett laughed in reply.

The quiet that set in as they pulled out of the lot was defining. Adrenaline's numbing effect dissipating with the lights of the compound in the rear window. Jasper began to sweat as the weight of the situation slowly sank in fully. He looked at Emmett and saw no fear, just a smile, almost in gratitude. Gratitude? Emmett had already been printed. His punishment was given. His record would be stained by his printing, but that was as far as the sentence went. *But then there was me, an analyst, who broke protocol, entered an off-limits room to meet with a man that I never confirmed based on expression. I condemned both of us. The body of evidence toward charges of obstruction of justice, corruption, or treason were obvious enough for even the worst investigator to press. His punishment was paid, and now I have multiplied it by ten.*

Jasper's mind raced once again, doing the math on the sentencing that his entering into that room warranted. Worried that Walsh had come to the same conclusion, Jasper tried to avoid looking at him as they drove. What was in that file that the inquisitor didn't mention? He could have a violent history—murder or battery. On an impulse, Jasper turned his eyes toward the other man for a brief moment, but it wasn't malice he saw on the older man's face. Walsh looked at him with compassion, as if he knew the conclusion that Jasper was coming to.

"I'm excited," Emmett said.

Jasper was so taken aback by the contrast between what he assumed the other man would say about the situation and what he did say that he paused to double-check the words he heard. Then he asked, "Excited for what?"

"Excited for you to get an answer to your question."

Jasper drove down the highway and began to process what to do next. *Ask him a question—that's what I'll do,* Jasper thought..

"What just happened? Who are you?" As soon as he asked, he realized how stupid the questions were.

"I could ask you the same questions," Emmett laughed, without a hint of scorn. "Let's answer the questions one at a time; I'm still figuring out the first one. I'm Emmett. Born and raised in Idaho. History and philosophy teacher by trade and apparent threat to the peace of the State. Or at least, that's what your friend in the interview room seems to think. As a facial analyst, don't you have access to the same file as Stockton?"

"No," Jasper replied. "In order to try and keep our minds free from bias, we only confirm what the interviewer asks. We look for signs of resentment, disgust, contempt, or fear in order to confirm malicious intent to disturb the peace."

"What did you see with me?" Emmett asked as he tried to squeeze his seat's armrests, testing if his hands were still tender. After a brief wince, he got his answer and turned back to look at the still sweating analyst. Jasper's mind was racing again, finding it hard to focus on one subject.

"I didn't see anything on your face, at least not those emotions. That's why I couldn't confirm the conviction."

"Seems like that irritated Mr. Stockton."

"How did you know he was irritated? Stockton is very good at appearing like a playful puppy."

Emmett turned his head to the window, looking out at the streetlights that bathed the hillside. "A man who finds his purpose in seeking other's fear and contempt can't keep actual joy in his heart. His demeanor may look like a puppy, but in order to succeed and have the stamina to continue, you have to be a jackal on the inside."

"That's the thing. He couldn't find that in you. I couldn't see it. That's what struck me! You were in handcuffs walking through the halls, and you smiled at me. You go into the room and are mocked and ridiculed by Stockton. No fear, no contempt, no anger. Then he convicted you without confirmation from me." Jasper stopped and thought for a moment before continuing.

After a few minutes of silence, Jasper began again. "After you... you know...were printed and everyone left, I needed to know...something. I don't know what was bothering me, but I felt this compulsion to ask you...something." He needed to ask a question he had long suppressed, a question he could not formulate. Emmett looked like he would ask a question, but Jasper continued to verbalize his thoughts before he could speak.

"Then I got to the room and"—Jasper once again found himself at a loss for the right words—"I couldn't speak. I still didn't know why I needed to go in there, but I had to ask you something. The words... any words I thought of to ask you just were—" Jasper stopped, bringing his hands up and gesturing to find the words. Without knowing why, he looked at his hands, free from the wheel. They were juggling air as if something was in it.

"Your words seemed like they were taken from your mind and spun around with many others? Like they were being juggled?"

Jasper put his hands back on the wheel before his momentary daze made him drive off the road.

"Yes, like a juggler. I could see it, but I couldn't find the words to speak, even though I wanted to." They turned into the residential section of Richland and stopped in front of the gray mass that was the exterior of the housing units.

"You knew what I mean by someone juggling my thoughts. I still have no words to describe it, but it seems like you know. What is it?"

CONCERN showed on Emmett's face as he undid his seat belt. "I'll tell you what I can, but it won't be long until they find me not there in the morning and the video footage of us together. They'll come here first. You can try and explain this away and maybe get a pardon. Or you can leave with me on a little trip. We can wait and talk here, but the longer we delay, the bigger the chance is that you will have your decision made for you."

There was no manipulation in his eyes. There was just COMPASSION. Jasper could see that Emmett seemed to understand the situation that he was in.

"I've got some packing to do," Jasper said.

Jasper and Emmett walked up the stairs to a gray door that had "225" painted on it. Jasper placed his hand on the scanner, and the door clicked, allowing them to enter. The lights automatically turned on with the signal of the motion detector to illuminate a simply furnished room with a couch and a desk at the far end. Next to the adjoining kitchen was an area for dining, but no dining table was there. Instead, it was covered in pictures. Thousands of prints of people's faces lay with no apparent order on the floor. Images of scenes from movies and photos of historic politicians and newscasters were spread out. As his eyes adjusted to the eruption of light in the room, he saw something written on the pictures. Lines had been drawn over the entirety of the photos—lines indicating muscle patterns on the facial expressions.

Emmett bent down and picked up one of the photos. It was in black and white, showing a woman sitting in front of a desk. She had a somber expression and a weary posture. Only one illustration was on her face—an arrow pointing to her left check and labeled ANOM. Jasper returned from another room as Emmett was inspecting the picture. Emmett looked down and found three more pictures of the same woman. In the first, she looked on the brink of tears. Lines covered her face pointing to muscles that had changed the expression from somber in the first picture. In the second picture, her mouth was open and her eyes bulged. The third showed her face set in stone. Her nostrils were flared and her brow tight. It looked like she wanted to kill something.

"She was a prisoner," Jasper said from behind him. "They started this program in the '60s where they would take war prisoners and subject them to visual and physical stimuli and test to see if they could get a consistent reading of their emotions."

"She's beautiful. What kind of international crime did she commit?"

Jasper turned, went to the closet, and took out two backpacks. "Look at the back of the print. It usually gives some context," he said.

Emmett turned the first photo over and read the words printed on the back. "Tanya Laskin, age 31, Russian KGB Assassin. Wow... didn't expect that."

Jasper smiled as he put cans into one of the packs. "You probably would have been a very easy kill for her then." They both smiled.

"Where are we going to go?" Jasper asked.

"I don't know. The State security has little presence anywhere north of here. They don't care that much about general security anywhere outside the cities. If we can get out by the river, we can follow it north where the highway meets the mountains. There's a junction there, and then nothing else for miles. It may be the best place to gain our heads and plan our next move." Emmett didn't sound entirely confident that it was a good plan, but it was something.

Jasper went into his bedroom to gather more clothing. Something caught his eye as he stuffed a pair of pants into his pack. A picture of his family taped to the wall. Jasper's father was a tall, lean man with wavy brown hair. He stood next to shorter, tawny-haired women of about twenty-five, a baby cradled in her arms. They both stood smiling at a young Jasper who had no front teeth at the time. He was reminded of the fact that he would likely not see them again. He picked up the picture and studied it for a moment. It was the image of a perfect childhood. A tear formed in Jasper's eye as he remembered that the familial bliss caught in the picture changed soon after that photo was taken, and it was all his fault. Jasper folded the picture in half and started to put it in the pack, then he hesitated and tossed it onto the unmade bed instead.

When Jasper returned to the main apartment space, he found Emmett sitting on the couch with his eyes closed. He was sitting forward, which meant he couldn't have been sleeping, and the younger man's attention was brought back to his preparations. Jasper continued to move into the kitchen, stuffing some food in whatever space was left in the packs. When he was done, Emmett had already stood and walked up to him.

"Ready?" Emmett said.

Jasper looked around his apartment one more time. He wouldn't miss it. "Yes," he said.

THREE

AS JASPER CLOSED the car door, he noticed that the mood had changed since he had last been there. He was about to leave his home, to run toward an end he could not picture. He couldn't remember the last time he'd experienced the two things that fueled him: exhilaration and wonder. He turned the key, put the car in drive, and pulled out of his housing lot. They had decided to go down to a golf course just south of Richland, where the town's edge met the Columbia River. Every car was outfitted with GPS software, which the State would easily track. They would park at the golf course and continue on foot, following the river.

Several questions were balancing at the end of Jasper's tongue throughout the drive, something that Emmett no doubt could tell. He sat quietly in the passenger seat, waiting for Jasper to order his thoughts enough to start the conversation. Before he knew it, Jasper was pulling into the golf course's parking lot. They parked the car, pulled out the packs, and started walking.

The moon was full in the night sky. It illuminated the mountains in the distance and the peaks with a dusting of white from early snow. It had been a while since Jasper had walked outside. The beauty of it all was staggering to him. There was an immense irony in the fact that the moment he could recognize beauty and wonder for the first time since he was a child was when his entire life was falling apart. He suddenly remembered his mother's face again and its uniquely compassionate expressions that Emmett showed as well. Her face had been lost to him throughout the years without her presence, but when he saw Emmett's expressions, his mother's face returned, freed from the blur of time into a clear picture. His life as he knew it was over. But he was free.

So many questions. Which do I begin with? Jasper thought. *Just spit one out, and maybe the rest will get easier,* he almost shouted at himself.

"How did you do that?" Jasper asked Emmett, even as he realized that there was zero chance of asking a question with more ambiguity. Before Emmett could begin an answer, Jasper clarified. "When we were in the room, and my brain was all jumbled. I was trying to regain control of my thoughts, and it was like I woke up, and I saw you sitting there with your hand on my shoulder."

Emmett nodded to acknowledge the effort Jasper made to clarify and calmly answered. "I didn't know why you came in. I didn't really know much of what was going to happen to me. I knew I was going to lose my job and have to move to one of the rehab facilities but not much else. You came in and asked me what you were doing there, which immediately convinced me that you might be there for a reason that you did not truly know."

Jasper winced at the absurdity of his question, but the tall man didn't make fun of it.

"You sat down in front of me," Emmett continued, "and my eyes were still adjusting to the light. By the time that happened, you were...growling. You made little sounds like you were being hurt. You pressed your hands against your head, and I did the only thing I know how to do in that situation. I talked to my Father."

It took a second for Jasper to register who he meant by "father." Religious studies of all kinds had been removed from the school curriculum several years earlier, after a string of attacks on government buildings by religious groups. With the removal of the curriculum also came the removal of private schools that could provide breeding grounds for the ideas that caused the attacks. Which the State deemed to be all of them. "You prayed?" Jasper asked bluntly.

"Yes."

Jasper allowed himself to remember what that moment felt like. The chaotic snow globe of thoughts came back to him, in the third person now. The image of his mind was more apparent now, and it bore the resemblance of a being. It had little structure, but its presence brought with it an eerie chill and a deep malevolence that he had never felt before. Jasper didn't want to speak the idea into existence, thinking it may lead to some more startling discoveries in the near future. But begrudgingly, he let out the only way he could describe it. "There was something influencing my mind."

Emmett nodded in acknowledgment that he understood. "Often when chaos is amplified is when we are the closest to a bit of truth. That influencer you were affected by goes by many names. The Evil One, Satan, the devil, Lucifer. But I call him the Juggler."

"I thought Juggler were supposed to be funny."

"This one sure thinks he is," Emmett responded. "I don't want to scare you, but I don't think it was coincidence that we met today. The Juggler tried his best to stop us from meeting. He slips into our minds and takes our thoughts and starts juggling them until we give up on that thought. Have you ever seen those old juggling-clown videos?"

"Yes," Jasper responded.

"Do you remember when the clown would be juggling lots of blue balls really fast and then added one red ball?" Jasper nodded in reply. "When the balls kept speeding up, what color were they, red or blue?"

Jasper strained to remember the children's cartoon.

"It was still blue right, just a little tint of purple, but it was still blue."

"Yes. This is what the Juggler does with our minds. He takes thoughts, facts, and truths from our minds and starts juggling them, making us confused. Then he slips in a lie, a red ball, a piece of logic that doesn't match up into our consciousness. Not only are we confused, but in the swarm of thought, we often have a lie within the things that are true, making the lie that much more dangerous."

Jasper's body remembered how to sweat even though there was a chill in the northwestern nighttime air. *How is he explaining what was happening in my mind hours ago?* Jasper strained as Emmett completed his explanation and attempted to look into his mind, as if that were physically possible. He imagined his feelings, something they taught him to do in his training to help visualize others' emotions. The young man saw a large amount of fear in his mind, accompanied by an odd cool feeling. Doubtless, his body was telling itself to warm up because the chill air was magnifying his stress sweating.

He thought for a moment longer, letting his body walk on but keeping his mind closed in his own head. He allowed Emmett's voice to become vague, intensifying his focus. There was a moment of peace, a brief feeling of calm from the absence of anything unworldly. Then briefly, a flicker of light. Subtle and muffled, the light began to move, back and forth, then in a circle. The circle reminded him of something, but he couldn't remember what.

"What's really concerning is when the fireflies start talking to each other, then the balloons burst into butterflies and bound toward the broccoli." Emmett's conversational tone crept back into his consciousness. It took him a second to realize the lunacy of the sentence he'd just heard. He turned to see Emmett smiling back at him.

"You really know how to get into your head. I stopped talking sense five minutes ago. I was getting worried that if you kept walking, you would have walked into the Columbia River." Emmett stopped walking and turned toward Jasper, who was glad it was too dark for the other man to see his embarrassment.

"This is a lot to take on," Emmett continued. "Two days ago, I was teaching in my classroom when I was arrested in front of my students, and now I'm here with you walking at four in the morning with no plan besides stay out of the camp. A day ago, you were just finishing work, and something or someone turned your life on its head."

Jasper usually had no problem finding responses, but the chill in the air and the anxiety racing in his heart made his jaw tighten. He gave Emmett an exhausted smile, which seemed to satisfy him, and they continued to walk, switching to a lighter topic.

They walked for another hour, noting the beginnings of light peeking up above the brown hilltops showing that their head start was coming to a close. Jasper thought that idea would be more concerning to him, but the realization was covered by the easy, light conversation he had struck with Emmett. He had known the man for fewer than twelve hours and had begun to trust him more than he thought should be wise.

Jasper's training had made him look at conversation as a game. A little battle that ends with a winner and a loser. The winner gave up little information and gained much. The loser provided insight and received nothing. Jasper excelled at the academy because he could read the muscle patterns in people's faces that flash in an instant and translate that into an emotion. He could know when someone was lying, and sometimes even why, without asking a single question. But with Emmett, it was different. It was almost as if he had turned off the need for investigation. They talked about many things. How Jasper hated swimming, how Emmett became a teacher, and even how Jasper was an intensely heavy sleeper. There were few limits to the conversation as they walked.

"They are going to label us both terror threats you know," Jasper said as he stepped over an especially thorny bush, wincing as it stung his calf. It was still very dark even though the morning would arrive shortly. In anticipation of the coming light, they cut over rough ground to make it to the Tri-Cities area's valley walls.

"What do you think that means for us?" Emmett replied.

"If Stockton sees this as a level-four threat, they will send heli's to find us and have a couple of cars looking. But if he can convince higher brass that we are a direct threat to security, he may get privileged satellite usage. Which could find us at night just by the heat contrast of our bodies against the cold ground. If that happens, we're in trouble."

Emmett laughed as he climbed over a dirt outcropping at the top of a hill.

"I think we're in trouble no matter what."

He reached out a hand to pull Jasper up the ridge. Turning to look over the other side of the bank they had climbed, Jasper saw the vastness of the Columbia River. A fresh morning breeze hit him, almost causing him to lose his balance. The air was crisp and refreshing. He had not been outside for this long in years. The river was large, almost a mile just in width. A sound came to Jasper's ears—a rushing noise that stood out in the budding light of morning. He swept his eyes to the right to find a dam.

"Is it automated? Would there be anyone working in it?" Emmett asked. pointing to the five-hundred-foot-high concrete fortress.

"Not likely. All the dams are worked by computers remotely."

"What do you think about heading in to find out. It may be the only place we can wait out the sunlight." Jasper nodded his agreement, and they began a nerve-racking track down the steep incline toward the dam.

As they approached the massive concrete structure, mist from the opposite side of the dam drifted on the wind to bathe their faces.

"No cars in the parking lot," Emmett noted. Now with enough light to see the whole structure, Jasper made out the shape of a green tree painted on the concrete wall.

"This is Evergreen State dam. It's pretty old, but they have probably automated it by now anyway. I think it is worth a try," he said, noticing the sun peeking over the rolling hills. He thought it had to be close to checkout time at the facility, which meant someone would have inevitably noticed Emmett's absence, checked the video, and realized that Jasper had let him out.

The dam's size became more apparent as they climbed the ladder up to what looked like a service door. There was slight vibration, but the vastness and perceived weight of the water on one side made Jasper conscious of the pressure the structure was enduring. He gripped the metal ladder even harder as he climbed, feeling the cold of the metal bite into his hands. They got to the top of the ladder and found themselves in front of a lonely steel door. Knowing that there was no chance of it being unlocked, Jasper tried the handle anyway. Sure enough, it didn't move.

He shot an unsure look at Emmett, which was returned by a shrug. Emmett moved around the side of the building, looking for a window. Jasper and Emmett searched for an opening into the structure for another hour before sitting down, frustrated. They remained for a moment under the sheet metal outcropping of the locked service entrance door in case Stockton managed to get precious satellite time.

Emmett turned to Jasper,

"You sounded optimistic that Stockton wouldn't be able to get satellite usage to find us. Why? Aren't there hundreds of satellites at the state's disposal?" Jasper blew on his hands, trying to regain their full use after a rare night in the cold.

"There has been tension between the States and the Far East Coalition for the last couple of years. Because of that, they have been devoting most of their space tech to that side of the world. Stockton is the regional director of security, however, so you never know how many strings he has to pull."

Emmett nodded his acknowledgment and stood up. He went around the corner of the building and sat down again. He was now out of sight, but Jasper could hear him.

"Father, thank You for this morning," Jasper heard him say vaguely. He slowly scooted toward the edge to listen more carefully to what Emmett was saying. "Thank You for allowing me to meet

Jasper. I don't know what Your plan is right now, but I am confident that You have something for him. Thank You for having me be a part of that."

Plan, what plan? Jasper wondered as he listened.

"In everything I do, please let it be to glorify You. Please be with Justice and Lucy back home. I don't think I'll be able to see them again, but I trust You have a way for them to know You outside of my involvement."

Jasper remembered the book that Bernie had thrown in the room. Those must be the names of his students.

"Please help us to find a place where we can rest," Emmett continued. "Whether your will is for us to leave or be found, we rest in your hands."

Captured, Jasper thought. *That's a stupid thing to say. In no way could that be a good thing at this time.*

This trail of thought was interrupted by a chopping sound that echoed throughout the river valley. Faint at first, it grew in clarity as well as volume. A helicopter was coming! No doubt it was for them. Jasper jumped up and grabbed Emmett by the arm. Emmett stood up and opened his eyes, acknowledging the reason for Jasper's panic.

"Got any great ideas, meditation man?" Jasper said.

"Not yet." He walked over to the steel door again. Jasper flattened himself against the wall trying to make out which direction the sound was coming from. The sound seemed to be reflecting from every side of the valley. Then suddenly, a thunderous bang erupted his ears! Jasper jumped to the floor in panic.

"Emmett!" Jasper whisper-screamed in no specific direction.

"Jasper, let's go." Emmett replied, standing in the doorway of the now-open service entrance. Jasper, visibly confused, scrambled to his feet and dashed into the poorly lit entrance. Emmett smiled as he passed in. He then shoved the door closed, cloaking them in thick darkness.

Both were breathing heavily, Jasper audibly more so. "You sound a little frazzled." Emmett said jokingly.

"You don't say." Jasper squeaked out as he recovered his composure. He began digging through his backpack, looking for the flashlight they had brought from his apartment. Once he found it, he illuminated the room to see Emmett's face with a wide smug grin on it.

"What is that for?" Jasper said, trying to gather his thoughts. "And how did you get the door open?"

Emmett let out some of the laughs that he was holding in while Jasper bumbled.

"I remembered an old metal door in my house when I lived in Colorado. It would work fine throughout the year, but when it got cold, it contracted, and it wouldn't close properly. I just tried to kick the door in the right spot that might make it spring open," he said as he began to examine his foot for injury. "The smug face is because I've never seen an adult wet themselves before."

Jasper couldn't believe it. It was true. He hadn't even noticed it until Emmett mentioned it.

"I thought I was doing to die," Jasper said in resignation. He swallowed his broken pride and began to laugh, which was accompanied by Emmett. "Now I wish I had," Jasper joked. Once the laughing subsided, as well as the echoing sound of helicopter blades, they stood up and walked into the concrete behemoth.

Emmett took the lead with the flashlight, more to avoid being downwind of Jasper than anything. The interior doors were unlocked, being that most of them had watertight compartments rather than locks. As they walked through the doors, they began to hear more and more diverse sounds. They walked through the turbine room, where six turbines too large for the flashlight to illuminate complexly buzzed. A wealth of machines was running, expelling a warmth that was pleasant to Jasper. He started feeling very tired and found himself longing to curl up next to one of the warm machines and fall asleep. "There is a bathroom over here," Emmett said as he pointed to a door with the flashlight.

Jasper desperately wanted to change clothes, so he shrugged off his daze and took his pack to attempt to wash his clothes. After soaking his dirtied garments and washing them with the hand soap, he laid them on one of the massive, warm machines to let them dry. He slipped into his only change of pants and walked back to where Emmett was sitting.

Emmett offered a smile. "I checked the next three rooms," he said. "They're huge. The first one is full of wires. It must be the controls and communication's center. There is a panel of instruments that are pretty well lit and some routers that provide Wi-Fi if you want to stream a movie."

Jasper smiled at what he assumed was a joke. He knew that all it would take was a minor abnormality to alert the authorities that there was somebody here that typically wasn't.

"I don't want to offend you. But are you a Christian?"

Emmett seemed surprised at the question. "Yes. That couldn't offend me. I'm a follower of Jesus Christ."

"Sorry if I sound ignorant, but not much is taught about Christianity anymore. Is that who you speak to when you speak into thin air? Do you characterize this...Jesus...as your father?"

"I'm happy to share. I worship the God of heaven. The One who revealed Himself to the Jewish nation and then to the world through His Son, Jesus. I call Him Father because He calls me His son and because He made me."

Jasper struggled with that. He had heard jokes about Christians when he was in school, but nothing that actually described what they believe.

"I thought you believed in the one true God. This sounds like two to me. Do you have any others hiding under the rug?" Jasper laughed. He knew these people were crazy. He should be relieved really. How could the whole world be wrong and one man be right? So why did he still have this nagging feeling of unease?

"I believe in one living God. There are many things that act as god. Money, influence, political systems, humans. But I believe there is One who lives, and by His will all things have their being. He created everything. One God, but three persons functioning within that God."

Jasper had been keeping up with Emmett's explanation until the last sentence. He could see that Emmett understood his confusion.

"I believe in one living, feeling, and all-knowing God who created me, as well as everything else. I use the Bible as a source to help me understand who and what this God is, as well as my own personal experience with Him."

"So, you've met him?" Jasper responded.

"Yes, I talk with Him every day."

It was obvious to Jasper that Emmett truly believed every word he was saying. He could not decipher any sign of deceit or ulterior motive on Emmett's face. He was either the best manipulator in the world or someone wholly convicted of the truth of what he was saying.

"The Juggler," Emmett continued, "you know the thing that gave your mind a visit back in the security building?" Jasper felt a chill go down his spine, remembering the feeling of his thoughts being played with. "He is the enemy of God—the adversary, the father of lies. He is so filled with pride, insecurity, and hatred that all he wants to do is turn people away from God. His ways are seductive, and he relies on deception to lead people away from God. He promises freedom, but his freedom leads to chaos and bondage to desire. He promises security and justice, but his way is the way of the power hungry and vengeful tyrant. He believed he could surpass God, but his way only leads to death."

Jasper wasn't liking where this conversation was going. He was starting to wish he hadn't started it. There was a heavy spot in his stomach building with tshe feeling that Emmett was going to connect dots and answer his unasked question. He was afraid of what that might mean. He knew there was something unnatural about what had happened. But worse, he could feel the long-suppressed questions and the long-suppressed guilt rising in him again.

Emmett didn't push. "I know this is a lot to take in, but I know of a One who loves you more than you could fathom and desperately wants to be in your life. I can't see His whole plan, but I know that we didn't meet by chance. You didn't come to my room by chance." He stood up and put his hand on Jasper's shoulder. "I don't know about you, but I'm willing to see where this story goes." He walked away with the flashlight to find a cushion to help them rest while they waited for evening to move on.

Jasper closed his eyes, knowing that sleep would come quickly, regardless of the bed he rested on. As he closed his eyes, he felt the warmth of the machines around him. The young man heard the sounds that surrounded him morph into a singular drone. Once again, he saw a light in his mind. Vague at first, it clarified into a purplish tone. It began to move back and forth. The speed intensified, and the back and forth turned into a figure eight. After a moment of watching the uniform dance, Jasper got the impression that it was suddenly startled. It faded, dissipating to bring back the typical inoffensive dark of sleep. He felt an odd tranquility fall over him as he fell deeper into slumber.

Out of the dark, a raspy voice entered his mind.

"Hello, gentlemen." Jasper stirred from his sleep. The voice—he knew it. Stockton? What was Bernie doing in his dream? "You boys gave me quite the shock this morning. Mr. Walsh, I must not have given you enough credit, considering you had a sympathizer to your cult that I didn't know about. Well done, indeed." *Wait a second,* Jasper thought. *This isn't a dream.*

"Jasper wake up!" He heard Emmett yelling at him. He opened his eyes to see sparks flying, and something was on fire. He jumped to his feet, wiping his eyes to confirm what he saw.

"What did you do, Emmett?"

"It wasn't me; your wet trousers dripped on that transformer. It must have shorted and started a fire. Stockton must have gotten an alert about the dam and got patched into the speakers." They grabbed their packs and went up to the communications room.

"To think I was about to leave the office. What luck!" Jasper heard the voice say from the intercom, and its implications shook him.

"What time is it?" Jasper asked as he followed Emmett up the steps.

"Almost seven. You were out!"

"Evening?" Jasper asked in surprise, but he didn't get a response. The emergency lights had been switched on in response to the fire, and they illuminated the corridors in red light. They got to the communication room where the computer screens had all been turned on to a face. A sadistic and frighteningly polite face schooled to instill a false sense of security.

"Come now, friends. I know you are there. Let's have a chat and work this out. Jasper, are you there? You can tell Emmett who you really are now. Tell him all about your mission to break him out of our facility just so that you could learn more about his terrorist cell."

Jasper couldn't believe what he was hearing. What mission? Then he realized what Stockton was doing. He looked over at Emmett and shook his head pleadingly. Emmett didn't respond; he was feverishly looking for something on his phone.

"If you're not going to talk, I'll have to become very impolite. We will send a team of heavily armed men in there with orders to shoot on sight. That wouldn't be very comfortable, now, would it. Or I could just blow the whole dam." Jasper noticed something wasn't right about that last comment. Everything else was said with jest. The typical lyrical pattern that Stockton used to comfort his victims into confessing. The last one was said with ANGER and, even odder, GLEE. His face on-screen betrayed his plan. Emmett was already picking up the microphone on the table, assuming that Stockton could hear the PA's signal. He started speaking into it before Jasper had time to confer with him.

"I hope you had a nice night's sleep. No need for guns and that sort of thing. We'd love to have a chat. Jasper is a good guy, and I don't think he will be troubling me much."

Jasper thought he may be insinuating that he had killed him already, or at least he hoped that was the case.

"Sorry about leaving," Emmett continued. "I thought I had already paid my punishment to society."

Jasper saw a twinge of disgust flash on Stockton's face.

"I had full confidence that you would be smart enough to enroll in our rehab program," Stockton replied.

"No," Emmett said. "I prefer more...natural remedies to my ailments."

This made Stockton visibly upset. However, he controlled his emotions quickly and returned to his grandfather-like reasonability. Jasper was desperately trying to get anything from his face that he could. None of Stockton's comments helped his cause at all. None of the answers would have led to reconciliation. This wasn't a negotiation of surrender. It was something completely different. Jasper tried to verbalize something to Emmett, but the man held up a finger as he spoke into the mic. Jasper turned to a pad of paper on the desk as Emmett spoke.

"So, what do you want us to do? What is your plan of making peace out of all this?"

Jasper scribbled two words in big letters and shoved the paper in Emmett's face while they were waiting on Stockton's reply.

Stockton looked pleased with the response. "As Jasper knows, I am a reasonable man, and all I want is a secure, functioning society. I may have to pull some strings, but I think if both of you enroll in our rehabilitation program, you can one day be released back to fulfill your debt to society. I believe in second chances and the vast potential that hard necessities bring on situations."

"I believe in a world that has gone under. I believe that a nation that was once the light to the world can find its roots, where liberty and freedom reign. I believe that the pseudo-reality that has been built by schemers, dictators, and narcissists is bound to crumble under truth. That one day, our children may see this nation re..." The transmission was cut off, and the screens went blank. An unworldly explosion rocked the mile-long structure. Its foundation quaked, and in one motion, the entirety of the dam gave way, unleashing three cubic miles of water, cement, and metal into the valley with awful ferocity.

Still catching their breath, Emmett and Jasper sat on the bank of the river in stunned horror. Emmett looked down at Jasper's scribbled note, which he still held. "HE'S STALLING," was written in frantic large letters.

"Thanks for the note," Emmett said to Jasper.

Jasper, still exhausted, responded, "I don't get it. How did he blow the dam? Why did he..." Jasper couldn't finish the sentence. Emmett looked out for a moment and pointed to a thinning trail of smoke.

"It was a missile. Looks like it came from the coast. Bernie must have some authority to authorize a missile strike on two guys that would destroy a dam."

"If I just hadn't wet my pants." The sentiment was funny, but the mood was heavy enough to stifle the attempt at humor. They collected the things that fell from their bags as they sprinted out of the structure to the other side of the reservoir. "What did you set up on the microphone?" Jasper asked. "I only heard the first few words before you pulled me to the door."

"It was a recording of a speech that I made for the past election. I had my class make videos of what their own speeches would be if they were running." The only words that Jasper heard before he was rushed out were "I believe." *What do I believe?* he thought. It troubled him that he couldn't come up with one suitable answer. He had thought he believed in...

They stood at the top of the hill parallel to the wreckage and looked at it one last time. The sunset was almost complete. The sky was a deep, reddish pink, casting a fiery reflection on the river, a sign of the death that would fall on many as the onslaught of water crashed down the valley.

FOUR

THE MOON WAS full as Jasper followed closely behind Emmett, attempting to channel his inner mountain goat. The ridge he was on was steeper than the one they climbed to reach the dam and was full of loose rocks that were actively trying to rob what little balance his legs had. Jasper had never encountered an adrenaline rush like this before. His body was unprepared for it. He felt like his insides wanted to be on his outsides, which was unfortunate given the terrain they were navigating at night.

This is all so absurd, he thought. *Why couldn't the fool just follow the free-thought laws and abstain from religious teachings? None of this would have happened. I'd be back at work. I would have my car.*

A creature skittered out of a nearby bush, jerking Jasper from his thoughts. Thrown off balance, he fell, then muttered several unfriendly things to himself as he sat checking his arms and legs for injury. Emmet offered him a hand up, and they continued down the hill. After a good part of an hour, they were faced with a plain. As they walked, a line of dark trees came into focus, marking the beginning of a mountain range. "We're not climbing, are we?" Jasper asked Emmett, as they sat to take a break on two rocks.

"I don't think we need to climb it. I'm just wanting to get into the cover of the trees so we can figure out what to do next and maybe even build a fire for warmth." Emmett stopped briefly, shaking his head as if trying to organize his thoughts. This was comforting for Jasper to see. Emmett always had a calm about him that amazed Jasper. A quiet confidence that put his own anxieties to rest in the dam. But now he looked human, confused, and though Jasper couldn't see much in the dim moonlight, he could make out his face enough to read it. SADNESS. Emmett lifted his head after the pause.

"Stockton must think we are dead. The speech would have only been halfway done by the time the missile struck. It would be impossible to find our bodies in the artificial tsunami that he created."

"He will make a media statement. Likely saying that we blew up the dam and that we died in it," Jasper said.

He registered the truth of what he had concluded only after he had said it. They were dead men. Everyone would know. His family, friends, and coworkers would all be notified that he had blown up a dam and killed himself in the process. He wouldn't get to say goodbye, and his only legacy would be whatever Bernard Stockton wanted it to be. He felt a lump grow in his throat. He tried to push it down, but soon silent tears were streaming down his face. This was the first time since they left that the magnitude of what they had done hit him. Wiping his tears, he looked up and no longer saw Emmett's feet before the rock in front of him. Before he could look around, he felt Emmett sit on the little bit of rock next to him and put his arm around him. Jasper looked up at his face. His eyes were calm, but below them was a solid stream of tears just like his own. Then Emmett closed his eyes.

"Father, I don't understand what Your plan is. I don't understand why all this happened." Emmett paused, and Jasper wondered if this was going to be when Emmett broke. *Is he going to curse his God?* "But my life is Yours," Emmett continued. "You haven't failed me yet. Please help us follow Your will."

Jasper didn't know why he was being looped into this "will." A day ago, that would have bothered him. He didn't know exactly why, but now it didn't.

They sat a while, letting their tears run out. Jasper was starting to grow a connection with this man. He normally pushed people in his life away because they would inevitably find out what he did for a living and separate themselves from him. He just didn't want to risk the pain. Emmett was a different story for reasons beyond their circumstances. He knew what Jasper did yet showed no contempt or fear of him. If anything, he displayed micro-expressions that were clearer than day to read. Jasper knew he was stupid to trust this man, but it mattered less and less as he spent more time with him. They got up and continued their trek through the forgotten farmland toward the line of trees.

It took about an hour to reach the beginning of the trees at the base of the range. An old wooden fence along a gravel road that they passed was a lonely sign of civilization. Once they entered the trees, the cold seemed to intensify. Jasper couldn't decide if the chill was from the trees or his own fear of the unknown. He had been in the hills outside town only a handful of times. The most significant change was the smell. When they entered the line of trees, there was a beautifully subtle fragrance of cedar and evergreen. Jasper found himself breathing deeper, welcoming the scent in as they walked deeper into the forest.

"Have you done much hiking?" Jasper asked after an hour of trying not to trip over tree roots while keeping up with the long-legged Emmett.

"My dad, sister, and I used to go backpacking every summer," Emmett said. "We'd pick a new place each year, leave my mom to herself, and set off for at least a week." As he explained to Jasper the different areas they backpacked, Emmett began gathering sticks. It made Jasper more comfortable that Emmett had some experience in the outdoors.

"So, you have experience in the Northwest?"

"Nope, never done much out here," Emmett said.

When he was young, he had watched videos online of what to do in survival situations, especially when encountering dangerous animals. He was beginning to realize that, unfortunately, knowing what to do was different from knowing how to do it.

The terrain had been becoming steeper for what could have been a half mile. They walked across a long face of rock at the base of this mountain range and came to a shallow opening in the rock face. Emmett stopped when they came to it and scanned the trees and surrounding areas. The trees were so thick that Jasper couldn't find the moon. "You want to stop here for the night?" Emmett asked after putting his bag down.

"It looks like a good spot to me. Can we risk a fire? My hands are freezing," Jasper replied, putting his pack down.

"I don't see why not, the trees cover us pretty well, and we can put it against the mountain to help insulate it." Emmett put down the wood he had gathered on their trek around the base of the mountain. "I don't think anyone's going to be looking for us anyway. We're dead men."

That truth drove another pang into Jasper's side. It was still so hard to believe. Everyone he had ever known would think of him as a lunatic who took his own life to spite the State.

Emmett looked at Jasper, concerned. "What are you thinking about?"

"Being dead. It's colder than I thought it would be." Emmett smiled at the joke. "I'm just trying to think of people who will miss me, and I can't really think of any," Jasper said.

Emmett picked up another stick and sat down next to the pile, drawing out the lighter they had brought from the house.

"I'm sure there are many," he replied.

Jasper became pensive and thoughtful as Emmett lit the edge of a ball of grass and sticks that resembled a bird's nest. As the fire grew, he added larger sticks to the flame. "We don't often see the evidence of who we are to other people," Emmett remarked as he leaned three logs together carefully and then slumped back against the stone contentedly.

"What are your parents like?" Emmet asked.

Jasper sighed audibly. "When I was a little kid, our family was amazing. I was an only child until I was five, and we were as happy as can be. When I was six my sister, Ziva, was born, and around that time is when my parents started finding out I could read their faces."

"You could do that when you were six?" Emmett exclaimed.

"Probably earlier, but I wasn't very great at it until I understood what I was doing more."

"It doesn't sound like this was a good thing," Emmett said as he blew on the fire. Jasper winced, uncomfortable with the story.

"They probably would have been better off without me," Jasper said. "Once my parents knew what I could do, they started to use it against each other. My dad started traveling a lot, and he became suspicious that my mom was cheating on him. It wasn't horrible for a while, but a couple of years later, he asked my mom if he was Ziva's biological father, and I hesitated when I looked at my mom's face." Jasper paused, looking into the fire. He seemed to get lost in it for a moment before shaking his head, returning to his response. "My dad got mad. He took my indecision as me wanting to protect my mom, and he kicked my mom and my sister out of the house."

Jasper's jaw was tight, and he didn't want to say anything else. He had never verbalized what had happened to him.

"Dad was never the same. Mom called me every once in a while, but I haven't seen Ziva since. Dad shipped me off to boarding school, and that's where I started on my path to the illustrious and noble career in lie detection and counterterrorism. What a mighty fine career it was." Emmett wasn't sure about the joke until Jasper smiled. "No thanks to you," Jasper said, which led to laughter for them both.

"Ziva is a Hebrew name," Emmett said as he threw a thorn from his clothes into the fire. "It means 'light.'"

"She definitely illuminated the flaws in my parents' marriage," Jasper stated.

"I'm sorry, Jasper. That must have been hard. The story is not over, though. You may get to see her again."

Jasper pulled out the can of olives from his pack and popped open the tab.

"I don't know what I would say. Sorry I didn't give the right answer when our dad was investigating if you were a bastard or not?"

"Well, I wouldn't start with that."

"Might as well," Jasper said as he popped an olive into his mouth. "Anyway, that's why they may have been better off without me."

They sat and shared the can of olives and a bag of jerky for a while before they realized that few food combinations were worse than those two and that their rationing couldn't have been more poorly planned.

"What is the reason for the religious criminalization? I was really young when it started. We learned in school it started with a string of domestic terrorist attacks and a sociological debate on the value of religion. Which led to its dismantling."

Emmett adjusted the bag against the rock, then chose his words carefully.

"There was a string of domestic terrorist attacks on US soil, and that caused a lot of fear in the country. Angela Garrison ran with the platform that she would protect Americans from that at all costs, and she won in a landslide. She started placing law enforcement in all churches and institutions, and they started collecting lots of information on potential threats. But at least people got to continue to practice their religion without being arrested."

"Then she brought her big plan to the floor in Congress. She had a supermajority in the House and Senate, so there was very little argument to anything she proposed. President Garrison presented evidence that countries that were the least religious were better off. And at the end she challenged lawmakers to draft legislation to capitalize on this fact, which ended with her famous phrase."

"'We can kill each other for invisible relics of history, or as united Americans, we can be god to this world.'" Jasper finished the well-known quote that was taught in school and posted on government buildings.

"Yes," Emmett said and sighed. "She was offering an ideology where we promote humans as a group as god. Not leaving the potential that there could be something greater than man. She got the idea from some old philosophers who believed we are to revolve around ourselves as gods."

"I don't remember learning about those people," Jasper said.

"Of course, you haven't. Not all of their views align with the State, and they are therefore viewed as dangerous. Only a select few are allowed to study their ideas."

Jasper was keeping up but struggled with a part of Emmett's explanation. "Where do you find 'truth' if not in yourself?"

"Well, that is part of the lie, isn't it? The State doesn't really want people to find the truth in themselves; they instead dictate the truth and punish those who don't fall in line. That is why we are here, isn't it?" Emmett asked.

"Does that mean we are to find the truth in ourselves then?" Jasper asked.

"The truth is that people need a mooring and anchor. They cannot exist without a foundation to stand on or a framework to build off of. That is probably why so many, having lost their faith, easily fall to the will of the State. The truth the State offers is a counterfeit. It doesn't live up to even its own standards of justice or equality. But I revolve around something else. Not my own or that of the state. His name is Jesus. I perceive, understand, and apply what is true based on who He is and what He has done." And that's where Emmett lost him.

"How can something you can't see or hear explain what is factual or not?" Jasper asked.

"I'm not talking about facts. I'm talking about truth. I can see clearly enough that these sticks are on fire. That's a fact. However, that doesn't give the fire meaning or tell me what to do with it." As Jasper struggled to find a response, Emmett continued, "There is the

Bible, which is a book that has spoken about God for thousands of years; however that was limited by fact until there was a special man who was prophesied to come in that book. His name is Jesus. He was born in Bethlehem, crucified under Pontius Pilot, and rose again after being dead for three days."

Jasper had heard this story before, but only when it was being told with ridicule and sarcasm. Emmett truly believed everything he was saying. There was no deceit or doubt in his mind.

"Not only was that prophesied in scriptures that could be dated back hundreds of years prior, but it was also backed up by more scriptural and archeological evidence than there was for the existence of Julius Caesar at all." Emmett paused, waiting for Jasper to catch up before finishing his point.

"Jesus died for a reason—to be the sinless, perfect sacrifice required to pay the debt for all the wrongdoings of mankind. By His death and resurrection, we know that He is who He said He was, and that He accomplished this task and offers eternal life through Him to all those who accept Him."

Jasper's mind began to race. His brain connected the dots that Emmett was laying out, but his thoughts became scattered as he spoke. Thoughts flashed through his mind of moments in life that he regretted, and after an onslaught of painful memories, his consciousness rested on one event. It was his mom's tear-streaked face accompanied by his father's stern voice.

"Is she my daughter?" He'd heard his father say those words as he pointed at his little sister. Jasper remembered his father forcing his face to look at his mother's. He hesitated, and in that hesitation his father's fears were confirmed. Guilt and shame took his breath away. He tried to shake himself from the memory but found his mind occupied with something else. Someone else.

He had felt this before. The Juggler was back. Panicked, he tried to tell Emmett to stop, but he didn't know how. His words just wouldn't come out. He looked up at Emmett, trying to display his frustration and fear on his face as they had to do in facial recognition exercises. The look Emmett returned was serious. He came closer and put his hand firmly on Jasper's now shaking shoulder.

"Jasper, I know you've known me for two days. But I tell you that it is not the scientific evidence of Jesus that stands out, not the archeological or historical miracles that convince me of His reality. It is the fact that I have a personal experience with Him. A relationship that goes beyond any that I could ever have on this earth. He is my God, my King, and my best friend, and He wants to be yours too."

Jasper was forgetting to breathe. This was no simple juggling of his thoughts; it was like a hurricane was confined in his skull. He didn't know what he needed to say, but he knew that there was one thing that the hurricane didn't want him to speak about. He took an intentional deep breath in, then released it from his tightly wound mouth. "Jesus."

His jaw loosened; his breathing returned to normal. It was a slow process, but the one constant was Emmett's hand remaining on his shoulder, supporting him. Jasper felt tired, but his mind was clear. Tapping Emmett's hand on his shoulder, he indicated he was okay and stood to his feet.

"Thank you." Emmett didn't know whether he was thanking him or Jesus, and if Jasper was honest with himself, he didn't know either.

"Are you sleepy yet?" Jasper asked.

Emmett looked at the moon briefly, judging to see if there was enough time to get some sleep before dawn.

"If we are going to, we need to keep the fire going. I'll go get some more wood," Emmett said. Jasper waited for Emmett to disappear down the hill, and as he heard the last evidence of his footfalls, he turned his head to the sky.

"Emmett's father, or Jesus, or whoever you are. I'm sorry I don't really know how to do this but—Thank you." He didn't know if anyone was listening or if it would only work with his head bowed and eyes closed, so he tried it just to make sure it worked. "If you are there...where have you been? Why did you let this happen to Emmett, and why would you rope me into this? I don't want to sound critical, but what the hell, man!" Jasper stopped, realizing the potentially offensive term. "I'm sorry, I didn't mean that. Why here? Why now? Have you been manipulating me my whole life without me knowing? Have I made any of my own decisions?" After asking another flurry of questions, which were answered by silence, he opened his eyes and looked to the sky again. "I don't know if you are a one question or request at a time kind of guy, but what I'm trying to say is, I think you are there. Show me more."

FIVE

EMMETT CAME around the bend holding a small armful of logs. He quickly and quietly set them on the ground and motioned for Jasper to be quiet. A hundred different scenarios flooded into Jasper's head. A bear! It could be a bear, or the State... Either way, Jasper felt a pang of terror rise up his spine. Emmett motioned for him to follow. They crept down the hill in the direction Emmett had come from. After going about fifty yards from the camp, Emmett put his hand on his friend's chest, halting him. He was listening for something.

Jasper was waiting to hear a howl of a wolf or call of an elk, but it never came. Instead, there was a voice, lyrical and soft. It rose from farther down the mountain like smoke. Emmett came closer and whispered, "I think this is when Gandalf comes out of the darkness and surprises us."

"What's Gandalf?" Jasper replied. The look Emmett gave him showed an exaggerated shock. Jasper thought it was a joke, but he looked on his face and saw genuine pain at his response.

They focused on the voice. Neither of them could hear where it came from. It sounded like it was above them, to the left, and also to the right. They looked at each other, confused. They walked together farther away from the camp, and the singing got marginally louder. It was beautiful. A soft, pure melody that had no words to constrict its sound but echoed different vowels in a cascade of notes. When they took a few more steps, the singing stopped, like a cricket when someone steps too close. They stood still for a moment in consternation. Then a new sound took its place, not singing, but more of a splintering, cracking sound. It no longer was vague in its direction. It was coming from right above them. They both looked up just in time to jump out of the way as a tree limb broke free and struck the ground where they'd been standing. Accompanying the limb was a girl, who let out a moan when she hit the ground. Visibly shaken, she saw the two men looking at her and tried to scramble away. Planting her foot to run, she cried out in pain and fell to the ground.

Emmett crouched down and raised his hands.

"Hey, are you okay? It's fine, we aren't going to hurt you." The girl gripped her ankle looking up at the two men. It was very dark in the trees, but Jasper could make out a girl's facial features, maybe twenty years old. Emmett jabbed Jasper in the ribs, encouraging him to speak, but he didn't know what to say. The girl remained on the ground, her ankle in her hands.

"I'm Emmett; this is Jasper. We heard the singing and came looking. You have a beautiful voice. That was you, wasn't it?" The idea that someone else was out around them unseen sent a chill down Jaspers back, making his hairs stand up. The girl nodded her head, breathing heavily, which brought Jasper some comfort.

"Like I said, we aren't going to hurt you. We can step back if that would make you more comfortable, but you look hurt." The girl was flustered. She nodded, and Emmett and Jasper stepped back five steps and sat down.

They gave her a moment to gather herself, which she spent examining her ankle and finishing with a sigh.

"We have a camp with a fire just up the hill. We may have something that you could wrap your ankle with. If you would feel more comfortable, you could stay here, and we can bring it to you."

The girl thought about that and shook her head, then spoke. "If you are bad people, it doesn't really matter if I'm here or there."

"Fair enough. Jasper, why don't you help her up the hill?"

Jasper was surprised and suddenly very nervous. He slowly walked up to her and realized he had no idea how he would help her up the hill.

Face to face with her now, Jasper came to an unnerving conclusion. She was less afraid of him than he was of her. He gave her a hand, and she awkwardly stood up and gained her balance, then put her arm on his shoulder steadying herself. Emmett knew what she was doing immediately, and he stifled his urge to correct the young, shaken man. Jasper turned around and squatted with his back to her. This confused the girl.

"I don't think I can really jump," she said.

Jasper, being the helpful man he was, squatted down farther, almost at a ninety-degree angle. Emmett covered his mouth to stop himself from laughing aloud as he forced himself back up the hill toward their camp. The girl repositioned her arms on his shoulders and began the piggy-back ride up the mountain. She wasn't heavy, and Jasper carried her with ease as they approached the camp.

Reaching the top of the ridge, they returned to Emmett, who was reorganizing the larger logs onto the fire. Jasper put the girl down, then looked up to see Emmett's face laced with mirth. Jasper sat down next to the fire beside her, warming his hands. He looked at her briefly as she reached out to the fire as well. She was pretty, that was easy to see. She had high cheekbones and a long face that was dominated by two large light-brown eyes. Her hair was long and had a curl at the end, and she was now looking at him as he looked at her.

Jasper forced his eyes away as she smiled, obviously not as embarrassed as he was. People always became awkward whenever they noticed his eyes on them. Even in a simple conversation, any hint that he was reading their facial expressions caused the conversation to end and an exit to follow. She was different. But then again, she had a hurt ankle and couldn't leave.

"Which bag was that roll of athletic tape in?" Emmett asked.

"It was in yours," Jasper replied.

Emmett grabbed his bag and searched the few compartments. "It's not here." He then dumped the remaining contents onto the ground. "As well as most of the other things we brought."

Jasper looked at the empty bag and then looked at the unnamed girl.

Shaking her head, she called out. "Cale! Come out." No response.

Emmett and Jasper looked at each other. Jasper rose to his feet in alarm.

The girl called out again. "It's okay, Cale. Just come out."

The bushes rustled, and a man jumped out. In his hand, he held a cruel-looking knife that sparkled in the firelight. Jasper stepped back instinctively. It took him a second to grasp what he was looking at, but to his surprise, the "man" wasn't close to five feet tall, and his face resembled a ten-year-old boy more than a full-fledged man.

"Put that down!" the girl said, and Jasper could hear fear and anger in her voice. The boy looked at the two men around the fire with undisguised distrust then back to the girl. Taking in her injured ankle and dirty face, he turned on Jasper in anger.

The boy charged Jasper, jumping over the fire's flames, knife brandished, looking for blood. Jasper tripped backward, trying to get space, and fell to the ground. As the boy swung at Jasper, he seemed to float and stop in midair. Emmett had been quick to respond and had grabbed the boy by the collar. He quickly but gently wrestled the knife from the enraged youth. Jasper, who had seen his life flash before his eyes multiple times in the past day or so, found this encounter the most frightening. Emmett helped Jasper to his feet. The boy stood between the two men and the girl, fists clenched. He put his fists up, readying himself for round two, but was pulled down from behind and hit the ground hard next to the girl.

"I said stop. They're friends, I think."

Jasper dusted himself off and turned to the two. "He tried to kill me!" he said, pointing a finger at the youth.

"I'm sorry. He thought you hurt me. This is Cale, my brother, and I'm Lake. I don't think I had the chance to tell you." The boy pointed at the ankle and cuts on her face accusingly. "I fell out of the tree," she said. The boy rolled his eyes and made himself comfortable next to her, keeping a close eye on the two men. "See, they're not so bad," she said, patting him on the back.

Emmett sheathed the knife in his belt and approached. "It's nice to meet you both," he said offering his hand. Lake shook his hand and had to nudge her brother to do the same.

Jasper searched through his bag and found that the majority of supplies they had brought were missing. "They robbed us!" he accused.

Lake winced. "Yeah...that was the plan. I'm really sorry, but we were getting desperate. We've been on our own for a couple of days now, and Cale's hunting skills are mediocre at best. We didn't know what kind of people you were." She tapped her brother on the back to get the stuff.

"I need something to wrap my foot," she told him. The boy stood and cast another distrustful glance at Jasper before disappearing into the bushes. "Please don't mind my brother. He's a little...different. He just doesn't want anything to happen to me." Emmett didn't respond to her comment, but gave a polite nod in reply.

"What are you two doing out here?" Lake asked. Emmett looked at Jasper, inquiring if he wanted to say, but Jasper was in no condition to speak.

"We had a misunderstanding with the State." Emmet thought about continuing, but let the air consume the sentence.

"How'd you meet him?" Lake asked.

Emmet looked at Jasper, "I guess you could call it Providence." Lake raised her eyes at the story. Before she could say anything else, a small sound caught her attention. A faded stretching sound, like rope when brought taught.

"Cale, no! Put it down. Cale, you have to trust me!"

Jasper's mind jumped back into survival mode. *Put it down?* he thought. *Put what down?* Then the boy walked intently toward them, a bow as long as he was high strung back with a steel-tipped arrow nocked, pointing directly at Jasper. His hands were struggling to hold the string back, and it was wiggling, making Emmett, Jasper, and Lake all duck for cover. One second later, the inevitable happened. The string slipped from his hands, sending the arrow flying straight into the rock face above where Emmett was standing.

"Give me the bow!" Lake said as she hopped over to Cale, who was attempting to nock another arrow. She took the bow from him and used it as a crutch to get back to where she was sitting. Jasper and Emmett slowly rose to crouching positions, looking up carefully for additional signs of danger.

Jasper saw Emmett's mind working, which usually meant he was about to say something he didn't want to hear.

"If you give us back our stuff, you can take whatever you need," Emmett said to the girl. Jasper almost exploded at the absurdity and threw a harsh look at Emmett who turned to him in response. "God will provide." His answer was hardly satisfactory for Jasper, who sulked as the girl mulled the peace offering. Soon she nodded.

"Bring the stuff we took, now!" Lake said to her brother, who walked sulking back into the bushes between the rock and the grove. Lake turned and smiled back at them. "We don't have any more weapons. Sorry."

The two men looked at each other, clearly unconvinced. Cale brought back a sack of food and other supplies he had taken from the two, and Emmett began wrapping Lake's visibly swollen ankle.

"How did you do what you did in the trees?" Jasper said, tearing off a piece of athletic tape and handing it to Emmett.

"You mean falling out of the trees?"

Jasper gave a laugh in response. "No, I meant the singing. That must have been a distraction. We couldn't really tell where it was coming from. We wouldn't have found you if you hadn't fallen out."

"That was supposed to be the point. My grandmother taught me the trick. Trees and rock deflect sound differently. She taught me how to angle my voice in ways that would make it sound like it was coming from several directions. My tribe was famous for it during the tribe wars. They would sit in the trees, sing, and fall on the enemy when they were turned around."

"You missed us when you fell," Jasper said, smiling. "Thank you for that."

She smiled back. "I'll be more deadly next time."

Seeing the twinkle in her eye, Jasper didn't know if she was serious about the deadly part, but for some reason, he didn't care. He smiled back until he got a nudge from Emmett, who had been patiently waiting for another piece of athletic tape.

After the ankle was supported, they brought out some food to offer to the siblings. They put some cans of soup next to the fire to warm as they all now sat next to the fire.

"We told you about why we are out here. Why are you and your brother all alone traveling with nothing but a knife, a bow, and two and a half arrows? Aren't both of you supposed to be in school?" Emmett asked the question the pair had obviously been anxious about for a while.

Lake took a deep breath and looked at her brother, who only eyed the sizzling soup in the can resting by the fire.

"We were honest with you. Please repay us with the same," Emmett said in expectation.

Another mental game seemed to go through Lake's head. Jasper looked at her face in the firelight, studying the expressions as she thought. Sadness Resentment Remorse. *We don't need to convince her to trust us enough to explain. She doesn't want to tell us because it's something that brings pain and remorse.* Emmett looked at Jasper, a question in his eyes. Jasper subtly traces his finger down from his eyes, resembling a tear. Emmett seemed to understand what he was trying to communicate—or at least pretended to. He inclined his head toward the girl. Jasper knew what he was saying, but he was scared to do it. Emmett did it again, and Jasper nervously got up, carefully eyed by the hungry but wary Cale. He crouched next to her and put his now shaking hand on her shoulder. Jasper didn't know why, but that seemed to comfort the girl. She took her can of soup out of the coals with a rag and sighed in resignation.

"Cale and I are from Umchin." Jasper and Emmett looked at each other, blinking in ignorance. "It's a Native reservation east of Pasco. It's in a valley right by the mountains. When the State was giving reparations to different people of color, they omitted Natives because they already didn't have to pay taxes. The reservation was our home for a long time, but when you turn eighteen, you are sent to one of the State's institutions. I watched lots of friends go, and when they came back, they were completely different. They didn't see our tribe as they used to. I reached out to one of my friends on my eighteenth birthday. I asked her why she didn't care for the tribe anymore. She lashed out at me, calling me lots of really hurtful things. I decided I didn't want to go. A week ago, my parents told me that there was a transport to the institute coming. It was supposed to arrive a few days ago, but I was already gone. I left the night before, after my parents went to bed." A tear began to creep down her cheek.

"My father had a celebration for me, but all I could think about was how I was going to slip out. When everyone was sleeping, I snuck out of the house with the supplies I had gathered." She looked at the bow, and another tear dropped from her brown eyes. SHAME Jasper noticed that when she looked at the recurve bow she showed shame. "And then this little monster followed me out. I didn't notice him for two miles."

Jasper looked at the boy, who was smugly smiling at Lake; it was the first time Jasper had seen him smile at all. "We were too far away for me to bring him back and arguing with him is impossible. So, it's been the two of us. We ran out of food, and have lost five arrows trying to get more, all in a few days."

Emmett stoked the fire, then looked up.

"Will the State be looking for you?"

"I don't know. The transport makes rounds monthly all over the State, and if I'm there when they come back, they will take me whether I want to go or not. If I refuse, they will print me, and I wouldn't be able to be on the reservation if I'm printed."

"I'm sorry that drove you to this, away from your family. What now?"

Lake sipped the hot soup.

"I don't know; I may just go back after a few days. The transport has to keep going. I'm worried my family will turn me in and send me anyway."

"Why do you want to avoid the institution so badly?" Jasper said.

"My tribe is who I am. My identity is in my tribe. Everyone who goes loses that. My grandmother is one of the few people on the reservation who understand the power of a unified tribe and how much value there is in that community."

Emmett and Jasper looked over at each other.

"Do you have room on the reservation? How much is the reservation dependent on the State?" Emmett asked.

Lake thought for a moment.

"Not very much. They tend to leave us alone. I remember a few years ago there were big meetings where people were very upset that there were groups of people getting help from the State and Natives didn't get the same help. But others said that nothing comes free and it is better not to be beholden to a government that doesn't really care about you. I don't know, maybe they were right. Still it hasn't saved us really. I mean look at me: class A example," she said with a bitter laugh.

Jasper remembered hearing about the issue. There was a bill that supplied reparations for different racial groups, but Natives were omitted because they were already exempt from certain taxes. She was telling the truth.

As Jasper was thinking about that memory, he noticed Lake lie down adjacent to him by the fire. Then he looked up and saw the source of that unnerving feeling. Cale's eyes were like lasers burning a hole in his chest. A silence held around the fire for a moment.

The sound of the fire was soothing. It had been burning long enough that the coals in the middle sounded like broken glass when moved. Emmett was the first to break the silence. "You both are welcome to stay with us if you are comfortable with that. We're not even sure what our next move is, so if you two want company while you figure it out you are welcome."

Lake was still sniffling and occasionally sipping the still-hot soup. She looked up at Emmett, then to Cale, who looked like he was attempting to break his neck, shaking it so hard. She returned her gaze to Jasper, who was stirring the coals and nodded with a hint of a smile.

"Thank you."

They finished their midnight dinner and then distributed blankets as they prepared to get some sleep before the sun came up. They lay down around the fire, finding the middle ground between getting as much heat as possible and not burning themselves. Emmett was the last to lie down. He had stepped away from the fire and slipped into the darkness for a time. Jasper found sleep as he listened to Emmett's voice, distant in the night.

THE MOUNTAINSIDE BLOCKED THE SUNLIGHT, so morning came by lazy light filtering through the trees. The fire had gone out, but there was still some heat left in the coals. Feeling the fresh morning breeze that smelled of pine, Lake decided it was time to wake up. She cleared the sleep from her eyes and sat up to survey the camp. Emmett's blankets were left by the fire, but there was no sign of him. Looking to her left, she saw Jasper still sleeping, blankets pulled tight around him. Movement caught her eye, and she saw Cale was walking from the other side of camp casually; he gave her an unobtrusive smile. The smile tipped her off that something was wrong. What should have alarmed her brain, which was still waking up, was the rock that the boy was carrying. It filled the space between his arms as he struggled to hold it, and it probably weighed almost as much as he did. Lake gave him a hard, questioning look. He continued on his way and stood adjusting his grip on the small boulder close to where he had slept, which was directly above the head of... Lake whisper screamed, "No, Cale. Stop! Get away from him."

He looked back, hurt.

"We don't need them," he mouthed back.

"I don't care; I like them!"

Cale frowned stubbornly, and Lake noticed that his grip seemed to be slipping as his arms grew weary.

JASPER WAS in the latter parts of a pleasant dream when something tickled his face and a noise interrupted his slumber. It wasn't the nauseating voice of Bernard Stockton this time; it was whispering. A girl whispering. A girl whispering as loud as she could. He undid his arms from the burrito-like wrapping of blankets and wiped his eyes to see a meteor hurtling for his head. He flinched and screamed, but the impact didn't happen. He looked back and saw that it was still hovering over his head.

"Jasper, get up!" Lake yelled. He quickly rolled off his mat and stood just as the meteor slipped out of the weary hands of a certain eleven-year-old boy. It crashed to the ground, shaking it. Beneath the rock was Jasper's makeshift pillow, the combination of socks rolled up in a shirt, flattened by the impact. Lake, already on her feet, was grabbing her brother by the arm.

"I told you no. I said not to hurt them."

Jasper heard the words and was still trying to piece together what had just happened. She told him not to do it. Which meant she didn't want her brother to kill him. That was a good thing, Jasper's still groggy mind concluded. The rest of it was harder to understand. He leaned against the rock wall, not trusting his back to the youth. *Why do people keep trying to kill me!* He looked at Lake, her eyes on the brink of tears, and saw anger and sadness on her face.

"Where's Emmett?" Jasper asked after a moment.

"I don't know; I just woke up too." Lake said. Then she turned back to her brother, his arm held tightly in her grip.

"What am I going to do with you!?" she asked her brother in exasperation. He looked around with a straight face and shook his head.

"What's going on?" Emmett said, coming from around the rock face. He surveyed the scene. Jasper saw him study Lake, who looked furious and on the brink of tears at the same time, holding her brother's arm like her life depended on it. Then Emmett turned to Jasper. He knew he probably looked worse than death, his eyes wild and his hair worse. As Emmett looked at him, Jasper suddenly realized he had no pants on and feverishly put on the pair of jeans that were in the blanket.

"Jasper, my friend, what's got you so frazzled?" Emmett looked at Jasper's bed and saw the stone where his head had been. He looked up, surveying the mountainside to see where the rock had fallen from.

"It wasn't the mountain; it was him!" Jasper said. Emmett looked to get a defense from Lake, but she couldn't deny it.

The tall man slowly walked over to the boy, and when he reached him, he looked at Lake to release her prisoner. She did. He crouched down to the proud boy, making himself almost eye to eye with him. "You held that rock over Jasper's head?" The boy hesitated, but when Emmett repeated the question, he nodded his head. Emmett waited there until Cale met his eyes. When he did, he raised his hand. "High five!" All three of them were shocked. "You can hold up a rock that big! That's huge! That's pretty impressive, man!"

Jasper was about to object, but a wink from Emmett stopped his interruption. "Here's the thing, though. I am not going to hurt you or your sister. I promise. I also promise that Jasper won't hurt you or your sister. I will make sure of it." The boy didn't look convinced, but his attention was gained. "If I can trust you not to hurt him, I may even give you your knife back." He pulled up his shirt to reveal the knife he had taken the night before, which was now in a sheath made of tree bark attached to his belt. "I want to see what you can do with it." He smiled at Cale and Lake, and to Emmett's surprise, Cale smiled back.

"Do you promise not to try and hurt Jasper again?" Emmett asked. The boy nodded. "A promise is a very serious thing. Are you certain?" Cale nodded again, turning serious again. "Will you shake on it?" asked Emmett, offering his hand. Cale reached out cautiously and grasped Emmet's hand. "Good man," said Emmett, thumping Cale on the shoulder. He stood up and turned to the others with a smile and said, "Well, if that is settled, should we figure out something for breakfast?"

SIX

THE CURVED blade cut into the bark, sending splinters into Emmett's face. He struck again, carefully, creating a V shape in the bark. He looked at the boy sitting next to him, watching carefully, impatient to possess his knife again. Jasper sat on a tree stump a few yards away watching the two. Emmett gave the knife to the youth and showed him with his hand the direction that he wanted him to cut.

Although Jasper had little reason to trust Cale, seeing the peace of mind that Emmett had with him helped. In the morning light Jasper could make out more features of the young runaway. He had long dark hair with a little curl at the end like his sister's. He was thin but athletic looking and had a seriousness in his eyes that Jasper had never seen in someone so young. There was a deep sense of responsibility in those eyes, silent, but communicative.

Jasper's mind wandered from the pair continuing to slice the tree open in an effort to collect sap. He started to think of Lake, who they had left to rest her ankle at the camp. It seemed he kept catching himself thinking of her. Why? Jasper forced himself to change the route that thought was taking. He had caught many girls looking at him in the past, but the looks would lead to facial expressions that cut him deeply. Disgust was the worst, and those moments made him curse his ability.

He walked farther down the side of the crag that they had climbed, walking in the patches of light that streamed through the tree-studded hill to take advantage of the warmth. Once he found an especially warm beam, he stood in it and closed his eyes in the comfort it brought. *I'm free, in the wild, and...do I believe in a god?* He laughed at the absurdity that the last few days were. He would have never believed he would have wanted, or ever be convinced, to make any of the three a reality, but for some reason he didn't mind it anymore. In fact, he felt happier than he ever had. He was like one of those adventurers he saw in shows when he was a kid. Free, and fear—

Before his mind finished the word, he heard a horrible splintering sound. He ducked to the ground terrified. After a second of rustling, he poked his head from behind the rock he had hidden behind and saw the biggest rat he had ever seen, with oversized yellow teeth eating a limb off of fallen tree. He stepped closer and realized the oversized rat was actually a beaver. He stood to his full height, thankful the danger wasn't what he feared and that no one had been there to witness this fear. He stepped closer to the tree until the beaver noticed him. And then it scampered away, leaving the freed branch in pursuit of safety.

Jasper waited, watching the beaver waddle over the next hill. He looked at the stick that it had left. It was at least two inches in width throughout the whole of it and virtually straight as an arrow. Knowing there was going to be traveling ahead, he picked up the branch and tested its strength as he attempted to bend it over his knee. He was pleased and displeased at the same time to find out that the branch did more damage to his knee than his knee did to the branch. Rubbing the pain in his bruised leg, he walked back to find Emmett and Cale wedging a long sharp rock into the hole they had cut in the tree.

Emmett greeted him with a smile, and Cale somehow forgot to acknowledge his arrival. They were soon satisfied with their work and began the trek back to the rock face they called a temporary home. That morning they had discussed a plan. They would wait a couple of days to rest Lake's injured ankle before traveling to Umchin. Once there, the men could get supplies, and Lake and Cale could explain how she went for a walk and got lost in the night after being chased by some wild animal —or something along those lines. She wasn't quite sure how she was going to be received, but she knew that she would be in trouble if the Institution envoys were still there. Jasper thought about this as they walked and made an attempt at gaining the trust of her very protective brother.

"Cale?" Jasper said invitingly as they walked. "I found this." He held up the branch; the boy looked unimpressed. "Your sister may want to get around, and if you use your knife skills to clear the bark and make it smooth, she could use it as a walking stick." He stopped, offering the stick and all the credit with it to the boy. Cale thought for a moment, seemingly deciding between being obstinate or taking the opportunity to help his sister. The latter won over. He took the branch without any sign of thanks and broke into a trot to catch up to Emmett.

It was almost noon when they made it to the firepit. The camp was not how they had left it. The blankets had all been folded, the gear had been put away, and that five birds'-nest-looking piles of kindling for the fire had been stacked beside the rock face. The two men looked at each other inquisitively, then looked at the young woman sitting on the ground.

"Did you manage to find a river?" she asked. "We are out of water. It's at least a day to Umchin, so if we don't find any water we would have to leave now." She rose testing her ankle, which left her collapsing again as shooting pain answered her unsung question. Jasper looked at Cale who had begun skinning the branch of its bark. Emmett turned to Jasper concerned.

"Did you see anything around the bend? You've gone the farthest in that direction. Any signs of water? Even snow would be welcome."

"No, there were just more trees. The rocks get bigger, almost like shards of the mountain that broke off. I did see a beaver though."

Emmett's eyes lit up as did Cale's and Lake's. They all understood what Jasper had failed to connect.

Emmett began to gather their containers and some blankets into his freshly organized bag. Jasper, who was embarrassed by the fact he had to have Lake explain the connection between beavers and water did the same. By the time they had gathered the equipment to go in search of the water, Cale had already stripped the branch of twigs and bark and cut each end, making an almost perfect rod. He walked over to present the gift to his sister, who graciously tried it out. She smiled at her brother and caught him in an embrace before he could dodge it.

"Can you two hold down the fort here until we come back, or do you want one of us to stay?"

"We will be fine," she replied, smiling. Jasper felt caught in her gaze for a moment, forgetting what he had asked.

"Jasper!" Emmet called from almost halfway down the hill. Shaking his head, Jasper turned and began jogging down the hill, Lake's laughter following him.

They walked for a while in silence until they came to the tree that they had cut open. "There is no way we are going to get any sap from that tree," Emmett said.

"How long does it take?" Jasper asked.

"Normally weeks to have enough to actually eat, but this isn't a tree that you can tap so... never."

"Why did you do that then?" Jasper replied as he stuck his finger into the cut in the tree.

"Cale has this drive toward responsibility that I haven't seen before. He wants to adopt a job, be useful, and do what's right."

"Do what's right?" Jasper retorted.

"He is eleven years old. He's a kid, so he doesn't always know what to do or how to channel his energy in a positive direction. But look at how he protects his sister. He doesn't know anything about us, and he is willing to fight two men, both bigger and stronger, just to make sure she isn't mistreated. He sees how she looks at you and thinks of you as a bigger threat to her safety. That's why I've been trying to gain his trust and give him opportunities to use that drive in a positive way."

They continued on their way down the hill. *How she looks at me?* Jasper thought. Emmett had confirmed what he had noticed several times. He didn't know what it meant and was trying to figure it out when Emmett interrupted his thoughts.

"How is your courage?" he asked.

"I don't know what that means." Jasper had never been asked that before.

"How is your will to fight on in the face of adversity?"

Jasper thought about it. "Better than it has been. I'm becoming more at ease with this whole situation. I recognize that your 'father' is real. I tried talking to him, but I still wonder what is next." He paused for a moment as they moved past the fallen tree the beaver had been gnawing.

"Lead the way." Emmett gestured, since Jasper knew which direction the beaver had gone.

"Why weren't you scared in the room?" Jasper asked the question that had been on his mind since that night. "People show fear when they are handcuffed and led into an interrogation room. They show fear whether they are guilty or not. You didn't. Why?"

Emmett continued walking. "When I was called in to be questioned, I knew why. They had raided my house to find my Bible, and I had seen it on my security cameras while I was at the school. I didn't know what my punishment was going to be. I thought I might be printed, lose my job, and be forced to go to a rehab facility. I was prepared to accept it all. Even if they killed me, I was ready. I know where my future lies, and I know that my Father has a plan. If this was part of it, then so be it."

Jasper struggled with most of what he heard. "How could you accept that? They were going to take everything from you if you didn't go to rehab or put you in a psych ward labeling you crazy."

"There are worse things than death, Jasper. I believe that there is life beyond death, and I am certain of my place in that life. I'd rather die in the light of truth than live for self-preservation born of fear, dishonesty, and contempt."

Emmett let Jasper think about that for a moment as they came around a rocky outcropping.

"How do you know that you will go to this place?" Jasper asked.

"There's one thing that separates us from God, and that is something we call sin. Rejecting His values and believing the lie that we are something less than He said we are. We are born into this proclivity toward selfishness from the first human, which means we can't live up to the standard of perfection. That's where Jesus comes in."

"We read about him," Jasper said. "He was a teacher who fought for the oppressed against the religious and political authorities, right?"

"That's what the adversary would love for you to believe, but Christ wasn't just a teacher. He was the Son of God in the flesh, who came to take on the penalty of sin."

"What is the penalty?" Jasper asked, stopping to catch his breath.

"The penalty of sin is death. You know this. We all die, but some never truly live. How can you live fully when you are burdened with all your past mistakes and chained to your habit of sin? We were made to be in communion with God, but that line was broken when we acted against Him in disobedience. We were cut off from Him— the very author of life. But Christ came and lived the perfect life, never straying from the ultimate standard. He died the death that is our due, but He did not stay in the grave. He rose again after three days. Christ put death to death and paid the price that we may be made whole and enter again into communion with God. Christ offers new life to anyone who believes in Him. The life He offers is not one burdened by guilt or fear, but one of freedom, peace, and joy. That is what sustained me in that interrogation room. I knew that denying Christ is death both today and for eternity."

Jasper thought of his mother, his father, and his sister. He thought of how he had wronged them. He recalled the countless times he had suppressed his discomfort in condemning the Printed and how he had eventually bought the lie that it was for the good. He knew that he had felt the consequences in his soul and seen them in the shattered relationships that littered his life. In the end he had been left utterly alone. Maybe there was something to what Emmett was saying.

THEY HAD BEGUN to hear a sound. Not a roar, but a trickle accompanied by a light misty splash. They looked at each other pleased that their hopes were likely to be rewarded. They climbed over a few boulders and then through a crack in the stone to find a mountain riverbed, and down its middle flowed a steady trickle of water. They tracked the source of the trickle to another level in the rocky mountainside. There was a path laden with sticks and debris on the right moving up. The water disappeared into a hole in the wall. They followed the path up to the next level.

"Another dam," Emmett huffed in exasperated. True enough: they stood in front of a large pool of water fed by a small waterfall spring that came from a hole six feet above the water line. The waterfall made a pleasant sound as it poured steadily into the pool. To the left of the entryway was a mass of sticks and debris piled in no apparent order against the inside of the crevasse.

It was quiet, closed-in, and peaceful. All things that had been at a premium for them the last few days. Jasper looked at Emmett, still taking in the beauty of what was in front of him. Emmett drank it in as well, looking at the source of the pool. Jasper took off his pack and sat down on a rock beside the pool, and Emmett followed his lead.

"Thank you, Father," Emmett said, and Jasper wondered, *What did he have to do with this? Why was Emmett thanking him for the fact that they found this source of water and maybe even shelter?* He didn't know if it was a rude question to ask, but at this point he thought that the relationship he had built with Emmett could absorb any miscommunication of ill-will.

"Why did you thank him?" Jasper asked.

Emmett didn't answer immediately, seeming to phrase his answer carefully. "I thank Him for everything. I don't know if He had a direct hand in us finding this place, but being thankful isn't just saying thanks to people who provide something for you. It's a lifestyle, a constant choice of posture."

Jasper gave Emmett a look that he knew his friend would see as an invitation to explain what he was obviously confused about.

"The reason we all have an opportunity to have new life is because someone had to die. It had to be someone who had never done wrong, which meant the only candidate who could save us was the only one who didn't deserve to die. That's what my faith is based on. Not the list of rules that your textbooks have talked about. Not the teaching of people in the old times who killed people who didn't believe what they did. Not at all. Christianity is based on a few simple truths."

Simplicity—that would be refreshing, Jasper thought.

"There is a problem," Emmett continued. "Humans are selfish, and this causes us to act in ways we weren't originally created to. The wages of sin are death, which means anyone who acted in this was condemned to death. The one who hasn't acted in this was Jesus, the Son of God, sent to take the sins of the world. Because He never sinned, He reversed what had been done by the first human when He died for us."

Jasper nodded his head, the point becoming clearer.

"But it doesn't end there, because if it ended just with Him dying, then we could have no hope that we could have new life. After three days Jesus rose to life again, and there is more evidence for that fact than there is evidence for the existence of most world leaders at that time. It's because of that death that I try to live with a posture of thanksgiving, because I know what He has done is worth my gratitude."

"Why haven't I learned any of this?" Jasper asked Emmett.

"You went up through the State's schooling system, correct?" Jasper nodded. "Twenty years ago, there was an attempt at equality within the curriculum public schools were teaching. They wanted to teach religious history but wanted to teach all religions equally. This was a problem because they found that faiths are not equal. There were ones that condone killing gay people, beating women, and threatening death to anyone who doesn't convert. They decided to eliminate whatever religious history was already included because they couldn't agree on a curriculum. This means everyone goes through school with no sign that religion has ever had an influence on the world."

"That's how I was brought up."

Emmett gave him a sympathetic smile. "How are you doing?" he asked.

Jasper smiled. "Good. It's a lot to think about."

Emmett rose, and it looked like he was about to go to the pool, but he reached out a hand to Jasper. He took it and found himself embraced by the big man. There was no awkwardness about the embrace. In fact, it felt like Emmett had become the brother, father, and best friend that Jasper had never known.

They didn't linger long at the pool, knowing they needed to get water back to their camp. As they discussed the potential of moving their camp closer to the water, they filled all their containers with the water flowing from the mountain. The water was cold, very cold, chilling Jasper's back as they left the spring.

When they arrived back at the camp, Lake was breaking sticks and creating a pile of wood next to her. Every time they had come back to the camp, they had found it more organized than they had left it. Her brother was sitting, diligently carving on the wooden staff for his sister. They both noticed Emmett's and Jasper's arrival, but Lake was the only one to acknowledge it.

"You took a long time. No luck?" she asked, swiveling on the log she was sitting on.

The men set down their bags with a thud in answer to her question. They brought out containers of water, and Emmett nudged Jasper to go and give one to Cale.

Jasper whispered his reply. "But he has a stick. You really want me to get close to him?"

Lake laughed audibly. Jasper eventually relented.

A little later, Jasper looked back at the two others crouched together as if they were filming a nature documentary. Emmett was whispering to Lake, who was struggling to keep her laughter at a moderate level not to spook the show.

"Right over there," Emmett's exaggerated Australian accent was barely audible as he leaned toward Lake. "That's a wild Cale. Dangerous when angered, and quick as a tiger with a knife." He wasn't making Jasper any more comfortable with the idea, and he continued his commentary.

"But the noble Jasper will continue his quest to cure camp dehydration even if it costs him his life." Jasper shook his head violently at the assumption and hesitated once again. "Valiant Jasper needs to hurry as the wild Cale is preoccupying his knife with a task instead of hunting for skinny tall males of the same species."

Jasper rolled his eyes and walked to the boy busily carving the rod and offered him the screw-top plastic bottle. Cale looked at the bottle, then turned his mind back to whittling the handle of the long stick. He could still hear Emmett's continued nature-show parody.

"Unlucky for the young Jasper; his offering was less than acceptable to the proud lad. Maybe if he was to connect with him in a more creative way, he could bridge the gap of pride and prejudice."

Jasper looked back to Emmett and Lake, both grinning and waving their hands for him to go on and try something else. He took a deep breath and crouched down to Cale's level to give it another try.

"So, I see that you took all the bark off the branch. That's pretty...cool."

He heard a slap behind him and looked back to see Emmett's palm smash against his own forehead. Lake was about to die if she kept her laughter in any longer. "It is appropriate to note that valiant Jasper is still a work in progress." Emmett finished in the accent. Jasper set the bottle next to the boy and returned to the two, who were now laughing together.

AFTER MUCH DEBATE, Lake convinced Emmett that she could walk well enough with the freshly crafted staff that they could make it to the protected pool in the mountain. Emmett had looked to Jasper for help, but it had become apparent that he would not get any. At first Jasper didn't say anything, but he liked the dammed spring and thought making it their base could be better than having to walk over there daily to get water. He also liked the idea of being able to wash at least part of his body. He had never gone a day without showering, and in his current state after days of travel on foot, he was desperate. Eventually he'd expressed his support of changing locations, which had earned him a skeptical look from Emmett.

It was midday when they convinced him. They collectively packed the camp, taking what firewood they could, and began the trek around the east side of the mountain face. Lake hobbled on the ankle, putting most of the weight of each step on the staff. It wasn't fast going, but before an hour had passed, they had climbed the last bit of rocks opening up to the dirt path that took them into the mountainside.

At every step, outcropping, and rock, Cale was in front of Lake the whole way. He provided no opportunity for Jasper to help her up as he would shimmy up whatever obstruction was there and use all his strength to help his sister up the hill. Lake, who gave a show of thanks, grew more concerned that he would cause them both to fall if one of them lost their balance for a moment.

Jasper and Emmett walked in front, leading the way. They didn't talk much besides the occasional acknowledgment of a certain bird or tree. More times than Jasper thought was funny Emmett took the opportunity to point at a hole in the ground and declare it the home of a deadly snake or spider. Coincidently this happened only when Jasper was standing right over or on top of it, causing him to dance back from it.

After one of these clever moments, Jasper looked back to check on the siblings behind him. "Has he spoken to you yet?" Jasper asked the big man.

"Not a word," Emmett answered. "Do you think he is a mute?"

"No, Lake said it's hard to get him to shut up sometimes. She didn't seem like she was kidding, but I haven't seen any sign that he can."

Emmett began to let the conversation fade, then looked down at Jaspers feet and exclaimed, "Snake!"

Jasper looked down, uncaring of the embarrassment of falling for the joke again. He jumped up, almost losing his balance and falling down the hill. There was in fact a snake by his feet slithering into a bush to his right. Once he found his footing, he skittered to the other side of the path. Emmett stepped closer, identifying the species of snake.

"Is it poisonous?" Jasper wheezed.

"Oh, yes. And there's one thing that's unique about them." Emmett got closer to the bush where the snake was and motioned for Jasper to come closer. Once he got as close as he possibly could, Emmett whispered to him, "They hunt in pairs."

In that moment Emmett threw the rock he was playing with behind his back into the bush behind Jasper, causing him to jump higher than Emmett thought was possible and fly up the mountainside, leaving two and a half laughing voices behind him. After finishing her fit of laughter, Lake drew her gaze to Emmett.

"Was it really poisonous?"

Emmett, still laughing, shook his head.

"Poor guy, that was too easy."

The three of them rounded the bend that opened to the pool after another hundred yards of hiking. Lake was amazed at the pool, and after seeing his sister safely to the ground, Cale left to scout. When they arrived, they found Jasper casually sitting by the bank washing his hands and feet in the water. His hair was wet and showed signs that it had been cleansed as well. He made a quick remark about how they took so long, and how the reason he ran off was because he wanted to ensure that no other travelers or bears had inhabited the area. Emmett and Lake collectively endured his farse.

After unpacking gear and food, the group split off on different errands. Emmett left to continue past the closed cove and look for berries and other edible foods. He had advised Lake to put her ankle in the icy cold water and to take it out at intervals. Cale's job was to take an empty pack and search for rocks to build a firepit. Jasper's job seemed menial to him. Help Lake with whatever she needed. He didn't know if this was Emmett's idea of another joke, but he endured it.

He enjoyed talking with Lake. She didn't have the same edge that most women showed when talking to him. She was transparent, genuine, and unafraid of what he might read on her face. That was refreshing to a human lie detector. She was also pretty, very pretty. Something he had noticed immediately. Something that her little psycho brother had noticed that he noticed. Knowing this, he viewed his job with a note of professionalism. Helpful, but not overly enthusiastic.

When Cale had disappeared above them and Lake had begun forcing her swollen ankle into the frigid crystal-clear water, Jasper let his mind wander to the earlier conversation with Emmett. What a thing to not fear death. All he had done in his life was to ensure his own comfort and convenience. He had pursued a solid, safe job that would keep him employed and relatively well off. His only hobbies were safe and mundane, things that would never add any risk to his life. He had perpetually lived to not die, and here was this man who was the opposite.

Emmett didn't fear death. Somehow that fact seemed to make him more alive—if that was possible. Jasper still hadn't read fear on his face, though they had been through enough frightening moments to last a lifetime in just a few days. Jasper couldn't help but laugh when he suddenly realized that everything that had happened in the last few days stood in such stark contrast to every life decision he had made to that point. Perhaps Emmett was rubbing off on him.

"I know where my future lies, and that is more influential than whatever my circumstances are." Emmett's message came back to Jasper's mind in waves. Jasper could feel his suspicions about what Emmett was proposing falling away. What was alarming to him was that he was realizing how deeply he wanted whatever Emmett had. He didn't want his fear of death to prevent him from living. He closed his eyes and whispered that same thought to thin air, hoping that whoever had pulled the Juggler from his mind could hear his silent call.

He stood there with his eyes closed for a moment until something hit his face. He wiped the wetness with his hands and looked at Lake, who had guilt written all over her face as she smiled at him.

"What were you doing?" she asked, as he walked over to her, shaking off the remaining water.

"I was talking to someone."

"The same person that Emmett has talked to?"

Jasper smiled. "Yes." He was glad that he didn't have to explain names, and that she only inquired if it was the same person that she had heard Emmett talk to the night before.

She reached in the water to splash him again. It was very warm for fall, but Jasper was not interested in getting wet until there was a fire to retreat to. He dodged the splash easily. Lake tried again, and he evaded the water again. She paused her onslaught as something above him caught her attention.

"Cale, be careful!" she yelled up at her brother, who was twenty feet above the pool with a pack full of rocks. "Why are you up there?" Lake called up again. The boy didn't answer with words but held up a softball size rock, just one of the rocks he had collected from the ridge above where the spring flowed from the mountain. Lake, throwing her hands up in exasperation, used this last moment to try and splash Jasper while he was watching Cale nervously. He heard the splash and was able to move out of the way of most of it, which made him feel pretty good about himself. Lake rolled her eyes and then offered him her hands, inviting him to help her up. He warily walked over to where she sat and looked into her large brown eyes as he grasped her hands to help her to her feet. There was something in those eyes. Something that sounded a silent alarm in his head. By the time he had seen it, it was too late.

Lake turned sharply and flexed her arms, pulling Jasper into the water with her. The shock was unreal as their bodies were submerged in the water. The pool wasn't deep, but it was difficult for them to get back on their feet and return their heads to the surface. When they came up, Jasper was standing on the bottom with his shoulders clearing the water line. Lake, who was only a couple of inches shorter than Jasper was standing as well, albeit less comfortably as her chin rested on the water. Jasper's surprise turned to fury, but that melted as he looked at the girl's smiling face. She smiled guiltily back at him, and there was a hint of something he hadn't seen on a girl's face trained on him before. DESIRE His mind struggled to connect the meaning, and in that time, she gave a quick laugh that made her eyes light up. Jasper was at a loss. He suddenly forgot the cold of the water. She took a hop forward toward the bewildered man so their faces were a foot away from each other. Time stood still. Jasper could feel his heart beating, his mind scrambling for what to do.

As they were caught in slow motion, they glimpsed something flying just over their heads. Not a bird, but something much bigger. Time regained its speed as they saw Cale flying past and crashing into the water at the base of the pile of sticks and mud keeping the integrity of the pool.

"Cale!" Lake shrieked waiting for him to surface from the water. Something was wrong. Jasper felt the water around his feet hiccup, and an undertow formed. The dam had been dislodged, and water had started pouring out of it. Panic gripped Jasper's heart as he lost his balance in the immediate surge of current. He fought it leaning back. He saw the panic in Lake's eyes and looked to where she directed her eyes. Cale still hadn't resurfaced. Feeling his panic and chill swept away, he grabbed Lake by the waist and threw her toward the bank, where she scrambled the rest of the way onto the shore.

Before she could say anything else, Jasper was gone. Under the water line, Jasper swam toward the collapsing dam, the water spearing him on. He came up for air just before where he had seen Cale land and dove his head down. He felt something struggle under his hand and opened his eyes to see, in the midst of white-wash bubbles, Cale struggling to pull himself from the hole in the structure. He faced Jasper, making it difficult for him to push himself against the current. Jasper dove down, wedging himself between the youth and the wall of sticks. He tried to push the youth out, but the current was strong enough to keep both of them under now. Feeling Cale's struggling falter, Jasper set his back against the sharp beaver-chewed logs and the ground and pushed the youth up with all his strength, feeling the wooden spears dig mercilessly into his back.

He felt the weight of the youth lifted, but the water continued to push him down into the ground and farther into the wood that had cut into his body in several places. The water pounded his chest as it ran, forcing his remaining breath to flow up in thankless bubbles. Is *this it?* he wondered. He tried pushing against the ground, but the gravity-induced water kept him seated between branches and the hard rocky floor. He attempted to spin but the spear-like wooden rods cut deeper making him want to scream.

He sat. Waiting. Waiting for his lungs to be starved enough to inhale the inviting flow of water. He concentrated, not knowing what to do. It seemed like an eternity. His limbs became stiff. He couldn't discern whether it was the cold or his body shutting down. Maybe he was already drowning, and he didn't feel himself take on water. He gave one more attempt at lifting, but his exhausted, malnourished body had had enough. He felt that he was finally beginning to understand this Father Emmett spoke of.

Closing his eyes, he brought his mind to bear. He reached out with his thoughts, calling out in his mind. *Father, I give myself to You! Let Your will be done.* A wave of peace flowed through him.

Jasper waited for the dark to come. The slow, slipping from reality that he had read in stories that depicted death. When it came, he was surprised at how it felt. It was like he was traveling up through a substance that he could barely feel. He felt a wave go over him that crept down his face to his shoulders. It melted down to his waist, and he took a breath. This pricked his mind. *Is there breathing in death?* He had never really thought about it before. It wasn't easy to breath in death.

Suddenly something touched him, and sharp pain exploded in his back. *There's pain in death too. What a rip off.* He thought, knowing it was ridiculous. He felt his body being moved and his face touched. Like a thunderbolt, light exploded into his eye. The beings he saw didn't match with his expectations either. First of all, it was a girl, something that Emmett was definitely wrong about. Light burst into his other eye, and he saw the mystical beings of the afterlife again, only this being was young, male, and breathing heavily.

Jasper blinked, looked again at the beings staring down at him. Bringing what he saw into focus, he realized the identities of the two individuals. He tried to sit up, but pain leaped up his spine, causing him to crash back, which invited two more jolts of pain into his back. One in his side and another in the adjacent shoulder blade. Reality returned quickly. He breathed out through his mouth hard, almost panting.

"Jasper, can you hear me?" he heard Lake ask, but his ears barely made out the sound. He shook his head, shaking out some of the water in his ears.

"Jasper!" Lake cried out, embracing his body as it lay on the bank of what had been a pool but was now barely a creek. Her embrace felt nice, except when her crying moved him enough to irritate one of the wounds in his back. He kept himself from crying out in fear she would step away. He looked at Cale, fearful of his response to her embrace, but what was on his face wasn't anger or contempt. Cale sat looking at him, his chest heaving, and his face apologetic to the point of tears.

Jasper closed his eyes, remembering his silent words spoken in the water. He opened them, looking at the sky, realizing his commitment and conversion. Tears began to stream from his eyes, and with his mouth contorting from emotion, he said, "Thank You, Father."

SEVEN

EMMETT BEGAN to run when he saw the empty pool that had reverted to a streambed. Seeing the three by the edge, he dropped the small bundle he was carrying and rushing to them. Lake welcomed his arrival as she was tearing strips of cloth from Jasper's extra shirt for something.

"What happened? Are you okay?" Emmett inquired, bending down to investigate.

"Splendid," Jasper responded in a very Emmett-like fashion.

The big man acknowledged what he was going for and awaited an answer to the first question as he looked at Jasper's back.

"I did it." Jasper said to the big man.

"Did what?"

"I gave my life to God," he said, hoping his verbiage was correct.

Emmett's eyes welled with tears, and he embraced the younger man. Jasper winced at the embrace, causing Emmett to flinch back. Lake was dabbing Jasper's wet shirt against a gash in the middle of his back. His shirt, which was a dark blue had become soaked with blood, and Emmett noticed two other punctures in his back that were blood stained, although neither bled as profusely as the one in the middle.

Lake and Emmett piled the sticks together with one of the premade fire-starting kindling nests Lake had made and soon had the beginnings of a fire started.

"Let's get him bandaged and by the fire. You and Cale too."

She nodded and was about to go back to tearing more strips, but Emmett stopped her.

"Tell me everything I need to know about Christ," Jasper said. "I have given Him my life, now what do I do?"

"There will be plenty of time for that tomorrow," Emmet said. "Now you need to rest."

As the fire began to burn brightly, Emmett spent time getting it large enough to warm the three wet bodies. The shade of the mountains crept toward the group, taking the little warmth the sun had provided. His biggest concern was getting Jasper warm. He had lost some blood, and he seemed to be more in shock than the others. After pulling him as close to the fire as he could, Emmett took the strips of cloth that Lake had prepared, snatched some blackened coals from the fire, and snuffed them into the middle of each strip, creating a trio of blackened, charcoal-filled bandages that he tied tightly around Jaspers back. After they were all in place, Emmett helped replace Jasper's shirt with the one he had been given when they were at his house. By now, Cale had placed a few dozen fist-size stones around the fire, insulating the heat and shielding it from the wind.

As the sun went down, they stayed huddled around the fire. Emmett and Cale were the only ones to stray from its light to get more wood. After Jasper was taken care of and he had checked the large bruising red spot on Cale's leg where he dislodged the rock below the waterline, Emmett remembered the bundle he had dropped when he first returned. He brought it back and handed the small bag to the three who were seated quietly, no one willing to break the silence. Jasper opened it to find the sack full of blackberries. Some were riper than others, but they passed the bag around, grateful for anything at all. Knowing how skinny Jasper was, and that he needed the nutrition, Emmett insisted that Jasper take his share.

There didn't seem to be a specific reason for the silence, but Jasper couldn't find anything that he wanted to say. He knew that he didn't like the melancholy that had fallen over the camp but didn't know how to break it. He looked to Emmett, who returned his gaze, awaiting a question.

When none came, he took the initiative in a very "Emmett" way.

"Jasper, when you were down at the bottom"—Jasper immediately regretted where the conversation was going, and he braced for many questions he didn't want to answer—"did you see any of the beavers? Like, did you have time to chat and maybe apologize for what you did? It was really quite rude when you think about it."

Jasper smiled. "No, they had the sense to get out of there."

The conversation flowed freely from there, lingering in jest. Wondering about how it all happened from the perspective of the beavers. One thing was certain. They all needed to stay away from dams.

Soon Jasper and Cale were curled up in their blankets close to the fire. Emmett and Lake sat quietly. Every night Emmett spent time alone talking to his Father, but this evening, Lake had stayed up as well, staring aimlessly into the fire. Emmett, who was already covered in his blanket, decided to talk silently instead of disturbing the group by leaving, and as he closed his eyes, a voice arrested his attention. It was quiet but clear. It sounded like someone was whispering. He opened his eyes to investigate and saw for a brief moment Jasper's mouth moving. Emmett smiled and listened carefully to hear what he was saying just in time to catch the last few words.

"Thank You, Father." Jasper said, concluding his whispered prayer. Emotion pulled a tear from Emmett's eye as he turned his head to the sky and whispered, "Yes, Father. Thank You."

Emmett opened his eyes to see that Lake had switched her attention from the fire to him. Though she'd offered a few clever remarks during the evening, she still seemed in a daze.

"Who is this person that you and Jasper talk to?" she asked. Jasper, hearing her question, had his attention pricked by her inquiry. He fought off sleep waiting for his friend's answer.

"My Father is God and the creator of the universe. He is not like the gods of old times. He is not made by human hands. He is not made to reflect the passions and desires of man. He is the Alpha and the Omega, the beginning and the end. He is not swayed, and He does not change."

Jasper snuck a look at Lake, who was following along without signs of sarcasm.

"He reveals himself by His creation; everything around us is evidence of His power and purpose. He reveals Himself in the writings of the Holy Scriptures. Lastly, and my favorite way He exhibits Himself, He has relationship and communion with us. He works in us, changing us in ways that are evident." Emmett stopped there, letting it sink in.

After a few seconds, Emmett offered a question to Lake. Lake thought for a while. Jasper fought sleep harder than ever, but the day's events had exhausted him. He struggled against the way sleep was stealing his consciousness, trying to hear her answer.

"Jasper," she said, struggling to get the word out.

This pricked his ears, and he struggled to make out her reasoning as he faded into sleep.

"The one thing I noticed about Jasper constantly was that he is scared of everything. Today, something switched in him. When he had the most right to be scared, there was no fear. I froze when Cale hit the water, and I'm not afraid of much. But Jasper acted. He pushed me onto the bank and dove in after Cale." She began to cry, and Jasper could hear the tears in her voice. "Jasper changed, or something changed him. The only thing that seemed to be the difference is this 'father' of yours. We were never taught about whoever he is on the reservation. Only about our traditions, but none of them changed anyone like that." She sniffled. "I want to know who did that, and ask if he can do the same to me." Jasper's sleep finally won over as the last sounds he heard were the crackling of the fire and Lake's declaration.

THE NEXT MORNING Jasper woke up to the sound of the crackling fire reignited after the long dark night. Rolled tightly in his blanket as usual, it took quite an effort to sit up. When he tried, stabbing pains in his back immediately reminded him of the previous day's encounter, and he was forced back down on the ground. He felt hands on him as he surveyed the camp. There was Lake who had come to his side following his ungraceful attempt at sitting up.

"Easy. Take it easy," she said as she began to unroll the tightly wrapped blanket. Something caught her attention, and she suddenly stopped. "Are you wearing pants this time?" Jasper blushed. She laughed, a resonant but light sound that made Jasper's embarrassment almost worth it. Almost.

"I don't know what it is, but I cannot sleep in pants!"

She laughed again and turned away, allowing him to slowly and painfully replace his pants, which he had pushed to the bottom of the blanket before falling asleep.

When he was dressed, he allowed Lake to help him sit up. There was no one else at the camp. Lake anticipated Jasper's question after noticing him looking around.

"Cale and Emmett went looking for more berries. My ankle is still swollen, and you may be in worse travel shape than I am."

"How many days do you think it will take to get to your home?" Jasper asked, taking one of the fist-size rocks lining the fire into his hands. The rock was very warm, but not hot enough to burn his hands. He held it to his side, where one of the punctures was, hoping the warmth would soothe the intense soreness the shooting pain had left behind.

"It took us less than a day to get in this vicinity. Cale and I watched you two at your camp for a while before trying to nick some of your food." She winced at her admission. "Sorry about that by the way."

Jasper acknowledged the apology. His quick mind came up with a response, but he didn't know if he wanted to step forward into it.

"It was worth it to hear your singing." He tried again. "I mean... the way that you can sing, I've never heard anything like it." Flirting, if that was his intention, was surely not his strong suit.

Jasper realized that his problem was that he didn't even know if it was his intention. He was about to clarify, but Lake came closer.

"Thank you." She put a hand on the side of Jasper's face and kissed his lips softly.

Jasper felt that sudden warmth return. He wondered if maybe he was very good at flirting and just hadn't known it.. Lake, who was on her knees, hugged him then, holding him as he struggled to keep upright. It hurt, but he didn't care for the moment. His mind wandered without order or pattern. Her hair had a pleasing scent to it. His thoughts turned to a picture of what would happen if Cale and Emmett came back at this moment. That thought was alarming, but only half as much as the last notion that brought him back to reality. *She kissed me. That's the first time I've ever kissed anyone.* Jasper was surprised that it took three bouts with death in order to be kissed by a girl. The circumstances were abnormal to say the least. She trembled for a moment and said something into his shoulder.

"I'm so sorry. This wouldn't have happened if I hadn't—"

Jasper interrupted her with another squeeze. She released her arms around his back and looked at him, tears in her eyes ready to fall, based on what he was going to say.

"I guess it was the push I needed. God works in mysterious ways."

THE NEXT TWO days were uneventful—a welcome peace as they recuperated and prepared for the journey to Umchin. They had decided it was their best opportunity to lay low until they found another plan. Jasper tried to seem pragmatic about going to Umchin, but if he was honest with himself, there was another reason for going there outside the bounds of safety. If Emmett suspected an ulterior motive, he was doing a good job of concealing it.

Emmett and Lake would change and wash Jasper's bandages morning and night applying fresh charcoal and checking for infections. Morning and night Emmet would tell Jasper the stories of Scripture, and Jasper would listen hungrily. Day by day he grew in faith and in strength. By the second day he had been able to walk around with little difficulty. He was sore to be sure, but his mobility wasn't severely hindered by his pain.

The next morning, after his wounds had been checked, Cale returned with another sack of blackberries. He set them down and then proceeded to the beaver dam, where he began pulling out thick sticks several feet in length. The boy stuck them in the ground, forming a diamond. After driving them down with a rock, he stepped back twenty or so feet and cast the rock at the beaver-chewed branches rising out of the earth. He hit one of them, grabbed another stone, and repeated the process. Emmett stood and took up a rock to play the game with him. It was a good game, and eventually they began to wager with the berries that were their main source of food. Whoever won the contest would get first pick of the berries brought back, leaving the loser, or losers, to suffer the more sour treats.

Cale continued to be a mystery to Jasper and Emmett. He had continually refused to say anything; however, the hawk-like glare that he had directed toward Jasper had faded since the event with the dam. His apparent fury and righteous defensiveness regarding his sister also seemed to have been washed away in the frigid waters. Cale's invention of the game had introduced some humanity to the boy, who before had seemed to want himself perceived only as a cold, robotic bodyguard.

BY THE THIRD day after the beaver-dam incident, the group had started to get anxious to be on their way. Lake had grown more confident walking with the aid of her staff, and Jasper had healed enough that none of his punctures were in danger of opening. They planned to leave the following day early in the morning and anticipated a hot meal when they arrive at Umchin. Lake assured them that they would be accepted back without any problems and that they could probably stay as long as they wanted. They agreed and prepared for the journey for the rest of the day.

Just before sundown, Cale pounded the wood logs into the ground again to start another game. The activity had become a common pastime, besides gathering berries and telling stories about their past lives. The game had no name, so it was always initiated by Cale setting up the wood and then looking at the others to play. Emmett obliged him and following him; Lake stood to join her brother in the game. Emmett looked at Jasper who was tending the fire to see if he wanted to play. Before he could say a word, Jasper heard a voice that definitely wasn't Emmett's.

"Come play Bad Berries, Jasper!"

The voice came from someone young who was using the deepest voice he could. Emmett and Jasper turned to Cale, who was holding out a rock for Jasper to take. Shocked, Jasper rose to take up the rock that was offered. He looked at the boy, who had been mute since they had met him. Jasper took the rock from Cale, but it was more than an invitation to play a formerly nameless game. It was the only apology that the boy could muster, and it was enough for Jasper. They took their mark behind the line Cale had made, all taking turns attempting to knock over the most sticks in two throws to avoid the Bad Berries.

EMMETT WAS ALWAYS the first to wake up, so he had the responsibility of waking everyone else to start the march of the day. They all filled up whatever containers they had with water and began down the side of the mountain. Climbing down the rock-strewn paths was uncomfortable, but the hike got easier as they got closer to the bottom. Lake seemed to be handling the hiking well, keeping pace with her brother and Emmett easily, with little show of discomfort. Jasper shrugged the soreness away as he walked, but occasionally he would have to balance himself, engaging some of the torn and damaged muscles in his back, which reminded him that he wasn't completely healed.

Lake took the lead when they got to the broken fence that Jasper remembered from the way up and took them north. The weather had turned colder, and they all felt the brisk wind they had avoided during their time in the spring-made mountain crack.

There was little chatter as they walked. It wasn't that they were afraid of being picked up by microphones or drones; they just didn't feel the need to talk. Jasper's mood was uplifted. Since the interaction with Lake, he had felt almost giddy. He didn't let himself think about the long-term implications of the kiss or the affection and side-long glances they had shared during the last few days. But he felt lighter and somehow more alive. Emmett had noticed the change in Jasper, though he didn't say anything outright. He preferred to let Jasper read his face and tended to use that as a form of nonverbal communication.

Their pace was consistent and quick for about five hours, but as the day drew on Lake seemed less and less confident that she knew the way to go. Jasper started to wonder how accurately she could retrace her steps the night she left, given the fact that it was night the whole time. They stopped and had a rest, berries as usual at hand. Emmett and Jasper attempted to draw out details that Lake could remember about the hills around her, and they finally set off again in a more northeasterly direction. They were banking on the description of Umchin as a tree-covered valley, thinking it must just be farther up the mountain range instead of on the other side of the lower hills. Soon their gamble paid off, and within an hour Lake became excited as she noticed landmarks she recognized. Cale hadn't said anything since his performance at the camp that indicated he was capable, but he too became restless as he saw more and more familiar sights.

They marched up a shrub-studded hill to find a dirt and gravel road stretching back into the mountains. Jasper and Emmett looked at each other.

"It might not be a good idea to be so visible to people driving this road. We're all looking a little disreputable," Emmett said, glancing nervously up and down the road. "Someone might think we're dangerous and call the authorities."

"This road is hardly used," Lake replied, easing their anxiety. "Umchin is almost completely self-sustaining, and people don't often have any need to leave it."

After crossing the road, Jasper felt the coolness that accompanies entrance into the woods. Trees quickly surrounded them, and the smell of pine and cedar wafted in the autumn breeze.

Lake, assured of the direction, broke the silence as the sun began to touch the edge of the horizon, creating an orange glow in the ceiling of clouds. "We don't have much here, but the community is close. Most of our families have lived in the valley for generations. I just hope they won't be too mad that I left."

A strange smell began to drift in their direction, replacing the fresh cedar and pine scent with the odor of decay. Lake and Cale didn't seem to think anything of it, leaving Jasper to assume that they were simply downwind of a dead animal.

Lake continued her description of home, laying out a picture of a community of single-story homes surrounding a lively town center. "We'll go in through a gate," she said. "There's a low fence surrounding the reservation, but it's more to mark the edges of our land. It wouldn't provide any kind of protection."

Suddenly, Jasper remembered hearing chatter about potential plans for a new military facility, and he realized that this tribal land was on the list of likely spots. They were looking for a place that would be difficult to attack from the air, making a valley in a major mountain range prime real estate for a multifunctional weapons depot. Jasper let the memory fade as the smell grew thicker. More than the smell of a lone dead animal, the smell was of earth, ore, and moisture-saturated trees.

Lake and Cale together picked up their pace as they climbed a sharp ridge. Emmett and Jasper had to jog in order to reach the top the same time Lake did. As Jasper reached the top of the ridge overlooking the valley, he heard a muffled scream and saw Lake, still as stone, a whisper escaping her motionless body. Suddenly she began to crumple, and Jasper reacted, catching her before she fell. He surveyed the valley and immediately saw why she was distressed. What was once a valley in the mountain range was now a lake.

Jasper's back screamed as his muscles worked to support Lake. The call from his aching body was dwarfed by the cry Lake unleashed. Her voice came out as a single note and grew to a forceful crescendo that cascaded off the valley's amphitheater-like walls of rock, coming back to the group in a harmony of agony. She began to cry, shaking as Jasper held her. Cale still stood solitary, unblinking at the sight. On the edges of the valley, tall trees lay uprooted and flattened, half-buried in mud and sediment. A hundred-yard lake filled the middle of what was once Umchin, dark enough to disallow any sign of structure beneath it. Water had come from one direction, flattened all in its path. Then left receding in the ground beneath and through small, newly formed streams down the way it came.

Emmett had approached Cale placing his hand on the boy's shoulder. With a brief shake, Cale instinctively tried to dislodge the man's hand, but he quickly succumbed and retreated to the big man in a tearful embrace. Lake did no such thing. Her eyes were fixed on her home, blinking as if it would end the nightmare. The sun lingered, its light illuminating the ridges of the valley's walls, offering its homily to the group standing and sitting on the edge of the ridge, or so it seemed to Jasper. He held Lake tighter now, his body joining her in her trembling as he understood this tragedy's origin. Like many times before, his eyes met Emmett's, both pairs laden with tears, realizing the nightmare was just beginning.

EIGHT

JASPER AND EMMETT picked their way down the mountain toward the unrecognizable reservation, steeling themselves for what they would find. Lake stumbled as her staff was less reliable going down the mountainside. The newly formed lake grew as they approached, seeming to emit its chill, grim apology to its former inhabitants. Lake grasped Jasper's arm as she walked down, leaving Cale to take the lead. The boy scampered down the slope to where the rocky ground met the sediment. Jasper watched him jog on top of the mud. He ran for about fifty yards, but as Jasper helped Lake step down a rock, he heard a surprised yell. Swiveling toward the sound, he realized the boy who'd been running across the sediment was gone.

"Cale!" Lake yelled, but Emmett was already running toward the spot where he was last seen.

Lake and Jasper ran as fast as they could to the spot.

"Hold it!" Emmett called, flinging his hands out. "If you come to the edge, come slowly. He is okay."

Jasper and Lake crept toward where Emmett was standing, and looked down to see the sorely offended Cale sitting down, rubbing his bruised leg. The boy was ten feet down from where they're standing. Surrounding him was what looked like a tunnel that stretched into the dark in opposite directions.

Emmett turned on his flashlight to examine the hole. "When whatever flood happened, it must have brought in all this dirt and mud and then receded making pockets of air under the surface." Jasper looked at him quizzically and was going to make a comment, but given the mood, he resisted. There were distinct stream marks in the bottom of each streambed. "Whatever caused this much flooding was enormous, and some of it left as fast as it came."

Jasper put his arm around Lake as she quivered at Emmett's explanation. "Are there any rivers nearby?" Jasper asked her.

Still under the effects of shock, it took her a while to reply.

"Yes. The Snake River." Her eyes widened. "Do you think this could have been caused by the dam?"

Jasper shot a glance at Emmett, who returned it with concern. He didn't show any sign of answering the question as he began looking for a way for Cale to get out, leaving Jasper to manufacture an answer.

"It could be. But the Evergreen dam is pretty far away. I don't think it could reach this far even if it completely gave way." Emmett shot him a look, not of anger, but of sadness. Jasper put a mental pin in it, saving it for a later, more private conversation.

"Evergreen dam?" Lake responded, not recognizing the name. "No, the closest dam is the crest..." She struggled for a moment at the name.

"Cresthill dam?" Jasper finished. He knew generally where it was, but it was a small dam that made a reservoir half the size of the Evergreen. It was downstream from the Evergreen dam, making it probable that there was a domino effect of overwhelming force creating a gravity powered inland tsunami that leveled the reservation and likely other towns and farms along the way.

"That's it. I have only seen it once, but I think it's the only one close to here." She looked at Emmett, returning to the brink of tears. "Do you think it broke and could have caused this?"

He didn't want to confirm her fear that a lightning-fast torrent of water had destroyed her town and likely everyone in it with no warning, no room for escape, but from everything that he could see, it was true. He gave an answer that someone had given him at one point.

"Hard to know," he said, trying to show his compassion in the phrase that had once made him very cross. She didn't seem too put off by it, but another pang of guilt stabbed Jasper's gut. He wanted to tell her, but fear of her reaction overcame his remorse. Lake let the topic go and looked around as if she was trying to figure out where she was in her home.

Emmett supplied Cale with his flashlight to see if there was any debris he could use to climb back up. Cale walked around under the ceiling of caked mud. He found a perforated metal pole leaning diagonally that disappeared back into the wall of mud, and after much pulling, and a spot of digging, he was able to free it. The pole was actually a street sign.

"Walluca Street," Cale called up to Lake, whose mind was retreating out of shock, a hard decision brewing in her brain. One that she never thought she would have to make. The moon was full, though it was little consolation.

"Cale, we have to see... We need to find our parents." Lake raised her head, tears still at the ready but stubbornly defying the same gravity that caused this monumental atrocity. Jasper bent and helped Emmett pull the boy up using the signpost and then marched through the minefield of mud.

The surface was speckled with debris. Every fifty feet there would be a bent electricity pole or wireless tower, but little else was recognizable. Knowing that there were pockets under the surface that could be dangerous, they went slowly, tossing the metal sign forward to test the integrity of the ground. It worked for the most part, until Emmett threw the metal rod down, and it broke through to a hollow area. A mistake. He burst through and landed ten feet below with a grunt.

Jasper looked down concerned, another injury was the last thing they needed. Emmett was okay and scanned around himself with the flashlight that had survived the fall. Jasper could see the big man's eyes light up at what he saw.

"It's a gas station. I haven't seen one of these for a while," Emmett remarked. Jasper heard a faint knock on metal. "The tank here sounds full. That may be good to keep in mind."

For some reason that sparked some hope in Lake's eyes, and Jasper wondered if it could be true. Could there be survivors? That brief glint of hope was snuffed by the look on Emmett's face when he returned to the hole he fell through. Jasper read DISGUST on his face. Emmett had often used his expressions to communicate with Jasper, and they had gotten quite good at it. Now, however, Jasper hoped he was wrong. Emmett must have found something there that had disturbed him to the core. He moved a battered trash can to the entrance that he had fallen through, and with a little assistance from Jasper and Cale, he was back up to the surface.

The moon was almost directly above them now, and they walked to where Lake believed her house to be. She had decided she couldn't do anything else until she knew if her parents had gotten away. She steeled herself for what she would find. The tall girl was performing an emotional balancing act between the probability that they were all gone and the chance that they had survived. She was careful not to fall completely on either side, at least not until she had proof.

Another half hour of slow, careful shuffling brought them to the side of the bowl-like valley, which was higher than the middle section where the water had not yet receded. Lake had stepped in front of Cale to help guide Emmett, who was at the front sweeping for sinkholes.

"We should be close," Lake said. Her voice mirroring her anxiety as her emotional tightrope was growing thin. "The next time you find a hole to the ground, let's go down and see if it's on the road or not."

"Are you sure?" Emmett asked. "Jasper and I can go if it would help." But Lake gave him a look that silenced that idea.

Soon the end of the signpost sunk deep and cracked the earth, indicating that it was merely a crust. Emmett hit the spot with the sign side, and it opened a hole in the ground four feet around. He struck twice more, opening the hole more, to give a better preliminary view of what was below.

Emmett shone a light below the surface, which illuminated a power-line post lying horizontally, snapped from its original vertical stance. Next to it was an old truck, or at least that was Emmett's best guess. It lay on its side, wheels pointed away, wedged deep into a wall of dirt. The cabin was flattened against its body as if run through a car compactor. The big man noticed a smell that didn't belong. It wasn't of fuel or rust but of decay. Emmett took a quick glance as Jasper, and the two hopped down. Beneath the flattened roof, he saw a cold, pale hand barely visible from their direction.

Jasper remembered when he was flicking ants off the ground. He couldn't imagine a force so fast and powerful that could match a hand from an ant's perspective. He was wrong. This was far greater a power, one that could have destroyed almost anything. And it had fallen on an unsuspecting town nested in a nearly forgotten valley.

Emmett motioned to whisper to Jasper. "Be ready." He pointed to the truck, Jasper almost thew up at the sight of the hand and what it represented but Emmett gripped his wrist hard pulling him back. "I saw another by the gas tank. They weren't running, they had no warning." He brought the younger man closer and whispered, "You need to be a rock for them. Get it together; I don't know God's plan, but we need to be ready for Him to use us here."

He slapped Jasper shoulder and strode back to assist Lake and Cale as they maneuvered. "Let's be careful what we push or dig. The ceiling may come down, and who knows what's in it." He gave his flashlight to Cale and invited him to lead the way. Jasper did the same for Lake, but received a cold silence as she took the light and stepped deep into the black with purpose. Jasper put his body between her and the flattened truck; she didn't give it more than a parting glance as she walked. Twenty paces into the tunnel there was a pile of metal mangled around a circular disk eight feet in diameter.

"This is our neighbor's house," Lake said, putting her hand on the small structure. It was a merry-go-round. No paint was left on it, and rust had consumed nearly every part of the visible metal. "We used to try and play on it, but it was so heavy we could never go very fast." Knowing that there was no way it could turn didn't stop her from giving it a light push, but it did not budge. "Our house should be just down there." She pointed down the tunnel, but did not move.

Jasper walked beside her and took her hand. "Emmett and I can go from here if you want to stay." Her gaze didn't wander from the opening where she was pointing. She squeezed his hand and stepped forward with resolve.

The opening grew narrower as they went farther north and the ground grew higher. More dirt and rock surrounded them than just dried-mud walls as they continued. They walked twenty or so yards led by Lake, and then they all stopped with her as she turned the flashlight to the left. There was an upturned sign in the front of a mound of dirt and debris. The sign was bent backward, and Lake gestured at the sign.

"Our house is here." She gestured to the wall, and Emmett and Jasper inspected the mass of sediment caught by the sign and beyond. Jasper's mind wandered as he looked back at Lake. He could see her clenched jaw and furrowed brow in the dim light. Seeing her like this caused a reaction he had not expected. Under waves of emotion, he felt himself strengthened and not stirred. Steeling himself he began to dig with his hands hard into the mound. Emmett joined him and soon after Cale gave his light to Lake and joined in the burrowing.

As they dug, the thick mud changed consistency. More and more rock and gravel introduced its way into the uncovered hole they were digging, making their nails sting. Nevertheless, they continued, driving into the wall as if someone was drowning on the other side. *What if there is someone drowning on the other side?* Jasper thought.

They feverishly dug until one of the strokes Cale made at the dirt was met with something much harder than the packed dirt.

They focused their efforts on the single area, slowly uncovering an angled white wall stained by the water and sediment. They opened it more until almost half of what looked like the front door of a prefabricated house. It, however, didn't stand vertical to the ground like most doors, but was leaning sixty degrees backward into whatever structure it was attached to. They uncovered a door handle with the traditional hinge, ungraced with the typical hand scanner that accompanied most modern homes. Emmett tested the handle a few times. It was stiff, but eventually gave way and turned. The lock was undone, likely due to the certainty that Lake and Cale were late coming home from the festivities. He pushed on the door, but it didn't move. It rested against whatever floor or foundation was behind the door.

"Is anyone in there?" Emmett called to whatever was beyond the door. He looked around at the others questioningly, but they gave no suggestions. Before he could say anything else, or even think, Cale drove his shoulder into the door. The door stayed put, but what Emmett had feared the most was causing the whole thing to collapse, which thankfully didn't happen. Emmett planted his feet firmly, and kicked the right side of the uncovered door at the lowest point he could. There was an audible crack, and when he delivered another blow a foot higher, the hinges gave way, causing the board to twist, and eventually snap. Cale gave Emmett the light, and the big man solemnly crawled through the entryway.

There was a brief moment of waiting before the rest heard from Emmett. "Come in if you want, but be careful. I don't think there's much keeping the walls from coming down."

The three crawled into the space where only the light of their two flashlights graced the room. It was the living room of a small, manufactured house, common in small towns like this. The kitchen adjoined the living room, though it was hard for them to get their bearings in a house that was tilting at such an acute angle. Lake and

Cale scoured the room, then slowly made their way down the hallway to where the bedrooms must have been.

Lake opened the door to her parent's bedroom and gasped, but she didn't step back out. Cale, however, did not follow. Instead he sat in a chair, taking in the room around himself for the last time.

A few moments had passed since Lake had disappeared into her parents' room, and both Jasper and Emmett grew worried. Like he had before, Emmett gestured to Jasper with his head to go and see how she was doing. This time, the young man didn't hesitate. As he walked, Lake came out of the room and met him halfway. The light in her hand pointed down, but he could see her face.

SHAME. SADNESS.

He saw her emotions weave through her face like poison in the bloodstream, all moving to create a visceral reaction in the body. She broke, tears flowing openly for the first time since they saw the awful destruction. Cale tried to move past her to see into the room, but she engulfed him in an embrace. Emmett walked over to join the party of weeping. The worst was confirmed.

After what felt like hours, Lake moved to one of the chairs in the joined kitchen, and Emmett looked to her for permission to go back to the room. Lake nodded, and he went. When he returned, his face was grim.

Lake struggled to get out the question that undoubtedly had been on her mind since she entered the room.

"Did they...suffer?" Lake asked Emmett.

The big man sat in front of her, offering a sad half smile.

"No, I don't think so. They had fractal patterns on their skin, and there's no evidence that they drowned. I think the water came in while they were sleeping, and there were electric outlets in the room. I don't think they would have felt anything." He said, hoping that it was some consolation.

The somber group remained together in the space for a while, Jasper sitting on the floor, Emmett sitting in a chair, and Lake and Cale together on a small sofa. Lake made the first move; Emmett and

Jasper had been waiting, wanting to ensure Lake and Cale had enough time to say goodbye.

"Let's go; I don't want to stay here," Lake said to the group. She stood up, took Cale's hand, and walked to the doorway. She left him there and Jasper and Emmett stood to leave as well. "Take whatever you may need from the kitchen. Cale, pack your things," Cale looked at her sorrowfully. "We can't stay here, Cale." She was on the brink again.

Emmett patted Cale's back. "I'll help you." Cale didn't smile back, but he listened and fled to what was his room to stuff whatever things he could salvage in bags.

Lake stood alone in her parents' room. Her mother lay still on the bed, and her dad lay on the ground beside it. Their exposed skin was laden with fractal burns like the lightning that flashes in the night. Their expressions were calm, and their eyes were closed, both of which she was grateful for. She drew a sheet from a drawer and laid it on both of them, providing a burial within the tomb of the broken home deep in earth. It was closure, something she hadn't thought would be possible until she was old, with a family. Not now. One of her tears dropped on her mother as she drew the sheet over her body.

"I'm sorry," she said to her mother and wiped the tear off her cold skin. She didn't know why she said it, but there was some need within her to have one last conversation before she said goodbye. The young woman didn't know if they could hear her, but she continued anyway. "I'm not sorry I left. I know it wouldn't have made a difference, but somehow it feels like it would. I hope you understand in some way." Another tear escaped and landed softly, causing Lake to pause and wipe it away. "I never cried much. I so wanted to introduce you to the people we met while we were gone. They're funny and were very nice to us and didn't seem to want anything in return. I think you would have really liked them." She wiped her mother's scattered hair to one side and noticed something she hadn't seen at first.

A necklace chain glinted in the faint light, one that, when she drew it out, revealed the round pendant that had graced her mother's chest as long as she could remember. In the middle, a deer made from yellow gold proudly stood atop a slope. Though it was a mere two-dimensional piece of jewelry, the deer looked noble. Its stance was confident, its eyes intent, and its feet sure on the ground where it stood. She had grown up seeing that side of the necklace; now she turned it over in her hand out of curiosity, not suspecting there would be anything on the opposite side. To her surprise there was an inscription on the back. It read, "ᛈ" and below that, "Be Noble." Lake took the necklace from about her mother's neck and grasped her mother's hand.

She had little idea what the inscription meant, but she knew that it had been an integral part of who her mother was—a part she wanted to hold on to. A warm feeling crept through her body, something she thought was odd in that moment, but she was grateful all the same. She said her last parting words to her family. Not many people were buried in their homes, and in some way, she felt like this was better than digging a separate grave for them. She closed the door behind her, salvaged a few clothes and supplies, and met the group in front of the house.

They continued to a home that Lake had known was uninhabited. The previous owners had left, and it would provide a place for them to attempt sleep in a place unencumbered by the stench of decay. They were pleased to find the house uphill had stood stronger against the tidal wave than most of the others, and the garage door had been unblocked by the flow of sediment enough to let them in without labor. They dropped their packs and lay on the carpeted floor of the empty house, which was a welcomed change for the group. Nothing compared to the warm dinner that was promised, but there was no complaint from anyone that night.

Lake and Cale slept close together. What had happened within the previous days had brought them closer than Jasper had ever seen any siblings before. Jasper's examples of kinship had been full of discord and resentment, but with these two it was different. Cale would die for his sister, without a thought, but he never would have imagined having a relationship like the one Lake and Cale had. Jasper pondered how his relationship with Ziva would have grown to be.

"Want to pray in the garage with me?"

Emmett had placed his hand on his shoulder, and Jasper nodded his head.

"Yes," he replied, and they stepped into the empty concrete garage so as not to disturb the siblings. They sat on the floor, and Emmett began in the conversational tone he always took with God. He thanked Him for another day and prayed for the hearts of Lake and Cale in their grief. He mentioned many other things, but Jasper got lost in what he was supposed to say. When Emmett had finished, and Jasper felt that it was his turn, he began.

"Father, I'm still learning about You, but I see how You are changing me. Thank You for making me into something...better than I was. You know what I mean. I don't know what is next, but while we are with Cale...and Lake, please help them to see evidence of who You are in us." He felt a hand on his shoulder and knew by its familiarity that it was Emmett's.

"Amen," Emmett added.

Jasper wasn't sure what that meant and finished his prayer with an abrupt, "Well thanks...and...bye."

Something didn't sit well with Jasper, but he found himself scared to ask. Emmett noticed his hesitance and initiated a conversation. "What's on your mind?" he asked.

Jasper paused, trying out different ways of asking his question in the least abrasive way possible.

"God is powerful, right?" Emmett nodded. "And He created the world, right?" Emmett's face showed he caught where the question was headed, but he simply nodded in reply. "So why did He let things like this happen? It doesn't seem like these people were bad. Why would He let them die?"

"God doesn't kill all the bad people, because 'being bad' isn't who they are but what they do. He loves all His creation, but because He loves us all, He must let natural consequences take place, otherwise we would all just be mindless robots controlled by a tyrant creator. He lets us come to Him or not. Sadly, the same is true with the consequences of life. He looks at the world with an eternal perspective, however. Focusing on our long-term well-being over the softening of present tragedy." Emmett paused, shaking his head. "I can't imagine the pain He feels from this tragedy, though."

"God can feel pain?"

"Of course. The Bible shows us many times that God displayed emotion. We are created in His image, in His likeness. He cries with us and maybe even laughs too," Emmett said with a half smile. Jasper felt some of the rift he put between himself and his newfound heavenly Father disappear. It comforted him knowing that he had similarities with the Creator of the world.

They walked out of the garage to the carpeted living room where they found Lake and Cale lying down unmoving. Jasper turned and asked Emmett a question.

"What does *Amen* mean?"

"It means, 'this is true.' It's a declaration that whatever preceded it is honest and based on something you believe with all your being. That's why I said it when you asked for us to be evidence of His reality to Lake and Cale. I agree with that from the bottom of my heart. So I said 'Amen.'"

They laid their new and dry blankets down on the carpet, and sleep crept in to steal their consciousness away.

NINE

JASPER SLEPT FITFULLY on the carpeted floor. Though it was a softer bed than he'd had since the night of the printing, it was unwelcome. He had gotten used to the ground with its little rocks and the fresh night air. He decided that if he had the choice, he would rather taste the fresh air over the mildewed interior of the home. Whenever he tried to force sleep, he was greeted by the now familiar light that danced in that moody figure eight. It unnerved him every time it began behind his eyelids. It had purpose, though he couldn't pinpoint what it was.

Morning light slanted feebly through the ceiling of debris. Cale and Emmett were the first to rise as usual. Jasper joined them with a yawn. They broke out several cans of food from Lake and Cale's house for breakfast. It wasn't hot, but it also wasn't berries. Jasper was the first to offer conversation.

"How long do you want to stay here?" he asked Emmett as well as the siblings. He wanted to figure out where their heads were and thought an open question of that sort could do it. He got nothing so he tried again. "I mean, I understand if you would want to stay. And I also would understand if you don't want to be here any longer." He turned to Emmett. "Do you think it is safe here?"

"No," Emmett said, a frown wrinkling his brow. "If the sides of the valley are saturated with water, they could slip down on us in a landslide." Then he turned to the two siblings. "We will be here with you as long as you feel you need." He looked at Jasper, almost for permission for what he was about to offer, but he didn't allow Jasper the chance to respond. "We would never attempt to replace your family. But we will try and act like one for as long as you need. We are here for you. If you want us to go different ways now, then we will do that freely. But if you want to travel with us, you are more than welcome."

Lake looked at Cale, back at Emmet, and then at Jasper. She nodded.

"Thank you. That would be really...nice."

They packed their things and left the house. They climbed from the wreckage and made straight for the side of the valley that was least damaged by the flooding. Slowly the now familiar smell of wet decay dispersed. The edge of the valley's bowl was defined by several layers of rocks that stood out from the edge of the cracking mud floor. Overnight more water had receded from the pool in the middle through the half-dozen streams leading out of the valley, and it was half the size that they had seen by moonlight the night before. Seeing it in the daylight now brought a myriad of emotions to the group. It was humbling, seeing the force that gravity and water had, taking a mile of earth with it. The air was still and mostly unbroken. Jasper felt sad thinking that there would be no one to rebuild the town Lake had called home. As they walked up the side of the bowl, Jasper noticed something different about Lake. She had taken a shoulder pack from her house, but that wasn't it. She had changed from her simple jacket and jeans to a winter jacket that was open revealing a black long-sleeve athletic shirt. She had changed from the old jeans into a pair of black athletic tights, but that was not what caught his

attention either. Around her neck, where there once was no adorn-
ment, hung a shiny gold chain that slid down into the front of her
shirt, leaving whatever was at the end of the chain hidden.

"What is that around your neck?" Jasper asked. She looked at
Jasper, and as they walked, she pulled the pendant out, revealing the
golden form of the proudly standing deer. "It was my mother's. She'd
had it ever since I can remember."

"It's beautiful." Jasper responded. "Does the deer mean something special to your people?"

Lake thought for a moment, as she navigated a slippery section of
rocks. "I don't think so. We never had much art with it or stories
involving stags besides when wolves would kill them." She touched
the deer with her thumb and turned it over. "What I don't get is what
it says on the back. "Be Noble." What does that even mean? And
even stranger, there is a symbol I don't recognize: ⚥. What do you
think it means? "

Emmett stopped walking at the front of the column and turned
back. After Lake nodded her consent, he held her pendant in his
hand studying it. A frown furrowed his brow and then dissolved into
a smile. He didn't say anything as the others stopped in anticipation
of his words. But he decided not to speak and simply smiled to the
sky, obviously realizing something that none of the rest did. He
continued walking, a little more bounce in his step than before.

The rest, still standing in confusion, dropped the conversation
and continued after him. Lake, however, didn't replace the pendant
in her shirt but held it with her left hand. For some inexplicable
reason, it offered comfort as she walked nearer to the crest that would
lead her out of sight of the only home she had ever known. They
came to the ridge and walked alongside it until they could find a safe
way down the other side. The plan was to trek north to the vacation
and hunting cabins that Lake had told them about. An added benefit
was that the presence of State law enforcement was lower in that
direction. If they were found, all four of them would be institutional-

ized or worse. It would be too far to go, but Jasper and Emmett had considered making new lives in the provinces of what was once Canada, although Canada had been split for some time now. Getting there would be almost impossible as the border was surveilled constantly. Long-term plans did not seem to be in reach, but it was a start, and all they could really do was put their trust in God and take one step at a time.

They found a ridge that they could navigate to the opposite side of the valley, and all said their goodbyes to the sad sight of Umchin. Emmett was the first to turn away, and as usual he was closely followed by Cale. Lake stood still, gazing at the valley. She took a deep breath in and closed her eyes. She imagined her home before the tragedy and stood still, eyes closed, remembering it as it was and not what it had become.

Jasper fought a compulsion to go to her. He eventually gave in and put his arm around her shoulder. She leaned into him, thankful for his support.

"Let's go," she said with a clear, unwavering voice. So they did. Jasper led her down the ridge, and she did not look back.

They found a path on the other side of the valley, which was welcomed by the group after hiking rugged terrain for the past day and a half. The path switched back and forth down to face miles of rolling pine-studded hills. As they continued down, the warmth and sunlight faded away as clouds drifted in to cover the sky. Soon a fog enveloped them.

At the bottom of the hill, they stumbled upon a shack. It was nested among the trees. They would have walked right past if it weren't for the two discernible tire tracks that went up to it from the path. Cale took the lead and scampered toward the shack to Lake's concern. But she held back from stopping him.

As they approached, they saw that what had looked like a shack from a distance actually consisted of double doors that were hidden by trees on both sides.

"These trees were planted here on purpose," Emmett said on inspection.

"What do you think that means? Why would someone try to hide it?" Lake asked.

"Maybe there is something illegal hidden in it. Like drugs...or weapons...or—"

"An alien!" Cale said in excitement. The boy rarely spoke, but he was definitely making his mark when he did. The three looked at the boy in consternation before Emmett came to his rescue.

"I guess if I had an alien, I would hide him in a shed." The big man shrugged. He approached the shed. "No lock." He pulled the double doors hard. They refused to open. Emmett's surprise leaked onto his face.

"Seems like coach needs to hit the gym again," Jasper said, unable to let pass the one opportunity he'd had to poke fun at the typical teaser. Emmett took the joke in good humor.

"You give it a try, Hercules."

That shut Jasper up, as his own masculinity was at stake. He steeled himself, then, grabbing both doors, he threw all his weight back. The young man flew backward as the doors opened effortlessly. He landed on his back with a groan.

"Wow, you really are Hercules! You opened them like they were nothing!" Emmett laughed with a wink.

Jasper didn't respond and focused on getting his newly rebroken body back standing.

Inside the shed were many tools hung all over the sides and back, and in the middle was an old SUV. A cloud of dust breathed out of the structure when the doors were open, causing them to wait before investigating further. Dust covered the weathered vehicle, and Cale was the first to step up to it, and wipe the nameplate free.

"Land Cruiser?" the boy asked. "What's that? I've never seen this before."

Emmett approached it and reached out to touch the dusty deep blue paint.

"It's an old car, probably from the '80s. I'm surprised there are any around. The department of transportation has been cracking down on gas vehicles." He used a rag he found on a nearby table to clean the badge. "It is a beauty isn't it. No offense, Jasper, but this car would have gotten you much more interest from girls than yours... Maybe that was your problem." Jasper let the comment slide, but it produced a sidelong smile from Lake that caused him to blush.

"Why would someone store it here?" Jasper asked. "If they were caught driving it, they would be charged."

"State officers don't come out here very often." Lake supplied. "We have...I mean, had people in Umchin who drove gas cars. I don't think they care as much what we do."

"Have you seen this car driven in town before?" Emmett asked while shining his flashlight inside.

"I don't think so." Lake said as she tried to remember. Emmett opened the door and looked into the glove compartment for indication of ownership. He pulled out a piece of paper from an old yellow envelope, seeming to find what he was looking for.

"Do you know a Dakota Sillers?" Emmett asked the siblings.

"Yes. He owned the gas station. He didn't really do much besides sell us candy because not many people had cars, but he was nice."

Emmett's demeanor grew grim.

"I wonder if he survived. Maybe he was gone when it all happened!" Lake's eyes lit up at the idea.

"Was he a shorter man with a mustache?" Emmett asked.

Lake nodded.

"Long hair that went into a ponytail?"

"Yes. What? Is there a picture of him there?" Lake asked.

The big man sighed deeply. "No. Last night when we were in one of the gaps in the wreckage, I explored a little when we found the gas tank and the truck. Further down I found Mr. Siller." He stopped, letting his silence answer the rest. Lake knew what he meant.

"Do you think we could use it? I mean, I think Mr. Siller won't mind." Lake turned to Jasper, who was rubbing his back. "I think Jasper threw his back out, and he may get complainy if we go much farther." Jasper rolled his eyes but was secretly grateful for her suggestion for he was likely going to be obnoxious as they traveled regarding his wounds.

"Do you need a key?" Jasper asked Emmett who had already opened the driver-side door. Emmett returned his question with exasperation.

"Yes. It's not a horse and buggy."

"What's that?" Jasper asked, but received no answer from the man.

"You're making me feel very old right now."

"If I stab you a couple times in the back, I think we could make you into a certified geriatric."

"You know what geriatrics is but not the horse and buggy?" Emmett jeered back. He flipped down the sunshade, and something fell into his lap.

"Hey, what luck!" he exalted.

"You found the keys?" Lake asked.

"No, better! A coupon for two for one on radishes." He waited for the others to laugh at his joke, but none came. He quickly assumed he had tried too many in an hour, and they needed their senses of humor to recharge. "Oh wait. What a bummer; it's expired."

"When?" Jasper asked.

"1993."

Jasper frowned and climbed in to search for a key with him. They searched for a matter of minutes and soon gave up.

"I had an old Japanese car once that I could take the key out of and it would keep running," Emmett said. "I would forget the key sometimes, so I made some copies out of paper clips and aluminum foil." He went to the table and pulled out a length of metal wire three feet long. He grabbed a hammer off the wall and hopped over to a metal vice that was attached to the wall. He began hitting the wire, shaping it into the general shape of a key. Finding no cutting devices around, he bent the long side of the wire into an asymmetrical pretzel shape that was concerningly sharp on the end. Feeling content with his prototype, he jumped into the driver's seat and placed the wire into the ignition key slot. It fit, but just barely, and he was unable to wiggle it around, so he took it back to the vice and tried again.

After several more failed smithing attempts, he was able to turn the key. A click sound startled the basking group. It was soon accompanied by a grating of mechanics. The grating sped up and built a tempo. Emmett pushed down the gas pedal and tried again. The tempo sped up and grew to a crescendo. Smoke poured from the back, engulfing Cale as he lay leaned against a half-torn old tire.

"Get in!" Emmett called to the group. "The battery doesn't have much, so we need to go somewhere if we are going to use it!"

The group didn't pose any more questions, not because there weren't valid objections to the idea, but because something exciting had happened that wasn't born of tragedy. That was enough to let them leave behind their fear and jump in the old SUV. Jasper opened the door to the passenger seat only to find Cale. He was greeted by a smug smile from the lad. Lake had already jumped in and thrown her pack in the wide trunk. Emmett revved the old six-cylinder engine, and then began to drive forward, leaving the shack alone again.

Emmett had never driven in this area before, so he took it slow. The rolling hills were covered with trees that would muffle engine noise, but he didn't want any locals to get upset and investigate. They drove through flowery meadows that connected each tree studded hill like they were driving through the clouds, if clouds were full of holes, rocks, and logs that could surprise you at any time. Nevertheless, the group rode excited and in good spirits.

Jasper didn't know if Lake or Cale had done this before—riding off the road, free in the hills—but judging by their expressions, he assumed this was a new experience. Cale sat bouncing in the front seat, his serious face was bumped off by the first large rock they drove over, leaving a grin that he hadn't seen on the boy. Lake, too, looked transformed. Normally she had a cheerful demeanor, but that had been put away by the utter destruction of her home and her loved ones. Jasper knew that there was still that pain inside, but it was good to see her smile replace the pensive sadness.

They drove north, staying far from the main roads and opting for navigating the wilderness instead of chancing an interaction with the State. Emmett didn't know how they publicized the dam explosion or if they were still looking for them, but he thought it a good idea to assume that they were.

Emmett, looking pleasantly surprised, noted that the gas-tank meter worked on the old car. It was, however, the only gauge that was operational on the dash. The previous owner must have filled it after every journey, because the tank was almost full when they found it, though Emmett said the muffler gave off a smell that indicated the gas was not up to the same standards that he grew up with.

They drove over pits and brush for several hours before the fuel level began to concern Emmett. They started searching for signs of farms, which likely hadn't made the full transition to electric equipment. Lake and Cale didn't know much about the area northwest of their home, which provided no help. They drove for hours until they found a place to stop and plan. Emmett automatically turned the key in the ignition once he'd stopped, cutting the engine. He had a brief moment of panic, realizing that there was the possibility of it not starting again, leaving them stuck.

They had pulled to the side of a meadow that showed early signs of the winter to come. The wildflowers were beginning their inevitable tilt as their stems weakened in the changing temperatures. The gray sky and floating mist around them made it difficult to keep the direction they wanted. At the same time, they felt an extra layer of comfort thinking they wouldn't be seen by anyone who would find them suspicious. They ate in silence for a time before Lake broke the quiet.

She took out her necklace and swept her finger across the front, hoping it would shine.

"Emmett?" she asked.

"Yes?"

She stepped over to the man and handed him the necklace that belonged to her mother.

"Does this have any meaning? I mean, does the god you speak to take the form of animals or..." She trailed off, not knowing how to finish the question. He understood it well enough, though, and seemed to construct his reply carefully.

"I guess He could, but I don't think He would. His presence isn't temporary. His Spirit doesn't leave and go off and then come back to check on you. The place where He resides is here." He pointed to his heart, which thoroughly confused Lake.

"His Spirit lies within us. We are a temple of the One who created us, of the One who created everything. We become that temple by asking Him to be in our lives. He isn't forceful; He wants to be invited to work and grow in your life." While he finished his answer, he inspected the pendant carefully. "This is stunning," he said, complimenting the heirloom that obviously meant a lot to the girl.

"So, this doesn't have any connection to your god? No magic or meaning?"

The man turned the pendant over, revealing the inscription on the back. "☧Be Noble." It was almost as if his mind had prepared for this moment but something held him back from beginning a lengthy speech.

"That marking was a way of secretly identifying yourself as a Christian. In the early days of Christianity, you were severely persecuted if you claimed belief in Christ. In order to meet and live as one, you had to find ways of identifying yourself and others, without nonbelievers figuring it out." Emmett paused for a moment, choosing his angle carefully. "Was your mother a believer?"

"She never said she was a Christian. At least not openly." Lake strained, thinking about moments where that information could have slipped through if true. Her thinking of her mother brought tears back to her eyes. "My grandmother and mother would tell us stories when we would go walking in the woods. Stories about people who lived before us. There was one about a man that got swallowed by a big fish...and one where a man killed a big cat with only his hands. I just assumed that those were ancestors from the tribe."

A smile appeared on Emmett's face.

"What?" Lake responded. "Were they wrong? Were they made up?"

"No. Those were true stories of people who lived before us. But they weren't stories from your tribe specifically. The men in the stories were early followers of the God of heaven." Lake turned her head confused. Emmett continued. "Did they ever tell you a story about a man whose walking stick would turn into a snake? Or a prisoner who was put in a pit full of hungry lions?"

"The first one sounds familiar, but the second one she definitely told us about. So you're saying those aren't stories from our families' ancestors?"

"I would be surprised if they were, considering there aren't any lions around here. I think your mom was telling you these stories to teach you about the God of heaven!"

Jasper could see the consternation on Lake's face. Then as she let the thoughts settle, tranquility displaced the consternation as the revelation became clearer. This idea that Emmett brought to the light didn't bring back her mother, but it helped her learn something new about her. A sensation that she found comforting.

"What do you think it means to 'Be Noble'?" Emmett asked Lake directly.

The girl thought for a moment, trying out different answers, then starting again. "I don't know," she conceded.

Emmett turned to Jasper and Cale and posed the same question.

"I remember reading about the nobility. They were people in the medieval times who were rulers of different parts of the land. They treated the people who weren't of noble blood horribly," Jasper supplied.

"Great! All right. How did you become part of the nobility?"

"I think people were born into it, weren't they?"

"Yes!" Emmett showed his giddy side again when he wanted to get to his point faster than the others could follow. "You were noble based upon the blood that you had. The family lineage that you possessed."

The group waited for him to connect the dots, but Emmett had another idea.

"Jasper, do you remember the book that I was talking to you about? The one Bernie took?"

"Yes."

"In that book are the words of our Father. His stories, teachings, and instructions all piled into one big book. "

Jasper, realizing the book's importance, felt a rock form in his gut —regret that he didn't take it on that fateful night.

"It is in the book God tells us about different qualities that we need to develop. One of them is to be meek. Some people believe being meek just means to be weak or unable to hurt anyone. But what it really means is that we need to become people of great competence and strength who know when to keep our swords sheathed. A deer with a full rack of antlers could do a lot of damage to almost anything, but it doesn't use them to attack or oppress."

Jasper thought about the idea, but before he could make conclusions, he noted, "It is standing on something."

"Yes, it is. Probably a hillside or mountain. Let me ask you guys. Have you ever known a deer to fall or lose its footing?"

It didn't take long for the two to find their answers. "No," they said almost in unison.

"Deer are sure-footed. They always know where each foot will step even when they are running away from predators. They know where they stand, where their help comes from. They only place their feet on solid ground. Ground that will hold their weight and support them forward. There is a man who lived long ago that we read about in that same book, who was a mighty king. With God's help he killed a warrior twice as tall as himself when he was only a boy." Cale grew more and more interested in the story. "He wrote a song about God and said that God gave him the feet of the deer and set him on the heights. What do you think that means?"

Jasper inferred the answer, but Lake beat him to answering.

"It means that God had given him feet that had solid ground under them and He put him in really important places."

"Yes. He was a king, and he spoke out to everyone that it was God who got him to where he was and that God had given him firm footing within his life. Something solid to stand on." Obviously this was coming together far more easily than Emmett had dreamed. He felt a warmth as he knew that his Father was guiding this conversation, leading them to new understanding.

"So, what does that have to do with what's written on the back?" Jasper asked.

Something clicked in Emmett's mind; he didn't know specifically what it was, but he just allowed his mouth to open and connect the points that he had been thinking of for hours. "What did it mean to be noble?" He asked?

"It meant you were supposed to have good manners and fight dragons, and you had to be born to a king...or something like a king." Lake responded.

"Jasper, you and I know why we call the God of heaven 'Father.' Another name for him is King of heaven. Creator of the world. Prince of Peace. If we are His children, what does that make us?"

"Noble?" Jasper guessed.

"Yes! There are many verses that tell us that if we believe in Him and receive Him, we are adopted into His family. It's not about having blood in our veins that is better than others and then using that to put others down so you can rise up. It means that opportunity is there for everyone. And all they need to do is believe in Him. Something you have already done, Jasper." He turned his gaze to

Lake. "And if I remember right, it's something that you mentioned, as well."

Jasper looked to Lake, whose brow was furrowed in thought.

"Why wouldn't she tell me if she did?"

"Maybe she was scared that you would be printed," Jasper supplied. Lake didn't get the connection.

Emmett showed her his hands. "They were going to send me to a rehab facility to be brainwashed out of my convictions. But good ol' Jasper here decided to break me out, giving me no choice other than to see why God had compelled this skinny boy to make me hike through the night and get ambushed by kids." He smiled, and lowered his tone for one last pass. "What I know so far is that the most important parts of being noble are that you know you are a noble son or daughter of the living God and that you share with others that they have that same calling."

"That's why you were praying for your students," Jasper inferred.

"Yes. I taught them the curriculum for the most part and didn't teach them about God in my class, but they would come to me looking for answers about life and about why I was the way I was. I couldn't lie. So I told them the truth. I am happy and fulfilled because I know that I am a child of the living God. And that's enough for me."

Jasper felt a wealth of emotion fill him at Emmett's last words. To his knowledge he had never felt more fulfilled than he did at that moment. And by the rest of the world's standards, he would have been in the bottom of the pit. He looked at Emmett, his eyes showing the emotion he was feeling, rose, and embraced the man.

"I'm a child. I'm His son!" Jasper said. He felt Emmett's embrace grow stronger at his words. He felt another join in the embrace. The tall, long-haired girl sniffled back tears and was enveloped by the two.

"Father, if you're there, I want to know You. I want to be your daughter."

They stood in that embrace for a time until they were startled by a sharp screech. They each flung themselves from the group hug and looked around in panic, only to find Cale the front seat of the SUV, hands impatiently waiting on the steering wheel.

"Let's go!"

TEN

THEY DROVE on for another hour. The SUV jumped and bucked over the holes as they continued off the beaten track. The excitement of the drive had worn off for everyone except Cale. Jasper and Lake in the back were visibly sick and had moments where they rode with their heads out of the window. In one of these moments, Emmett drove over a rock at the very time Lake was sticking her head out the window. The bump slammed her head into the pillar of the rig.

"Are you okay?" Jasper asked, not knowing if he should laugh or not. Emmett stopped the car and got out. Lake was stunned by the strike. She took her hand to the side of her head that was throbbing, and when she took it away there was no sign of blood.

"Lake. I never thought I'd have to say this under the circumstances," Emmett said as he opened the left passenger door that she had head butted. "This is the only transportation we have, young lady! Why would you try and knock it down!" He was massaging the pillar tenderly, checking for signs of distress. Lake was unimpressed, and one look from her stifled the budding laughter that welled up in Jasper and Cale. Once he was genuinely sure that Lake was okay to continue, Emmett jumped back in the driver's seat and continued.

They drove through several fields of brush, much of it getting tangled below the car, but the old SUV drove on unperturbed. They came upon a creek about two feet deep and six feet wide. Jasper had never seen a car go through something like that, but trusted that Emmett knew what he was doing. He looked at the creek, sized it up, and returned to the car looking serious.

"Cale, do you think we can do this?" he asked as he tightened up his seat belt suggestively. Cale followed suit.

"Yes!" the boy said excitedly.

"Onward!" Emmett yelled, as he drove the car forward. He continued his yell as they effortlessly powered through the water and back onto weed strewn ground. Cale giggled from the excitement and looked at Emmett with glee overwhelming his face.

"I've never seen anyone do that," Lake whispered to Jasper.

"Do what?"

"Pull that much joy from Cale's heart. He is so good with him," she said, her heart in her throat. Jasper didn't answer, but instead looked in the angled rear-view mirror at his tall friend's face.

REGRET

Why does Emmett show regret as he laughs with the child? he wondered. Emmett's face smiled, but something pained him to the core.

Jasper's thoughts were cut short by his own insides wanting to be on his outsides, forcing him to focus on not allowing what little food he had had to come up.

After a short while Emmett had begun to look nervous, and Jasper followed suit when he saw what his friend was anxious about. The fuel indicator. Instead of continuing in the steady northwestern direction they'd been taking, he began looking for a place to run out. As he drove up the side of a ridge, he prayed both that there wouldn't be a cliff on the other side and that they wouldn't run out of gas on the way up. The needle was a quarter of an inch past E. Emmett had had no idea the car would continue this long.

They crested the ridge, and Emmett let out a sigh of relief.

Instead of a cliff, a steady and steep decline into a thick forest came into view. The relief vanished as he noticed something a few hundred yards into the trees. A subtle but clear pillar of chimney smoke. He had no time to think. At the top of the ridge, they would be easily made out from anywhere below. He inched the car to the edge, threw it in neutral, and let it slide down the steep hill to the tree line. The passengers were confused but were shushed by the big man when they came to the bottom and halted. He turned the engine off.

Nobody spoke, though everyone was thinking the same question, all except Emmett who was carefully listening outside the open window. They heard nothing but the chorus of forest sounds: wind, trees, and birds. After a moment Emmett seemed convinced of something and lowered his guard.

"When we got to the top, I saw chimney smoke that way. We couldn't stay at the top, so I had to idle us down to get out of sight." Emmett said, still looking around warily. They exited the car carefully.

"I can go and scout it out to see if we can get around it," Emmett said.

"Maybe they're friendly!" Cale supplied. The three let the naively optimistic suggestion slide without comment.

Lake stepped forward and tested her ankle with a few jumps and turns. Satisfied with its stability, she brought up a different idea.

"I'm quieter in the woods than you two. I can figure it out and not be heard or seen better than you two," she said with a bit of finality, which made any counter idea an insult to her, something Jasper was thoroughly unwilling to do. Emmett wasn't convinced, but he shrugged it off and conceded.

"Give us a yell if you get caught," Emmett said.

"Try and convince them that you have a whole crew of burly men ready if you are mistreated," Jasper added.

"So that when we show up, they will laugh to death at the contrast." Emmett jested.

Lake laughed at the joke, dropped her bag, and moved in the direction Emmett had indicated with almost no sound.

Jasper's nervousness intensified as the minutes ticked on. After thirty, he became restless. After an hour, his restlessness grew to anxiety.

"She should be back. Should we go after her?" he said while stretching, hoping that his back wouldn't give out in a prospective fight. He had never been in one, so he doubted he would fare well if he encountered one.

"She's fine. I'm concerned too," Emmett said. "Let's say we will go and check once the sun hits the top of that tree." Jasper looked at the tree he had indicated and assumed that was just another ten or fifteen minutes. After five, Emmett and Jasper noticed Cale, who was sitting on the open tailgate of the cruiser holding in laughter. They rose from their places on the ground and looked at the boy, who, when noticing this, shut his mouth into a forced neutral face. Jasper and Emmett looked at each other, bemused by the boy, then shrugged it off. It happened again, only this time the boy let the laugh out.

"What's the matter with you?" Jasper asked him.

"What's the matter with you?"

Jasper flinched from the voice that had suddenly appeared behind him. He spun to confront Lake, who was collapsed in helpless gales of laughter. Both Emmett and Jasper were frazzled by the sudden appearance, and it showed.

"How long have you been here?" Emmett asked, his heart pumping hard from the fright.

"I don't know. How long have I been back, Cale?" Lake answered.

"Since you two decided to wait until the sun hit the tree. Which I didn't get at all because if the sun hit that tree, we would all be burned up," Cale answered scientifically.

"I was going to wait until you went after me, then surprise you."

"Wouldn't that be dangerous? What if whoever is over there

heard you startle us?" Jasper asked. The girl shook her head deliberately, her lips still drawn in a mischievous smile.

"There's only one person there and a dog," Lake explained.

Emmett seemed pleasantly surprised by that, but Jasper was unnerved by the dog. He had never gotten along with them and wondered if maybe they didn't appreciate having their emotions read.

"The dog seems nice, and the woman does too. I didn't get too close because I didn't want the dog to smell me, but she was by herself, cleaning and gardening."

"Old?" Emmett asked?

"No. She looks about your age. She's got skin that's a little darker than mine, and she's a little shorter than me, but not by much." Emmett and Jasper built the profile in their minds.

"She looked very comfortable. Almost like she knew that nothing dangerous could be out here. So, that could mean that we are really far from anything dangerous, or..."

"She's not planning on being alone for long," Emmett interjected.

"No, I was just thinking that she may not be scared because she can defend herself from anything that may be out here. Bears, mountain lions..."

"Maybe she knows that trick where you lure people in, then break the limb you are on and fall on them," Jasper said.

They bantered on for a while about strategies but eventually settled with the plan of waiting to see if anyone else came and then politely introducing themselves as weary travelers looking for shelter for the night."

They waited until the sky began to change color to go and slowly scope it out together. They crept through the trees and brush that covered the area for a few hundred yards, attempting to make the least amount of noise possible. Emmett, who was the largest, had the hardest time with this and stepped on several large sticks, drawing blistering looks from Jasper and Lake.

Soon the building came into focus amid the trees. It was a large house, two stories built on top of a basement by the height of it. It had two garages attached to the side of the house, and its front was adorned with windows displaying a well-lit modern interior that contrasted with the woodsy rustic exterior. They saw no cars, and Jasper assumed that whatever car the woman brought was in one of the adjoining garages. Something nagged at the back of Jasper's memory. There was something he was missing that he told himself to be aware of.

To the side of the front parkway was a row of garden boxes, work-shops, and greenhouses. All things that Jasper had never really had much contact with in his life. A noise arose from one of the sheds—a bark. Jasper had forgotten about the dog. Fear jumped into Jasper's heart. The dog ran barking from the shed and up to the concrete patio next to the front door of the house. The dog was big, at least a hundred pounds. It was mostly black but had patches of red and white adorning its face, legs, and tail. Even from a distance, its face didn't seem ferocious or malevolent, but then again neither did those girls Jasper tried to date, and they were the epitome of malevolence.

"Let's wait for the woman to come out, and the dog to not be alone just in case it's territorial." Emmett took back the lead, and no one objected. Jasper noticed something that concerned him. He saw Cale directly behind Emmett, and in his hands was the bow that was once aimed directly at himself. Arrow knocked. Ready for a fight. At that moment, Emmett and Lake also noticed and told him sternly to bury the bow in the leaves.

The dog stood by the door and barked impatiently. The large windows gave the group glimpses of a woman coming down the stairs. In a moment she opened the door to let the dog into the house. The woman lingered outside, looking into the tree line.

"Hello," Lake called. The woman looked startled, but Lake stood up from the trees and walked toward her, taking initiative that Jasper hadn't seen from her before. The woman, who was visibly surprised by the random call from the trees, became less defensive when she saw the young woman.

"We've broken down, and we're lost," Lake said, neither of which was completely false. She gestured back to the tree line, beckoning for the rest to stand and follow. When the two men stood from the trees, the woman regained her defensive stance halfway through the door. The tension could have been cut with a knife. The woman could barricade herself in the home and call the authorities, who would inevitably find them. Something needed to be done to calm her. Lake was already on it.

"We won't step any farther if you say the word. We're just looking for some help, but if you are uncomfortable, then we will leave." She stopped where she stood, true to her word, and waited for a reply. Jasper realized that it was the same response that Emmett had given when they found her in the woods. She was giving the frightened person control of the situation, hoping that would prevent her doing something rash. They stood still, all at different distances from the house. The woman was thinking, but she didn't leave the security of her doorway. Finally, they got an answer.

"Are there any more of you?" the women called in a smooth alto.

"No. Just the four of us," Lake replied as the ambassador of the group. The woman stood for another moment, but gave in and invited them to come to the patio, a place where she could still defend herself if there was malicious intent. They strode out from the last of the trees and walked along the large driveway to the patio. The woman had walnut-colored skin and wore a sweatshirt with a pair of athletic leggings. Her face showed concern but no immediate emotions that would make Jasper think she was going to flip the switch into panic.

As they grew closer, her face took on a spike of surprise, which bemused Jasper. He looked to his right where Emmett had been walking alongside to find Emmett frozen ten yards behind him. Jasper looked behind at the man. who seemed struck by fear. Emmett turned his body and started walking casually back in the direction they had come as if he was a forty-year-old mom doing power-walk classes and attempting to look casual doing it.

"Emmett Walsh?" the women on the patio said in astonishment. He didn't stop walking.

"Stop!" the woman commanded. "Emmett, is that really you?"

Trapped, the man turned around to face his confused companions. His eyes were filled with more than fear. They were filled with pain. A sorrow not unlike the one Jasper had seen when he was joking with Cale in the car.

Who is this woman? Jasper wondered. He brought his gaze up to the stranger, who stood now several steps from the door, her hands clasped together, and her mouth open in bewilderment. Silence gripped the air. Nobody dared to speak until Emmett forced out a trembling reply.

"Hi, Sophia," he said as if the words were crushed glass in his mouth. The woman's breathing was irregular; Jasper could notice even from a distance away.

"You've never called me that," she said as she walked toward him.

"It is your name," Emmett said, unmoving.

"It's never been my name to you," she said, passing Jasper as she approached Emmett. Though he was just two feet from the woman, Emmett cast his gaze down at his shoes. Sophia laid her hands on his face and brought it up to look her in the eyes, then saw how it pained him to look at her. A tear slid down from her eye, and neither made an effort to catch it as it cascaded off her cheek. The woman released his face and gripped him in a tight embrace, one that Emmett gingerly returned.

"What happened? The news said you were—"

"This is Jasper and Lake and Cale," Emmett said quickly, cutting Sophia off before she could finish.

Sophia released him from the embrace, feeling rejected, and nodded by means of introduction.

"What is going on?" she asked.

"Emmett and I were on a bit of a trip, and we found these two along the way," Jasper explained.

"The yellow brick road is that way," she responded mockingly. "Emmett, I think I found the only human worse at lying than you. If you tell me what is going on, I'll let you in and you can have something warm to drink," she said coaxingly. Emmett conceded the facade.

"We don't want to get you in trouble. If you were seen with us, or if a camera picks us up with you, you would be in big trouble," Emmett said.

"There is one camera here, and it's in my room. The rest has no surveillance. Devon never comes out here. This is my sanctuary. Now tell me, what is going on?"

"God brought Jasper and me together," Emmett began.

"Oh, I'm very happy for you two."

"Not like that. Anyway, the State and that lunatic Bernard Stockton hunted us. I think he believes that he killed us, and so we've been on the run ever since. We found these two who had run away from home just before their whole town was destroyed by a flood." Sophia raised her eyebrows understanding the bits that Emmett had left out. "We started driving north, hoping to find a place to stay or at least see where God leads us next, but we drove over the ridge and ran out of gas just over there. Please, Sophia, don't turn us in."

As the woman took in what he had said, she looked to the others, taking a quick inventory.

"Are they all believers?" she asked, and before Emmett could answer, Lake and Jasper nodded their reply. She looked at the boy compassionately.

"Even you?"

"He doesn't talk much, but we assume yes," Emmett responded for the boy. The woman stood still, arms folded, thinking for a moment. Jasper looked at her face, but the emotions in it kept moving and changing. RESENTMENT. FEAR. ANGER. SADNESS. The wave was hard for Jasper to follow, and he decided that he needed to look somewhere else.

"All right. On one condition," the woman proposed. "Call me 'Soph.'"

"You're married." Emmett said defensively.

"That shouldn't change this. Go on."

It clearly pained him to say it, but he relented. "It's good to see you, Soph."

She smiled, introduced them to the big dog that was eager to meet them, and then entered the warm house.

ELEVEN

JASPER SAT ON A SOFT COUCH, waiting impatiently for the hot cup of tea to cool to a reasonable temperature. The rest had already taken their places around the living room, happily sipping on drinks. But Jasper was ill at ease. The warmth that permeated the room was foreign to him. Even before he had left civilization, he had never felt this kind of warmth. The conversation was light as Sophia took care to make them feel at home. She asked Lake about her home and her childhood, and they spoke of the town that was not more. Jasper had been afraid to bring up anything that may trigger the pain of the loss of Lake's home and family. But Sophia spoke with grace, and Lake seemed to grow almost eager to tell stories of home.

Emmett sat quietly. Jasper noticed the absence of his jokes and humor. He looked back at his friend, wishing he could help bear some of the burden that was evident in the big man's heart.

The storytelling was eventually passed to Jasper, who told a few tales of his childhood to satisfy the room and happily conceded to whoever would speak. Sadly, it was the one with even fewer social skills than himself.

"How did you two meet?" Cale asked. Lake refrained from

holding her brother back because she was just as interested in learning the answer as he was. Emmett and Sophia obviously had a history, judging by his reaction to meeting her outside. The three knew the question was likely uncomfortable and even rude, given the circumstances. But they sat, sipping their drinks in anticipation. Sophia looked at Emmett, who didn't return her look.

"We grew up together," she said. "We were a part of this kids' group where we would sing songs, go camping, and learn different skills. Emmett was the first in our grade to achieve Voyager status."

"Wow, you were a Voyager?" Jasper said in feigned disbelief.

"Yes, he was, and he got a very pretty maroon scarf because of it," she said, smiling at the big man, who responded with an uncomfortable smile for no one in particular. "Anyway, we grew up together. We went to the same church and school. We became very good friends." She struggled with the word *friends*. Jasper saw that while her face didn't indicate a lie, it showed there was more to that word.

"Do you want to tell the rest? I think this is as far as I should go," she said.

Emmett hesitated but eventually opened his mouth to speak.

"We became very fond of each other. That tends to happen when you spend lots of time with a child of God. You find things to love about them." he said quietly. No one in the room breathed, just to make sure they were able to hear whatever words came next as clearly as possible. Jasper chanced a glance at Sophia's face. She was nervous, and he saw a mixture of regret and shame on her face. Emmett cleared his throat before continuing.

"We were very close, but we failed to communicate, and...we grew apart." The story was not finished, but it was evident he was done telling it. Sophia's face had changed dramatically. What was shame and regret turned to sadness. Tears began to fill in her eyes, but she held them back.

"That's all history now." Though no tears fell from her eyes, they flowed in her voice. "You all must be very tired. You are welcome to sleep here for the night. The one camera in the house is in my bedroom, so just make sure you don't go in there. You may sleep in any other space."

She held back the sniffle as she retreated to her room, and shutting the door, she left the group in a heavy silence. The dog, however, remained and was a pleasant distraction for Emmett as the rest took advantage of the extra shower in the house. Timber, as he had been introduced to them, lay next to the trio of boys on the living room floor while Lake opted to be in another room. As in many of the fire-lit nights, Jasper was on the edge of sleep when he heard the conversational whispering of Emmett's bedtime prayer. Jasper had learned manners well; however, one that always had slipped was eavesdropping. He listened in harder as the big man began his familial conversation.

"Why? Why? Why me? Why her? Why now, Lord?" he said, his quieted voice breaking. "I did what You told me. I did what You said was right. I know that means it hurts sometimes, but Father, why do You torture me again?" He stopped for a moment, working through something in his mind. "Thank You that we have a place to stay tonight. Thank You that it was someone who wouldn't turn us in." It took him another second to spit out the words that completed the 180-degree turn he had taken.

"Thank You that it was her. Thank You for her health and for her graciousness. I don't see where You're going with this, but I trust You." Emmett's words trailed off as he finished, but something else caught Jasper's attention. The door that Emmett's childhood friend had disappeared into was cracked open. Only at that moment did it shut.

JASPER'S SLEEP was accompanied by random dreams about waterfalls and beavers, birds and rocks. But one thing that had woven its way into each interlude was that familiar light that danced in the figure eight.

He had had several rude awakenings, but the next morning's rivaled even the intrusion of Bernard Stockton's chilling voice.

In his sleep he noticed that it was likely close to morning, but he refused to relinquish his sleeping state and open his eyes. That all changed when something punched forcefully in his gut. His back ached, and he couldn't breathe from the blow, but the fist didn't retract as most punches do. It pressed stubbornly into his gut. He opened his eyes to see Timber's vast body standing over him looking outside, one paw firmly planted in Jasper's stomach. The newly awakened young man crankily shoved the beast off and caught his breath sitting up.

Cale was nowhere to be found, and neither was Emmett. He heard a noise behind his head, and turned to find Sophia and Lake quietly making something on the stovetop. Jasper's curly hair had regained its volume after the shower he'd taken the night before, and after sleeping on it, he imagined it was quite wild. Lake had also noticed it and giggled as he rose.

"The lion sleeps tonight!" She declared, drawing a similar smile from Sophia. Jasper fled to the bathroom to fix his mane-like hair with little success.

"Where's Emmett and Cale?" Jasper asked, wiping the sleep from his eyes.

"They went out to see the animals, I think. Emmett likes to get out in the morning," Sophia said as she mixed something in the bowl.

"I'm sorry about the question Cale asked last night. That wasn't right of him," Lake apologized, though it was in essence a lie because she earnestly wanted to know more about this odd reunion. Sophia continued her stirring, but her eyes strayed to the window and its view of the tree line where she'd first seen them.

"It's okay. It was going to come eventually." She looked to see if there were any signs of the boys returning, and after not finding evidence of it, she continued. "We were more than just fond of each other. We were in love. We had all the plans in the world to get married and have a family. Emmett was very generous in his recounting. One night I decided that I wanted to take our relationship to the ultimate level physically. One that Scripture says to save for marriage."

The stirring stopped and was put down as she spoke.

"I thought we were ready, and the moment felt perfect. I loved him more than anything, and I wanted to be with him forever. I wanted him to be the father of my children...but he rejected me." A harsh weight fell upon the room. "He told me that he loved me too much to follow any path other than the one he believed God had laid out for us. I got angry and asked a question. 'Who do you love more, God or me?' He said the former, and I couldn't take it." She resumed stirring more aggressively than ever.

"I hated God, and I hated him. I left and found someone who was unlike either. I didn't want to be reminded about him at all. We never spoke. Devon asked me to marry him, so I did. He provided me with all this." She indicated the house, but it was halfhearted. "It's taken a long time for God to work that hate out of me. I'm just now starting to realize what I've wanted." She looked out the window to find Emmett walking with Cale around the fountain that adorned the middle of the concrete driveway. She smiled, and a lump in her throat caught her voice in a brief moment. "I want people around me, who even when they have every right to shame me, refrain and act gracefully."

Lake and Jasper knew what she had said, and Jasper felt a knot build in his stomach in empathy for the woman. Emmett's nobility had continued to amaze him, and this was a clear example. He thought of their conversation the day before, about the deer's antlers. How they are dangerous and competent like swords but are only unsheathed when absolutely necessary. Emmett could have defended his past with a sword, but he recounted it with honesty and compassion.

The two men entered, and they enjoyed eggs with bread and fruit that Sophia had prepared. It was easily the best meal they'd had in days, and they were liberal in their consumption. After breakfast, they took a walk outside in the brisk mountain air. To the north of the house were two gardens spanning thirty yards each. As they continued from the home to the right, they saw a shed that rivaled the house in size. It had two enormous sliding doors and housed a plethora of machines and tools.

Farther down the concrete road were several animal pens, which were occupied by goats, chickens, and a solitary brown cow. They moved directly north away from the road, and walked through the forested hillside. They had driven north far enough that the trees they saw had become more diverse, and they were greeted by a floor of red, orange, and yellow maple and oak leaves that created a mosaic on the ground. Suddenly the forest had opened to reveal a body of water that calmly reflected the beauty of a mountain straight ahead of them. The water was clear and blue and seemed to sparkle in the morning light. It was a misty morning, and the fog hovered over the water's surface. Behind the clouds rose a sharp, snow covered mountain that jutted like an arrowhead. In awe of the lake's beauty, the group took a moment to sit on the gray stones that lined the lake's edge. The water was still, and there was no sign of civilization around its circumference. Though they had rarely spoken, the childhood friends sat close, watching Cale jump from stone to stone. Inevitably, he slipped off a slanted rock, took several steps in the frigid water, and produced a childish yell that they had never heard from the proud boy. Emmett smiled at the boy and noticed that Sophia was watching him.

"It's so beautiful here," Emmett said.

"There was a major road that was built between Seattle and Spokane. It had branches that helped build towns in the middle of the state, when it was a state. When I married Devon, he was already treasury secretary for the region. I had told him that I wanted a place to go while he was off on business, and he let me choose. There were a few houses down the lake a mile and a half, and he didn't like the idea that I would spend time living alone in the same area as people he thought were degenerates. So he convinced the department of transportation that the roads to this lake were losing money, and they cut them off. There is a dirt road that goes to the south that I use to get here, but everyone else moved away." She pointed to the end of the lake that pointed south.

She sighed and gave a self-deprecating smile. "I thought that having a place to be alone would help...with everything. I was bored. I spent so many hours studying to earn my degree, only to marry someone who was rich enough for me to never have to use it."

"Did it help?" Emmett asked, skipping a rock over the calm water.

"I guess. I built this place up. It gave me something to do, something to produce. Whenever I've shown Devon, he's just said that we could've paid professionals to do it faster." She took the opportunity to cast a rock over the lake's misty reflection.

"What did you study?"

"Engineering."

"You were always better with that type of thing. I always envied that," Emmett said.

"I always wanted to trade with you. You were much better with people. You had a real gift," she replied.

"The world doesn't run around people anymore. It's all statistics and algorithms. Are you sure you'd want to trade?" Emmett said.

The young woman sighed and thought for a second. "Without a doubt."

The group walked back toward the house, but by a different route. After following the lake up toward its northern tip, they hiked east up a path that was only minorly overgrown. The foliage was different on this side of the lake than where they had hiked before. Bright red leaves speckled with bright yellow covered the ground and green bushes lined the sides of the path. Sunbeams fractured by the mist washed over a small wooden bridge of cedar so that it glowed like orange fire. The bridge stood over a small creek that flowed down the hill toward the lake.

A wealth of smells washed over them—wet cedar, fresh mountain mist, and pine sap, and though it hadn't rained that day, there lingered the smell of fresh rain. The detour eventually brought them back at the house. Sophia seemed comfortable with the group and didn't inquire when they would be leaving. Jasper took this as a possibility that they could stay another night. He asked if there was anything he could do to help, and she promptly instructed the young man to go and check the chickens for eggs.

Lake decided to join him in this, and armed with a basket, they set off down the road to where the chicken coop was. It was less of a coop and more of a mansion by standards for a chicken.

"Have you ever gotten eggs before?" Jasper asked.

"No," she answered. "But I think it shouldn't be too hard. Even if they don't want us to take them, they're only chickens."

Jasper hadn't thought of that. He thought it would be like an old video game he once played where chickens just popped out eggs wherever they were and left them unguarded. He had never assumed they would defend their eggs. They opened the door into the structure, and the chickens nervously moved away from them. As they searched for eggs, Jasper thought this would be a good opportunity to hear how she was doing without the pressures of others listening.

"How have you been holding up?" he asked, wishing he had Emmett's gentleness and humor.

"Up and down. It comes in waves." The irony was noted but not acknowledged.

"I'm sorry again about what happened." He found himself again knowing what he wanted to say. "But I am glad you are with us. That you're still with us." He was going to try again, but Lake's brown eyes stopped him. They were very pretty eyes, but they felt unnervingly direct. He had been taught to soften his face and his gaze in order to avoid tipping people off to what he was doing. She made no attempt; her eyes were direct.

She stepped toward him, and his heart skipping a beat.

"What does my face say, Jasper?" she said challengingly, her mouth half open and one side lifted up in a half smile.

Too busy looking into her eyes and attempting to control his heart, Jasper was late looking at her whole face. It showed a little nervousness, but one thing was clear. ATTRACTION. His heart began to beat faster and stronger. He tried to come up with a different emotion that he might have seen.

"I see...uh...happiness?" He didn't try to say it like a question, but that's how it came out.

"Seems like you weren't very good at your job," she said, as she leaned against one of the walls. "How about I give you another try. But this will be your last chance." Her eyes were bright and teasing.

Jasper didn't respond with a word but stepped toward the girl with all the courage he could muster. He dropped his basket and placed one hand on her shoulder and the other on the side of her soft black hair. She tried for a sense of grace in the kiss, but the girl had none of it. She latched her arms around him and to Jasper's dismay didn't let go after the kiss was over. They lingered there for a minute, and then the young woman detached herself from him.

They picked up their baskets and without another word, gathered whatever eggs they could find and returned to the house. When they arrived, all except Cale noticed the time they had taken to return after a simple errand, but none spoke of it. Jasper did however receive a sidelong questioning smile from Emmett.

Sophia cooked the eggs that they had brought back, and they feasted on vegetables and eggs for lunch before sitting down to discuss the future while Cale went outside to explore.

Emmett began. "We really appreciate what you've done for us, Soph...but we don't want to overstay our welcome—"

Before he could finish Sophia, eyebrows raised, cut him off. "What is your plan? What is the next step?" She looked at him keenly and seemed pleased by her old friend's inability to come up with an answer. "You have no plan; you've been moving from place to place to wherever you won't be arrested or starve." Emmett reluctantly met her eyes

"Do you believe in God?" she asked.

Emmitt was taken aback and looked defensive. "Of course, I do," he replied.

"No, do you really believe? Because I remember a fairly reasonable young man telling me years ago that what you believe in can only be confirmed by the action of living as if it is true. You ran out of gas at the top of the ridge next to the only home in miles. Not only that, but the owner and sole inhabitant is one of the only humans in this country that would take you in." Emmett was speechless. Sophia didn't relent.

"Look at the evidence. I've barely thought about God since I was married because I was afraid of what my husband would do. But seeing this has provided me more evidence for His presence than my whole upbringing. What are you afraid of that makes you not want to stay here?"

Emmett sat with his hands clasped together and placed firmly on his mouth. After a moment in which the only sound was Timber's heavy breathing, he cleared his throat and spoke. Jasper and Lake could tell the climax of the conversation was coming, and though they would be interested in hearing it, their respect for the two begged them to depart, leaving Emmett and Sophia alone with Timber. Before they could leave, Emmett spoke.

"I loved you. I always did. I saw a future. A life. When we made the decision that ended us, I was broken. Every fiber of my being wanted to take the step, but I said no. That maybe my faith would be rewarded by something better. That moment made me rely on Him more than ever in my life. When you got married, I was gutted. The hope that following my conviction was going to create a better relationship for the two of us was gone. I still love you and will always love you."

Time stood still. No one spoke for a moment. Even Sophia had been stunned out of her attacking stance.

"That's why it hurts to be here. To know that you are right here but are miles away."

"Because I'm married?" she asked. He nodded. She looked like she understood and used a tissue to wipe the single tear that had escaped. Turning back to him she had a much different posture.

"I've never felt...married. I'm grateful for my husband, but we've never been in the same place for more than a few days. Marriage was a drug. Not some stimulant that brought me a feeling of ecstasy, but a depressant. Something to numb the pain. Seeing you all has let me see more light than I have in years. If that means having to be only friends like we were, it's worth it to me," she said, and her eyes waited on Emmett for him to respond.

Before he said anything, Cale burst into the room at the worst possible moment.

"I like Timber," he said to everyone. "Can we stay with him for a while?"

Emmett looked at the boy who was petting the head of the massive dog and smiled. "I guess if the nice lady will have us, it would be rude to say no." They all smiled, grateful for how the conversation ended as well as the assurance of comfort on a higher level than a few berries and a campfire.

Sophia led them down a stairwell behind the kitchen that led below the ground level, proving Jasper's assumption was right; there was, in fact, a basement. It had the musty concrete smell and sported two old couches, a kitchenette, and a queen bed in the corner beside a wood burning stove.

There was a brief fight about who was to sleep in the bed. All three boys were comfortable sleeping with one another in the queen bed, but Jasper and Emmett were too polite to take on the comfort. Over and over, they argued for the other to have the bed. Emmett reasoned that Jasper should have it because of the condition of his back, and Jasper responded citing the man's age and how, because of his age, he should be the one to have it out of respect.

As the conversation came to a climax, Cale jumped into the bed, with his muddy shoes still on, which ended the debate altogether. After getting settled they returned to the main floor where they were met by Timber, Lake, and Sophia, who had already organized things with Lake's housing situation in the guest room.

The security camera was placed only in Sophia's room, which left it the only area that she deemed off limits, though she was unconvinced that her husband would bother to check it. There was an office space next to the master bedroom that consisted of two bookshelves lining the side walls and an expensive looking desk carved out of solid wood. On the desk were several books, ranging from novels to botany manuals.

On the bookshelf stood a stand that housed an old 1911 pistol, hung by a rod in the barrel.

"Don't be alarmed by the gun. My husband wouldn't let me out here without having some way to scare off bears and wolves," Sophia said, as she blew the dust off the weapon. The cold chrome finish on the sidearm glinted in the light from one of the home's many windows. Its handle was of dark wood that had unique coloration in the grain. Jasper was required to take a basic weapon-safety course, though in his line of work he would rarely be called to use it. Guns had become more outdated after bill D47, which had outlawed lethal bullets.

Lake gave Jasper a mischievous smile as they exited the room and used the small doorway to affectionately touch her cheek to his shoulder as he passed without anyone noticing.

Sophia had several chores to do as they day progressed, which gave Emmett, Jasper, and Cale opportunities to be useful to their host. They spent the rest of the day squishing bugs in the garden, harvesting ripe vegetables, and exploring the rest of the property. Sophia thought it would be a good idea to move their vehicle from the forest edge, and they used gas from her backup generator to drive the SUV carefully through the trees. There were several close calls as miscommunications between the two men were at a high, and in several moments the vehicle almost rolled over shards of rock that could jeopardize the integrity of the tires. They parked the outdated vehicle in the second garage spot next to Sophia's electric SUV, which was beyond top of the line.

Sundown eventually began to creep up on the day, granting the men freedom from their chores. They sat on the concrete patio in front of the house with different kinds of tea in their hands, discussing what the childhood of Bernard Stockton would have been like. Cale had set up stakes in the first line of trees beyond the concrete to play the game he created. The sound of the soft streamed television played in the room behind them loud enough for them to acknowledge it but not enough to distinguish what was on.

Lake had taken a shower and was preparing for the night meal the last time Jasper had seen her. He was feeling satisfied with how the day had gone. After the torrent of threats and tragedies that befell them in the last two weeks, he felt that they had made it through. He had made new friends, learned he could do more than he had ever thought he could, and met Lake. She was something else entirely. He had never admitted it to Emmett, but he would if the older man asked. He was attracted to her, and the fact that she wasn't frightened of him filled Jasper with a hope his mind had never before let his heart indulge in.

He heard footsteps behind him, and the door to the house opened fully. Jasper was excited every time he saw the young woman, and in anticipation he swiveled the outdoor chair to cast his eyes on her. What he saw made a chill run down his spine.

Lake stood in the doorway of the house, pointing the gun at him. Her face was pale with shock, and a torrent of conflicting emotions spilled across it. Jasper saw rage and horror and a deep despairing hurt. And under it all, he could see conflict as her heart seemed to be screaming, No! Her soft eyes were hard as agates, and her lips were curled back in an animal-like snarl unveiling tightly clenched teeth. She breathed heavily, and her body trembled,

"Lake?" Jasper said questioningly.

"Shut up!" she said through gritted teeth. Something caught his gaze behind her. Looking at the screen in the living room, he could make out three main objects. He couldn't breathe. There was his face, Emmett's face, and a repeating video of the explosion of the Evergreen dam. His horrified attention returned to Lake's face. She wasn't herself, and Jasper knew it.

Everyone seemed frozen in place as Sophia came down the stairs and surveyed the situation. She glanced at the newscast on the screen and noticed the young lady pointing the weapon at Jasper.

"You killed everyone." The words were spoken softly and were all the more piercing by their implications. Jasper was speechless. What could he say? He quickly decided to at least say something to calm her down, to explain.

"No. We—"

"No! No lies." She yelled now, freeing her voice from her tightly clasped teeth. Her hands shook as she gripped the weapon even tighter. Tears ran down her face. Jasper noticed Sophia slowly approaching, careful not to spook the girl.

"You lied to me. You killed my family...and everyone!" she yelled again. Jasper opened his hands in an effort to reason with the girl.

"No, we didn't. It was..."

"You killed them, and you kissed...and I..." Her emotions seemed to race across her face, and her mouth opened as if in a silent wail. Jasper looked into her eyes, hoping to communicate his plea to her, but it was returned by a cold look that stung him. He began to rise from the chair. He saw the pain in her eyes reach a new extreme, and it was accompanied by her squeezing the weapon, still pointed at his chest.

Suddenly, Cale was calmly walking to his sister's side. He placed his hands on top of her hands and pulled the weapon down toward the ground. His sister's face was still filled with rage, but Cale had introduced a challenge to the rage. She closed her eyes and appeared to relax, but pain erupted on her face anew, and she attempted to raise the gun again. Cale's hand was still holding it, and in the struggle, it went off.

The projectile hit Jasper in the leg, which exploded with pain.

However, to everyone's amazement, there was no outpouring of blood. Instead there was a small cut accompanied by shards of plastic and wax. Cale took the weapon from Lake's hands. Jasper grasped his leg.

"I'm sorr..." His apology was cut short.

She tackled him to the ground, and his back pain found new fiery life as his puncture wounds reopened. She began to hit him in the chest and the shoulders. The blows came faster than he could block, but their speed mitigated their strength. Eventually Sophia and Emmett brought the girl up, now crying. Jasper groaned and rolled over. Lake was stunned by the blood that his back had left on the patio, but before she could say anything else, Sophia took her into the house.

TWELVE

HIS BACK WAS WET, he knew that well enough, and there was a throbbing pain that echoed from the reopened cuts in his back. This was accompanied by a fresh cut in his shin. His breath was still fast and uncontrolled. Every time he tried to calm it, Lake's face reemerged and brought panic with it. The look on her face was animal. Primal. The bright and lively girl had, even in her sorrow, been a stable and consistent figure in the group. Whenever Jasper's ever overthinking mind drew him away from reality, her caring eyes kindly brought him back, but what he saw behind her fists was a tempest of anger. RESENTMENT. SORROW. He hadn't seen anything like that in the security buildings. He looked at the big man who sat, bandages at the ready.

"You really should stop being so reckless with these wounds. Your luck is going to run out, and they are going to get infected." Emmett said as he picked up a small carboard box full of plastic coated wax bullets. "Speaking of wounds, how are you feeling right now? These are meant for scaring off animals without hurting them enough to make them ornery. Do you feel ornery? Angry? Like you want to rip apart whoever shot you?" His real question was hidden in the satire.

"No, she had every right to feel the way she did." Jasper said, ignoring the jests. He glanced back at the man and was met by a concerned look.

"Be careful with her," Emmett said softly, his tone changed. "I know you care for her. Be honest, and maybe you can salvage this friendship." Emmett got up and went across the patio to the front door.

"Where is she?" Jasper asked, testing his ribs for breaks.

"Sophia brought her inside and is calming her down. She will explain what happened. How we aren't the suicide bombers that Stockton framed us to be."

A question popped into Jasper's head that he felt he should've had much earlier.

"If Sophia saw the news, then how did she know that we weren't what they made us to be?"

"She saw that we were alive. She had a hard time believing I would do that in the first place, but us being alive proved to her that we weren't suicide bombers. After she saw us, she looked at the film again and saw the missile trail. If you weren't looking for it, you would miss it. Us being alive is our biggest argument for our innocence. She will show Lake the footage. Hopefully whatever satellite or drone they used to record it didn't pick us up on the bank."

Jasper hadn't thought of that possibility. *Could they still be looking for us?* he thought. He felt again that cold feeling of dread that came from being hunted. Jasper lingered with his thoughts on the patio after Emmett checked on the others inside. He cursed his inability to tell her the truth. There had been so many opportunities to explain, but fear had shackled him every time.

No one shooting missiles at them. No helicopters that meant life in prison. No chilling voice in his dreams to shock him out of slumber. For once they were in a safe place, but Jasper realized that no one can outrun the lies they are too afraid to confront. There was no escape. Fast, accurate, and painful. Just as they had found something to be encouraged about, the pendulum had switched and brought hell with it.

Jasper came in the house and sat alone on the couch for an hour with only Timber for company.

Sophia sat at the end of the couch.

"I'm sorry I turned the screen on. I thought they were done publicizing it. Typically, they only have a story on for a day before they find something else they want to convince us of. But they have kept the dam video on for quite a while. Must be a serious point they want to make."

A door opened behind them, and out came a tear-streaked Lake, who quickly fled to the bathroom at the end of the hall without looking at Jasper. Once the door closed behind her, Jasper found his reply.

"It's not your fault. I didn't tell her what happened. She had already guessed that the flood must have come from one of the dams collapsing, but I couldn't find the right way to tell her that we were responsible."

"You weren't responsible. You were unarmed fugitives. They knew where you were. You didn't provoke an airstrike on a dam that would kill thousands."

It felt good that someone neutral was trying to make him feel better, but there remained still a question in his consciousness that nagged at him. He sighed.

"Why didn't we just leave it all alone at the compound?" he asked nobody in particular. At that moment Emmett returned to the room and stood leaning on the couch behind him.

"Is that still not clear?" Sophia said, surprising Jasper. "You were left in the dark, thinking that life was only about the State. It's what your life was surrounded by. It's obvious that God wanted to show you something greater. So He put Emmett in your path," Jasper looked to Emmett, wondering how she learned of this.

"We talked while you were getting eggs," Emmett said. Jasper turned his attention back to Sophia.

"I see that, and all it's seemed like is that my only purpose has been to survive missiles, random people in the woods, floods, and beaver dams," Jasper remarked.

Sophia looked at him quizzically at that last one.

"I'll tell you later," Emmett responded, encouraging Jasper to continue his thought.

"What now... We've survived... But what now?" he said in resignation. Right on cue, Lake emerged from the bathroom and strode to the middle of the room, tears lingering on her face. Jasper stood trying to find the right words. Finding none better, he spoke the only ones he could think of.

"I'm sorry," Jasper and Lake said in unison. They were both taken aback by the other's word, but their confusion was lost as they embraced. She squeezed Jasper hard. Then they both relaxed their arms and stepped back to look at each other.

"Sophia explained everything to me. I'm sorry for doubting you," Lake said quietly.

Jasper returned the apology again.

"Now that we all understand each other, can I take a look at how they are covering this tragedy?" Emmett asked. Sophia and Lake both gave slight nods, though Lake seemed unconvinced. Emmett turned the stream on anyway.

It took only a few seconds to find the regional information stream. It revealed a compilation of ten interviews with people who were speaking out against the two terrorists, Emmett Walsh and Jasper Wood. Several of the interviewees gave testimonies about their belief in God, but they were deterred from the belief because of the atrocity that was caused by those who destroyed in His name.

"Unbelievable, isn't it?" Sophia asked the room. "Don't let it get to you, guys. These are probably actors posing as genuine former Christians." The words didn't improve Emmett's expression. He was almost in a daze, as if there was something that he was missing.

"Has the coverage always been like this?" Emmett asked her.

"For the most part. There was a documentary tangled together of the history of massacres justified by religion."

"Have they shown any footage of the destruction left by the water?" Jasper asked, unsure if he wanted to know the answer. She thought for a moment.

"No. There hasn't been any video. Only of the destruction of the dam itself. They've mentioned the death toll as well as property damage that you two caused, but never showed footage." This irked Jasper, and he could tell that he wasn't the only one.

"Why?" he asked.

Emmett paced across the room and back.

"When Garrison's administration was elected, there was constant news footage of riots and attacks that they laid at the feet of religion. They used every second of video to teach people to be afraid of religion. Why not now?" Emmett asked.

Sophia gave no reply as she saw where Emmett and Jasper's minds were going.

Jasper had heard something, recently, from Emmett that was at the edge of his mind. A conversation they'd had. Something in his brain was screaming at him to remember it.

"No one paid real attention to the reservation. Maybe they don't want anyone to know that it existed," Lake proposed offhandedly.

It finally registered. "That's it!" Jasper exclaimed!

"What? That they don't want anyone to know we existed. Are we that useless?"

"Yes... No... I mean..." Jasper's mind was going faster than his mouth could speak. "Let me explain. When I worked at the compound, we heard about a building project being signed off on that would create one large State rehabilitation ward. It was rumored to be a huge project and would combine a military compound with a rehab and interrogation lab all in one facility." Sophia and Cale looked at him thoroughly confused. Sophia didn't know where he was going, but she nodded indicating she had known about the project.

"My husband signed off on the project. It cost a lot, if I remember. They hadn't begun construction because the land they wanted was occupied. They offered to buy it, but their offer was..." As Sophia's words fell, Emmett latched onto the growing idea.

"Their offer was rejected. They still wanted the land—" Emmett knew where he was going, but he was distracted when Sophia left the room. Soon she returned with a tablet from the office. She began typing and soon motioned for the two men to see.

"Our internet is encrypted, and my husband is cleared for basically all searches." She typed several key words and found folders of data already on the subject of Umchin and Evergreen Dam. Both files were organized in a larger file that was named 'Soteria.'

"Does Soteria mean anything to you?" Sophia asked the group but received nothing.

"Why is it capitalized?" Jasper asked.

"Because it's important!" piped Cale, excited to give support whenever he felt he could. Emmett wasn't satisfied, however.

"I think it's a name." Emmett responded.

"Not English is it?" Sophia asked.

"No. It sounds Greek." Emmett resumed his pacing trying to remember the word's meaning.

Sophia returned to scouring through the files all labeled "classified." She opened a subfolder that had been tagged with the word *Umchin*. In it were three contractor reports. One from a lake in what had previously been known as Idaho. Another from a desert valley south of Pasco, and lastly, from the Umchin reservation.

The first report showed that the plot of land considered for construction was prime and would be worth bidding for the price of the land. At the bottom was an indication of denial that confused Sophia, but she dropped it and continued to the next. The report of the land south of Pasco indicated it wouldn't be cost effective and also ended with the red denial marker. The last report read that Umchin was a valuable option given its proximity to the mountain that would provide protection in the case of aerial warfare. At the bottom was a digital stamp of approval "upon purchase of land."

"Umchin was one of the options for the compound," Sophia said, confirming the chatter Jasper had heard. "They offered housing in Westfield and four-hundred thousand dollars to each household if they were to sell." Emmett whistled at the amount. The mood grew cold as each person understood what had gone on.

"They didn't accept the offer, did they?" Emmett asked heavily. Sophia shook her head.

"The only other option was at a lake, eight or so hours from here." She returned back to the denied report. Her eyes grew as she looked at the buyout list.

"It was denied, because the regional governor's cabin was on that lake," Sophia admitted in shock.

"So they only had one option—Umchin—and they didn't accept the buyout," Jasper reasoned.

"So they were likely ecstatic when two fugitives were hiding in the largest dam in the northwest that was just a few miles away from the land they wanted to build on," Emmett deduced.

"And that's why they didn't show footage of it. They didn't want anyone to know they destroyed the dam so they wouldn't have to pay or kick out the people on the reservation to get their house of horrors built."

No one spoke. Jasper looked at the faces around him, expressions from anger, to disgust, and finally...resentment.

"How could he have signed off on this?" Sophia asked and began to cry. All sat in the room quietly. The sun went down, and Emmett left his seat on the couch with Sophia to start a fire in the fireplace.

"What is the purpose of the compound?" Emmett asked both Sophia and Jasper.

Sophia handed the tablet to Emmett, unwilling to chance finding more damning realizations. He scrolled through files and made several searches about the content.

"It looks like they are planning to consolidate all their rehab centers in one location per region. Instead of using the security centers as re-education facilities for threats against the State, they want to have one large one that has military security," Emmett said.

"What's the point of their rehab? How many of the people who go there are cleared to leave?" Jasper tapped on the tablet, searching the government's databases.

"Twenty-three percent," he said, surprised about the number. Emmett lit the fire, and after it had grown, he returned to his seat.

"What's the data of the last few years between rehabilitation success and people arrested on charges of religious affiliation?" Emmett asked.

Jasper tapped on the tablet once again, his hands remembering the database navigation he learned in the academies.

"In the last few years, the rehabilitation success rate has dropped 15 percent per year. The number of people who were printed and entered has grown 44 percent each year since it began."

Emmett thought for a moment, an idea brewing in his mind.

"They're not trying to rehabilitate people, otherwise their numbers would be higher on both ends. It's obviously not deterring people from practicing their faith, otherwise the numbers of printed would stay similar or go down." He was thinking. "They don't want to turn people away from their faith convictions, because they know that if they are convicted about it, they won't. They want one big prison to make these people disappear. Erase the history of faith, by erasing the people who keep that history alive."

The logic clicked for Jasper. He was surprised by his ignorance throughout the years. He was taught that religion had been omitted from education because it was an illogical waste of time. He had believed religion to be the root cause of evil. That it was the greatest threat to the State's security. *That*, he was right about.

Something caught his eye on a file. He saw the logo of the State's party at the top of the transcript. A green infinity sign that was shaped by arrows pointing in at themselves. It was the light. The light that danced in his mind during his sleep. That constant horizontal figure eight that had confused him many times in the previous week.

"Emmett? What is the State party's logo supposed to mean? Why not do an animal like the Democrats or GOP?"

Emmett came over and investigated to make sure he knew what logo he was talking about.

"The State party preached unity, which is why they wanted to dismantle state borders and run the country as one big State. The slogan at the bottom supports that. 'Only together can we survive.'" Emmett shook his head. "Anyway the arrows pointing in to create an infinity sign were meant to indicate that as long as we turn our efforts inward and keep them to the State, we as a country will survive. It makes a lot of sense to a people who are scared and full of division, but soon after Garrison was elected and all the influence was in the party's hands, then they began criminalizing any allegiance that wasn't to the State. Religion, ideology, those sorts of things." Emmett stopped his political explanation and sat down. His face showed no anger, but sadness was left in his eyes.

"There was a man not too long ago who believed people should cast away convictions to anything outside themselves. Then they could live free, revolving around themselves as their own true sun. That's the thing: people are flawed, so they can be horrible things to revolve around." He looked up at the others and gave a half smile. "That's why I choose to revolve around a different kind of Son. The One who is perfect and always with me and died for me."

He looked up to Sophia who had tears reborn in her eyes.

"What's wrong, Soph?" Emmett asked, not getting up from his seat.

The woman wiped her tears with her sleeve working on a response. "So many years. I'm so sorry... I"—she faltered—"I've wasted years of my life pushing away the only thing worth holding on to."

"It's never too late?"

"It's too late for a lot of things. It's too late to take back my marriage to a man who never wants to see me. I'm sure he has another." Now she was weeping. Jasper and Lake were taken aback by the accusation against her husband. Lake stood and put her arm around the woman as she cried. Emmett took this moment to rise as well, but he didn't go as far as putting his arm around her.

"What do I do?" she asked him.

Emmett returned a smile. "You know what to do if you want to. Just as well as I do."

She lifted her hands up as if she were a child asking to be taken up by their parents.

"I choose you, Father," she implored.

The group took positions around her in a group hug as they all saw a modern prodigal come home. They stood together for a while, and then, after many hugs and thanks, Sophia went to the kitchen to make something to eat.

"My husband will kill me if I tell him." she said to no one in particular. Then she laughed and cleared her eyes as she pulled out pots and pans to begin dinner.

"So does that mean you won't tell him?" Emmett asked?

"No, I don't think I will."

"Do you think that will be an easy thing to keep away from him?"

"Yes. We don't talk unless he needs me to sign something or ask what I'm doing." She grew somber talking about it, then brightened in an attempt to change the subject. "So what should we do now?"

"We?" Emmett responded skeptically.

"Yes, we. We all must have a part in what the Father is doing here. You said it yourself. The State is trying to snuff out any allegiance that isn't to itself."

"Is your network using blockers that disallow people from knowing where you are searching from?" Jasper asked.

"Yes. My husband had it set up. He didn't want anyone snooping in case he did work from here. He had that whole office built but only used it once."

Jasper began searching his media accounts. They had very little following, given his work hours and inability to hold friendships. When he looked at his profile, he found it flooded with messages and comments. He scrolled through and found that they were all grave insults and curses made to play on his inhumanity and demonic morals. Hundreds of messages ranging from celebratory messages at his death to a fury-induced letter saying they wish he survived so they could slowly and painfully murder him because of what he did. The shock was overwhelming, and he began to feel the blood pumping hot where the bullet had struck his leg.

He was forgetting to breathe and made himself consciously take a breath in and out as he had when his parents fought when he was a kid. He didn't want to read any more, but he felt a push to continue. More and more deadly curses stung his heart. He then came to a message that showed dissonance. It read,

---

Dear Jasper Wood, You don't know me and will never know me. But just to give you some context, my wife, Gena, and daughter, Susanna, loved to hike, ride bikes, and go canoeing. It was something they could do together as a mother and daughter, so I let them have their alone time. It just so happens that the night you blew up Evergreen dam was the night that they were testing the wonderful new canoe that we had been building for a year. It was beautiful, with bass and cedar strips that made it look like a tiger on the water. It was a little heavier than I thought, which made it harder to fight the current of the river. I wanted to get pictures of my girls slipping down the river in their creation, so I climbed Pine Springs hill to catch them rowing down the river at sunset. Then the ground shook, and when I looked down the river, I saw a tsunami, and I couldn't believe it. Nothing I could have done. Too big, too fast. I've tried drinking. I've even tried drowning, but for some reason I just can't die. I'm trying this other way, something my dad taught me a long time ago. I forgive you, Jasper. All this pain is still here and probably always will be, but I hold this not against you. God rest your soul. ~ Louis Antonio

---

Jasper looked at the profile picture of the man. The man had black skin and in the picture stood tall between a woman and a younger girl. His head was shaved, and a smile brightened his face. Next to his picture was his name. Louis Antonio. Jasper stared at the message, reading it again in consternation. The weight that had built in his heart was dissipating. Not because the messages weren't heart-breaking, but because the sharp contrast of this man's words sparked a fire built by wonder.

He refreshed the page, remembering the name, and as if it was stolen, when the page refreshed, the message had vanished. This was odd considering all the other posts were still where they were supposed to be. He paid it no mind and saw another message pop up. It was a private message from the night the day after the dam. Fresh chills ran up his spine as he read the message from the pictureless profile.

"I know you're alive. ~ B.S"

Frozen, Jasper didn't flinch when Lake sat next to him and peered at the tablet.

"Who's B.S?" she asked.

The question caught Emmett's attention, and he looked at Jasper pointedly. Jasper's mind was like an overloaded computer. Both men were visibly shaken, and this gave Sophia a chance to repeat the question, now very intrigued.

"Who's B.S? Bull....?"

"Banana Split?" Cale piped in.

"No...Bernard Stockton. He knows we're alive."

THIRTEEN

THE NIGHT TOOK on a surprisingly relaxed tone, given the day's events and findings. After dinner they sat quietly around the fireplace. It was late enough that Cale had given up on staying awake and left down the stairs to the basement. The fire crackled in the fireplace, and the room was silent except for occasional pops from the sap within the logs.

Jasper had never been into tea, but he grew a liking for the warm drink's subtle flavor. His mind felt calm and less scattered after he drank it. He even began to assume Sophia had dissolved some ADD medication into it to keep his nerves from bursting whenever something surprising happened, which in the last few days, was almost always.

He caught Emmett examining his hands on the couch adjacent to him. The big man rubbed them together, feeling them, studying them with intent.

"Does it feel different having new prints?" Jasper asked.

"No. I thought it would. I notice that something is different, but when I look at them, they still are my hands." He touched his fingers together. "It's interesting how we flock to identifiers to indicate our personhood. Every human is different in so many ways, yet we found our way to synthesizing ourselves down to fingerprints and retina signatures." He held out his hands to the three. "Emmett Walsh is gone. Whatever they classified my new print signature as after I was printed is now who I am to the world."

Jasper thought about the message from Bernard Stockton. *Emmett Walsh continues, at least in the mind of one man outside the room.* Before he could change the trajectory of his train of thought, Lake spoke for the first time since they'd sat down. She was rubbing the top of her necklace, making the gold gleam in the firelight.

"When we were talking about being noble, you focused on the deer. How it stands, prepared for a fight but not instigating. What does that mean for what we're doing right now? There is so much evil...just the fact that tens of thousands of people can be wiped away without evidence that they ever existed makes me wonder, Is it enough to just grow figurative antlers?"

The question sounded like a critique, but by her tone Jasper knew it wasn't. Her desire to do something was a fire burning in her.

Emmett thought about her question, and all sat in expectation.

"My dad was a pastor. When he would come home, sometimes he'd talk with my mom about people he was ministering to. He often told stories of tragedy and triumph, but there was one story that stuck with me. He spoke about a young man who had grown up in our church, and my dad baptized him when he was in high school. After he graduated, he fell in love with this girl. She moved and went to a college far from the one he attended, and they grew apart." Emmett sighed as he continued.

"The young man started drinking and eventually got a different girl pregnant. He came to my dad first, asking for advice and help. My dad steered him away from abortion and encouraged him to marry the young woman or put the child up for adoption. The woman was unwilling to give the child up, and the young man married her soon after, though reluctantly. My dad used to come home often and discuss the matter with my mom. I only heard bits from my room, but from what I remember, the marriage wasn't going well. He came over once and talked alone with my dad. My mom stayed with me in my room when he came so they could be alone, but I remember hearing the man scream once, 'God! Just release me from her! Take her away!'" Emmett spoke with a lump in his throat now. He took a sip from his tea and set it down to finish the story.

"I hadn't heard anyone pray something like that before. My mom reacted as if she hadn't, either. Later my dad talked with my mom and told her he believed what he said. He was so angry at his circumstances that he went so far as to prefer her death to gain his freedom. After that I didn't hear much about him for a while. After a month or so, he began meeting with my dad again, and it seemed like things were better. My dad even introduced me to him once, though I was really young and can't remember his face. His marriage was improving, and he seemed excited about being a father. About a month later, my dad came home and was very distraught. His face looked like he had been crying, and he had red marks on his arms and face. Later I eavesdropped on dad talking to mom about how there were complications in the delivery, and they lost the mother and child both."

The words came out of his mouth like breath on a frozen day, the vapor floating in the air as the group fit pieces together.

"He was in disbelief and attacked my dad when he was trying to comfort him. I never really heard from him after that. He never showed up at the church again. He blamed himself for their deaths, thinking God had granted his wish that they be taken away from him." He turned to Lake but addressed the room. "He looked into the human capacity for evil, personally. It frightened him and gave him a new perspective. Instead of it driving him to turn to God, he rejected Him. I don't know what has happened to him, but we can learn from him. Our capacities for evil are great, but that means our utility for good can be even greater. Standing firm on our beliefs regardless of ground or storm is an immense undertaking. Knowing who we are and standing in that identity is what we've been called to do. A truth in this chaotic world."

"But it seems like we are surrounded by evil. What gives us any hope that our being good will do any good?" Lake stared intently at the fire, seeming lost in the flames.

Emmett looked into the heat as it danced on the glowing coals.

"When it's daylight outside, if I had a fire, a lighter, or torch, what could you tell me about it from fifty yards away?" Emmett asked, opening up the question to the trio.

"From that far away, unless we can see the lighter itself, we couldn't know that much," Jasper responded. Sophia smiled, somehow knowing the direction Emmett was going.

"What if it was pitch black outside, and we had colorants to make the flame different colors? What could you tell me?" he asked

"Well...we could probably tell you the color of the flames and how big there were," Lake answered.

"We may also know if there was any wind, based on how the flame moved," Jasper added.

"Really? All that, in pitch black darkness?" Emmett questioned. His point ready to be made, the two waited as he found the words. "The Bible uses light as a metaphor for truth. Truth illuminates our path. When we don't have light, we stumble on things unseen in the darkness. But truth reveals the path even in the darkest night. Like you guys said, light is even more evident in the night. Think of darkness as lies; God's truth penetrates through the lies. You have His truth. Just knowing who you are in Him makes you a beacon of that truth." Emmett looked at them individually with tears in his eyes.

"I don't care what the State has," he said, putting his hands on Lake's and Jasper's shoulders. "Two children who know the truth can be the most dangerous thing in the world." Emmett stood and looked at Sophia, whose eyes once again brimmed with tears. Jasper felt warm and renewed with purpose as he locked eyes with Lake.

"How do we know the truth? And what do we do with it?" Lake asked earnestly.

"Well, telling the truth is always a good start, but we have something even better. Christ told us in John's Gospel that if we are faithful in following His word, we will know the truth and the truth will set us free. So we must follow the teachings of Christ. This, of course, is not enough. We cannot keep this to ourselves, we must tell others that they are called to live in the truth too."

"How do we do that? Do we get special noble bows to shoot truth arrows?" Jasper asked. Emmett laughed and looked at Sophia, who grinned as well.

"That's a thought. But I think the first thing is that we need a safe place where people don't have to fear a psych ward just for following God." Emmett looked at the data pad. Open on its screen was a blueprint of the building plans for the rehab compound. "I'm guessing they will begin building it within the next month or so." This brought a reaction from Lake, whose fists tightened at the thought of the State using her old home they had turned into a graveyard for such a purpose so soon after its destruction.

"Should we burn it to the ground right after it's built?" she asked. If he wasn't a facial analyst, he would have brushed it off as a joke, but Jasper saw from her face that she was dead serious.

"I know it must hurt to have that building be there, but they would only build it again," Sophia responded softly to Lake.

"If we had a safe place to take people, however, we could help people...'disappear' from their religious rehabilitation," Emmett proposed.

"But we don't have a safe place," Jasper said, hoping to slow the train of action down. Emmett nodded, acknowledging Jasper.

"What if that safe place was here?" Sophia proposed. Emmett looked at her with skepticism.

"No, really," she insisted. "I can't think of a better place. There is only one road here, which almost no one knows about. It's almost uninhabited, and we could build larger underground structures to expand." Emmett looked at her, eyes softening.

"Soph, that would put you at risk with us."

"I wouldn't be acting in nobility or truth if I did anything less. I know what I am getting into. Look on the bright side. I would finally get to use my education for something valuable."

"Have you forgotten that you are married to one of the most powerful State politicians in the country?"

"No, I've tried but...no." She stopped and thought about that for a moment, then spun back with an idea. "There is only one room with a camera. As long as nothing odd happens in the room, then we should be fine." Emmett didn't look convinced. Sophia made an effort at thought. "We would need some way to get building materials."

"But wouldn't new structures be suspicious?" Jasper asked.

"Yes, but we would build underground structures that the satellites couldn't see and helicopter patrols would miss."

"Ahh," Jasper said.

"But won't your husband notice something was off?" Lake asked.

"Not likely. He usually just gives me a budget of what I can spend, and I visit him once a month or so. He usually ignores me when I do, but I do it more out of principle than affection."

Jasper saw a relaxing in Emmett's jaw at that fact. Though the man was visibly uncomfortable with the reintroduction to his first love, he had grown less so in the hours they had spent together. Jasper's mind raced as he was taking in the information, a wealth of possibilities and hindrances coming to mind. This idea was crazy, maybe even impossible, but it was worth a try.

"It's done. I've made up my mind. I always wanted this place to have a purpose outside of giving me and Timber a place to stretch our legs and breathe clean air." Sophia looked bright, confident, and almost giddy during her declaration. Emmett exhaled, smiled at the woman, and for the first time since they had been there, initiated an embrace with her.

"If God is for us, who can be against us?"

THE NEXT MORNING Jasper woke fresh and renewed. Emmett and Cale had, as usual, beaten him upstairs, and he found them wrestling with Timber on the patio. Outside the many windows in the house was a bank of mist that moved throughout the trees. Jasper had never been an outdoorsy person, but he found that he missed the fresh smells of morning in the open air. He put on one of the jackets that belonged to Sophia's husband and strode through the back door.

He walked through the fallen leaves that painted the path red and orange as they fell in the morning breeze. As he breathed in the misty air, he pondered the insanity that was the change the last two weeks made with regard to his life. He had been an analyst, likely to do the same job forever, get paid the same, and live in the same place, never looking beyond his life of simplicity and security.

He had almost died twice, but now he was in the most beautiful place he had ever seen, something that he would've never sought out on his own. He came to the edge of the lake and listened to the subtle waves lapping on the dark gray boulders that made much of the shoreline.

He walked up the shore stepping from stone to stone. After a few hops he realized that he was in danger of looking silly. Even if the only audience was the fish of the lake, he was determined to protect himself from any embarrassment. Instead of stopping the balancing act, he decided to put his hands in his pockets as he kept his balance from rock to rock so he would look as cool as he thought possible.

He followed the shore for a half mile and then turned back toward the hills where they had been led before. The mist hung thicker as he navigated the trail toward the small cedar bridge over one of the mountain creeks. Squirrels were out, announcing his approach as he walked below them.

What a life it would be to be a squirrel, he thought. *Storing up food, chasing each other around. That sounds like a preferable way of life. Rather than responsibility, you have play.* As if the squirrels could hear his thoughts, several pairs danced around, chasing one another with reckless abandon. Jasper stopped to watch the pair and felt a smile creep onto his face at the scene. A shrill screech from above interrupted the picturesque moment and brought him back to reality. The squirrels scattered from the circling red-tailed hawk above, finding their homes to escape the ruthless creature.

It's more than an arbitrary life of chasing and foraging; they need a constant wariness of predators in every direction. The notion brought him back to the chilling message from Stockton. The days after the dam were horrible, but he'd felt bolstered by the fact that no one would be chasing them. But Stockton wasn't convinced. Maybe he saw them escape on the satellite. Either way, the curtain of comfort had once again been lifted. It had happened many times in the past week, but Jasper realized something different about this awakening.

Though the message chilled him to the bone, it didn't discourage him. Every time another event had gotten in their way, he'd thought about giving in. But in that moment, he felt no compulsion to hide or run. It almost startled him that he felt that way. Realizing that a feeling of freedom was growing in him made him feel high. It wasn't a feeling like some psychedelic that pushed him from reality; instead, he felt like he was a character in one of the video games he played. As long as you stay on the story line, your character will survive. He knew he was on the story line, and that was enough.

The red-and-yellow-leaf-covered trail led to the red cedar bridge Sophia had shown them. As he came around the bend, he found Sophia and Lake sitting on its damp planks, their legs dangling over the stream that cascaded down from the mountains. He stepped quickly behind a rock, hoping not to disturb them.

"Jasper, it's okay! You can come," Sophia called. Jasper turned back but when he came around the rock again only Lake remained on the bridge. She acknowledged him but resumed her gaze into the trees and creek below. Jasper sat on the damp orange planks next to her and let his legs dangle as she did.

"Where did Sophia go?" he asked.

"She wanted to get started on sifting through her bedroom to take out anything that she wouldn't want destroyed. She's very smart, you know."

"I can tell. What were you two talking about?"

"Lots of things." She looked down and around at her surroundings. "She built this, you know." She touched the bright wooden bridge.

"It's very nice." Jasper said, and he noticed the same color of wood in the stream bed as well as behind him. Shards of the bright wood were all around him, and he had to turn almost all the way around to find the source. A tall cedar tree had snapped toward the mountainside, and its base was just by the creek; it had splintered thoroughly throughout the area.

"It looks like someone blew up the tree. Its color is really bright," Jasper noted.

"It fell in a windstorm. There are a couple more like it. She milled the wood for this from one that was closer to the house." It sounded like a lot of work for just a simple bridge, but Jasper assumed that she'd had the time for it. They stayed in silence for a moment, neither exhibiting the ease that they once had when together. He knew they had questions for each other. He realized, however, that there was a difference between having a situation that requires questioning and knowing which ones should be asked. Like he'd done several times before, he decided to throw one out and hope that it was better than nothing.

"So... Where are we?" Not a strong effort at a question, and Jasper knew it. Lake gestured all around her as if that was the answer he was expecting.

"I don't know about you, but I think we are in the most beautiful place on earth," she said smiling. "But I don't think that is what you were really asking."

He nodded and gave a self-deprecating smile. "I meant us. Are we okay?"

"I tackled you, Jasper. I could have killed you! And you're the one asking if we're okay?"

"But you didn't."

"Still, how can things be the same between us?" Lake asked as a flash of shame crossed her face.

"Well..."

"So obviously we wouldn't be okay!" she said, louder now. "Jasper, when I saw the dam with your faces on it, I was more angry than I've ever been in my life. Angry enough to react in violence before even asking for your side of the story." She sounded like she was about to cry, but no tears came. "You should've told me the truth about why you were there. I trusted you, and you should've given that to us, as well." Her emotion grew as her words continued. "But that's no reason to...you know."

Jasper, seeing her falter in speech, began to respond but she waved him off. She wasn't done yet.

She took out the necklace with the deer nobly standing atop the heights. She rubbed it, and it glimmered in the morning light.

"It took me a day or two to forget what I had decided to try and become. I can't imagine what my mom would have said." She stopped herself. "Actually, I can imagine what she would say. It wouldn't have been too nice, though."

Jasper leaned toward her and reached out, asking to hold the pendant. She took it off and placed it in his hand. He didn't know what to say; he didn't even know what he wanted to say. Knowing that he didn't have to ask out loud to his Father, he gave it a try and asked for help.

"Now I know that there is a purpose for me outside my town, my family, but I was so mad, I was willing to end yours. I forgot my commitment to act with nobility, and it made me forget yours too," Lake said, her voice full of emotion again.

Jasper felt a compulsion to say something. "Lake. You're right; I should have trusted you with the truth. I didn't hide it intentionally at first, but once we discovered the full weight of the destruction, I just couldn't find the words to tell you. I felt responsible and was afraid you would never forgive me. I didn't know if I deserved your forgiveness, but I didn't want to lose you." The words came to him alarmingly clear. He didn't have time to wonder if he truly believed what he had just said, but the look on Lake's face banished any further thought on the matter. Lake's big brown eyes brimmed with tears at his words. She leaned closer to him, and he followed. As their faces grew closer and Jasper's eyes were about to close, she stopped.

"Don't make me push you into the water," she said smiling. Jasper laughed awkwardly, but before he could recover, he felt her lips plaster to his smiling face, where they lingered for a brief moment before she pulled away. Speechless, they sat together on the bridge looking out at the creek flowing below their feet to the lake beyond the tree line. Her head lay on his shoulder, which was uncomfortable for him, but he didn't care.

"Imagine if we had told our story to a relationship counselor," Jasper proposed jokingly. Realizing he had said more than he had meant to, he turned to clarify, but she beat him to it.

"Relationship?" She said, her head tilting questioningly.

"I didn't mean—" he started, but his gift came in handy as he saw the spark of annoyance in her face at his apologetic tone. She relaxed her face and returned it to his shoulder.

"I like how that sounds." Jasper looked up acknowledging the work of another as he sat next to one he had begun to love more than anything else he could think of. He opened his eyes wide and, assuming God could read facial expressions, moved his face to show the most gratitude he could muster. He'd never assumed God wanted anything to do with romantic endeavors, but given Jasper's former success in romance and his current circumstances, he knew that only the God of the universe could conduct such a narrative.

They stayed on the bridge for hours, telling stories from their past lives about petty school fights, bad teachers, and what Cale was like before they went on this adventure. The conversation never wavered, and Jasper realized that as he spent more time with Lake, he learned more things that he loved about her. They strode among the trees, and after noon they finally returned to the house eager for lunch.

They arrived on the back road and soon found the large shed's doors open and the sound of a grinder on metal awoke curiosity in the two. When they investigated, they found Sophia skillfully sharpening Cale's knife that he had taken the night they left. Cale was wearing a welding shield on his head that was much too big, requiring him to hold it in place as he watched Sophia's skilled labor. When it was done, she inspected her work and returned it to him. Forgetting who she was dealing with for a brief moment she turned back quickly to the boy.

"Be careful it's shar—" But like most boys his age, the first thing that he did when the tool was returned was check its edge. To his surprise, it was razor sharp, slicing a cut into his curious thumb. The metal was additionally very hot, and the fresh cut burned, making him drop the knife. He cried out and cradled his hand like it had been cut off, but when he turned and saw Jasper and Lake in the doorway, he stiffened and casually shook the hand, shaking blood on the table as a consequence, and walked down the road to the house as if nothing had happened.

"You have so many tools in here!" Lake said. Sophia took off the leather gloves she was wearing and looked around.

"Yes, they're my tools for my many projects. They pile up after a while," Sophia said as she wiped the table used for sharpening.

"It's almost like you could build a spaceship with all of it!" Jasper said jokingly. Sophia thought about it longer than Jasper thought was necessary and turned back.

"Not a spaceship, though that would be a fun build. I'll stick with an underground compound for convicts." Her finger shot up, realizing something she had forgotten. "That reminds me!" She strode to the wall and picked up a handheld propane torch and a mean looking bolt cutter. "I've never really destroyed anything. I don't know how I feel about it."

"Are you really going to set a fire in your house?" Lake asked.

"Just my room, and just enough to convince whatever recording my husband has that the house burned down."

"What is the point of that if he doesn't come out here anyway?" Jasper asked.

"If I make a lot of purchases on building material and other things, he will get suspicious and may want to come out and investigate. If we can convince him that the place burned down, I can ask for all the equipment and resources we would need."

The explanation didn't convince Jasper or Lake, but Sophia seemed confident enough with the idea.

They met Emmett back at the house. When they walked on the concrete driveway, they found him beating mud out of his shoes. His hands were caked with dirt, and his knees showed similar symptoms. He looked at the torch and the long-handled bolt cutters.

"What did you do to Cale? He just rushed into the house on the brink of tears."

Sophia lifted the torch and flicked the gas on. Blue flame rushed from the end, and she posed sinisterly with the tools.

"He touched my lathe, so I torched his hand," she said, straining to keep a straight face. A brief look of horror flickered on Emmett's face, but it was short lived as a smile returned.

"What have you been doing?" Jasper asked.

"While you were out exploring, I got bored and saw some weeds in the gardens." Emmett shrugged casually.

The night closed in on them as they stayed in the house, researching building plans in the folder mysteriously labeled "Soteria." Emmett spent much of his time pacing, attempting to remember the meaning of the word. Knowing that it would drive Emmett insane until he remembered, Jasper took a moment to look up the word on the tablet.

"Doesn't Soteria mean 'salvation'?" Jasper asked, after he handed the device back to Sophia. He made a pose of deep thought, and Emmett turned, frustrated that he couldn't remember.

"Yes! How did I forget that!" He then looked accusingly at Jasper. "How did you know that?" Jasper, who had distanced himself from the tablet, opened his hands in innocence.

"I'm a knower," he said, flashing a smug grin at the big man, which earned him an eye roll of biblical proportions.

"I guess it makes sense. The State believes that they are 'saving' people by removing what they believe are veils from the eyes of their people in religion and faith. Salvation to them is the State, because they are the providers, and there isn't any room for anything else if it is to stay that way." He sat, placed his face in his hands in exasperation, and breathed a heavy sigh. "Lord help us."

THE NIGHT WAS quiet and dark. Lingering clouds in the sky covered the fluorescent stars above, creating an eerie feeling. Sophia lay in her bed, eyes closed, welcoming sleep as it came. She made a practice of thinking about what she wanted to dream about while she was still conscious, but that night she had her mind fixated on one thing. A man, the one she had envisioned through books and paintings when she was a little girl, was reaching out a hand to her. She walked on green cliffs that reached over the ocean below, and in taking the hand of the man, she was invited to take a step off the edge of the cliff. She knew what was below, and fear crept into her heart, but as she kept her eyes on his face, she grew confident. She felt the hand of the man and held on tighter as she stepped into open air— and remained aloft. She smiled.

A light burst into her consciousness, so bright in the darkness that it blinded her. She woke up staring at angry licks of fire spreading furiously, consuming wood, furniture, and the curtains on her window. She rose, pulled on a T-shirt and athletic shorts and used a pillow to beat futilely at the flames. Terrified and in panic, she cast away the pillow and fled the room, coughing from the smoke. Her bedroom became a torch in the black of night.

FOURTEEN

JASPER COUGHED, but was unable to cover his mouth since his hands were full with an extinguisher and a set of bolt cutters.

"Did you cut the right cable to the camera?" Sophia said from the hallway.

"Yes, I think so. The camera light flickered and didn't come back on," Jasper said awkwardly, wiping his itching nose with the bolt cutters. Emmett came back from the blackened room holding a security camera.

"It had a battery on it, so it probably streamed for a little longer, but the battery broke for some reason."

"What happened to the battery?" Sophia asked.

"I hit it with a hammer." Emmett flashed his smug face at the two, satisfied with his work. "No footage of any of us was streamed out. Are you sure this plan is going to work, Soph?"

"It has to now; we don't really have a choice. I'm going to call my husband now and tell him the house was damaged by an electrical fire, and that I'm okay and the fire was contained. I'll ask for money and supplies to rebuild, and we can use that to expand the basement underground for people who are fleeing officials like Stockton. I've never met him, but from what you guys have said, I hope that I never do."

Sophia looked disheveled, which was the point. It was her idea to stage a fire in her bedroom to communicate through the camera that the house would require repairs. It would also explain her absence from her regular home for the foreseeable future, something she assured them that her husband wouldn't bat an eye at if there was even a vague excuse.

She went out the front door to the shed and closed the door behind her, dialing her phone.

Jasper went downstairs and picked up the tablet.

"I don't know if you should use that," Lake said, behind him. "I know the State can't track what we are looking at, but do you think they can see if the signal is being used?" Jasper looked up, surprised, at the astute observation from someone who had chosen to avoid most technology throughout her childhood. He thought about it and, realizing they may have a problem, he put down the device and sat outside waiting for Sophia to come back from breaking the news to her husband.

Emmett joined him and sat in one of the chairs. Their breath showed in the air, lit by the house's porch lights. Jasper's mind wandered. Everything had gone according to plan, almost too well. So far, it seemed that they had just been running from danger. They were always the ones reacting, but now they had a plan, and they were the ones acting. It was exhilarating.

Something pricked up the hair on the back of his neck. There was something wrong about this whole situation—or maybe something right about it. Jasper thought about Sophia and her response to their arrival. What would he have done in that situation? What was surprising? He thought back to the message left by the initials B.S., indicating that someone had hope that he was alive and not in a good way. What if this was all a setup? A way to find how much he and Emmett knew about the State's plans?

What if the idea to stage a fire in her room was a setup for her to call in the State to come and arrest them? Not only for terrorism, but for arson and attempted murder, as well. It all began clicking in his mind, and a chill ran down his back as he began to sweat and his mind filled the gaps of logic in his hypothesis. *I have to warn Emmett,* he thought!

Sophia returned from the shed, a shotgun between her arm and her hip as she strode back. His thoughts began to move, mingling together in an unholy symphony of insecurity and fear as they danced.

Jasper knew something was familiar about the feeling, but his response was greater as the woman walked toward them on the concrete driveway. With every step she took, his mind became increasingly distracted and confused. The dissonance made him close his eyes to make it stop. Jasper attempted to calm his breathing, taking deep breaths in and pushing them out, though his mind continued to race.

"That was harder than I thought it would be. I really don't like lying to anyone, let alone him," Sophia started, with a catch in her speech. Jasper took the words with a grain of salt and had his eyes on the shotgun.

"He told me that I had to sleep with this just in case any animals or people came to investigate. He is sending a trailer for me and a shipment of materials to start rebuilding." She hefted the gun. Jasper flinched back as she did, but it seemed like no one else noticed. "Are there actual shells in here?" Sophia said with a hint of humor.

She offered the weapon to Jasper, which disrupted his train of thought entirely. *Why would she do that?* he thought. She could have them now. He suddenly had an urge to point it at her, and a wave of intense anger flared in his mind. She flinched back, more out of surprise than genuine fear.

"Jasper. Don't do that; I was serious!" She said, putting a hand to block the firing line. Jasper continued holding the weapon aimed at her, his mind telling him to eliminate the threat. He closed his eyes, and after a deep breath, he reached out to his Father. In a second, he heard a silent voice calm the storm in his mind and leave a message.

Die to self; live for me.

Clarity rushed back into his mind. When he opened his eyes, he saw no one in front of him, as Sophia had moved away and now stood beside him. She was shaken, but she didn't look angry when he saw her face with his eyes. Emmett, however, looked quizzically at him, and a tinge of worry framed his face.

"I'm sorry; I wasn't thinking," Jasper lied, for he was thinking. Thinking more than a human ever should. Emmett looked at Sophia with an understanding expression, and she rested a hand on Jasper's shoulder, squeezed once, and returned to the house. After she left, Jasper pushed on the chair to rise, but Emmett pushed him back firmly.

"Jasper, I'm not trying to infringe on your thing, but I saw your face. You were definitely thinking something, and you aimed at her for a reason. Why?" Jasper turned to see if anyone else was in earshot and told him how his hypothesis started. Emmett was surprised but followed the idea to the end without interruption. When Jasper had finished, Emmett asked a question that surprised Jasper.

"So why didn't you pull the trigger?" Emmett asked. Jasper thought about it.

"I don't know. My mind felt like it had when the Juggler had come, but it was different this time. Instead of jumbling my thoughts around, he brought new ones, ones that seemed to fit so well. Ones that made me afraid. When I closed my eyes, I reached out to our Father, and I found myself again." He felt embarrassed and shuddered at how it must have looked. "I'm sorry. Did I ruin everything?" Emmett turned back to the woods.

"No, I don't think so. But next time you get an idea, let me know before you let it almost kill someone who is trying to help us."

Jasper nodded, acknowledging the advice.

"I heard something after He...cleared the chaos." Jasper said, trying to remember what the voice sounded like. The voice had been silent, but clear. He remembered the words, but the tone was void and forgotten. "'Die to self; live for me,'" Jasper recited to Emmett. "What does that mean?"

"Sounds like you were dealing with fear. Something you've always struggled with. It crept back into your heart with one errant thought, the idea that Sophia could be working against us for the State."

"What does that have to do with the words that I heard?" Jasper asked.

"Die. Problem solved. Die to yourself." Emmett said pointedly.

"Commit suicide? That's what you want me to do?"

"No. Better. Immensely better." His vocal tone grew as his passion inflated. "Dying to yourself frees you from the fear of the world. Surrendering yourself to the Father and His plan means that you die to your own will and align it with His. When you let go of your own will, you just say that His purpose for you is what you want and that yours is dead." Jasper thought about the words, and Emmett stood to return to the house, leaving him alone in the dark and the smell of fire that lingered over the house.

Jasper sat in the cold night for an hour, eyes closed, thinking about what Emmett had said. He leaned his head back and had a conversation with his newfound Father.

THE NEXT FEW days seemed to race by. If there had been a rift created between Jasper and Sophia, she showed no evidence of it. After the fire in the room, Sophia worked tirelessly for two days to create another internet antenna so they could use the internet while keeping the impression that the whole house, including the internet modem, had been damaged in the fire. In order to keep potential satellite surveillance satisfied, she had told her husband that the roof and general structure had been damaged but not destroyed.

She went to where the road met the inlet that apparently only she knew of and retrieved the mobile home her husband had insisted on. She brought it back to the lot and unveiled its wonder to the group. The thirty-six-foot-long RV was decked out with comfortable seating, a kitchen, a small theater, and a bedroom at the back that rivaled the size of Lake and Cale's former home. Sophia checked the trailer for cameras. After finding none, she offered the trailer for the brother and sister to inhabit.

Cale jumped at the idea with excitement, but Lake insisted that it would be for Sophia, as it was her room that was sacrificed for the cause. The deal was settled between the two that the ladies would live in the mobile mansion, and the boys would live in separate parts of the house. The night after it had come, Jasper went to the trailer to deliver a basket of extra blankets the girls had requested from the house. As he walked by an open window in the RV, he heard his name spoken, followed by girlish giggles that made him very uncomfortable. He, however, was overcome with curiosity, wondering what they were laughing about concerning him as they relaxed in the mansion on wheels.

Jasper slid alongside the back wheel directly under the bedroom windows and crept toward the midsection to where he had seen the outlines of the two from the interior lights. He got as high as he could without lifting his head in sight of the window. He could hear muffled conversation through the open window and pressed his ear against the cold metal and listened.

"I made a huge mistake with Emmett. I have wondered for years ever since that night what would have happened if I had reacted differently," Jasper heard Sophia say.

"So if you could do it all over again, what do you think you would do?" Lake's muffled voice replied.

"I would have swallowed my pride, married him, and we would have a bundle of kids now!" Both of them giggled girlishly at the idea. "How are you feeling about things with Jasper?" Sophia asked. There was a pause, or at least it seemed like a pause in Jasper's mind, which had begun rushing in nervous anticipation of the answer.

"Eh..." Lake causally brushed the question off. *Eh?* Jasper thought and was confused just as much as he was hurt by the comment. "I like him, and he's fun, but I don't think he sees me as someone he'd like to marry." *That's not true,* Jasper thought. In fact, she was the only girl he had ever interacted with that he did see that way.

"Does it bother you that he can read your facial expressions?" Sophia asked seriously.

"No, because I like to play with him using them. Just wait until he finds out that I can read him even better than he can read me."

Jasper's heart raced, an internal panic building. He had learned more than he wanted to know, and it was getting worse by the second.

"If it's not a long-term option, then I suggest you break off anything further sooner rather than later," Sophia suggested. "It's better to head those things off before he would be too crushed."

Outside the vehicle, Jasper waved his hands to no one in particular in the universal crossing motion for No!

"That's a good idea, but how do I break it to him?" Lake asked. There was a pause, and Jasper assumed Sophia was thinking of a reply.

"Well, it would definitely be a disruption to the group's dynamic if you broke things off with him. So...for the good of the initiative to make a place for people to escape religious persecution...we have to get rid of him." Jasper's blood ran as cold as the steel his face was plastered against.

"How are we going to get rid of him?"

"We could throw him in the lake," Sophia said with a calmness that frightened Jasper just as much as the suggestion itself. *How could they?*

"That's a good idea, but Emmett would be upset if we did that."

Jasper heard nothing for several minutes and considered flight, but he wanted to hear their plan for his demise so he could head it off.

"I know!" Lake explained. "We can tell Emmett that Jasper tried to seduce you! Emmett would kill him for that. Problem solved!"

Jasper would rather have been shot. He began to shake violently and knew that he had to talk to Emmett before the women had a chance to level their accusation at him. He raced from the RV and burst through the house's front door to find Emmett and Cale roasting marshmallows on sticks in the fireplace. They turned and saw his face, paler than usual.

"What's up?" Emmett asked, looking back to his marshmallow to investigate its sear.

Jasper, whose lungs were pumping, began his plea. "You guys have got to believe me. I mean it," Jasper huffed and tried to control his breathing.

"Believe what? Did you eat something you are allergic to?" Emmett responded, attention now on Jasper.

"Whatever the girls say...it's not true! They are making it up!"

Right then, the door creaked open, and in stepped the two young women, both changed from their daily work clothes to ones suitable for sleep. Their faces looked serious. Jasper backed away from them, turning his body to see both the women and the two by the fire. He braced for the accusation that he didn't have time to counter. Emmett rose from his seat.

"What's going on?" Emmett said intently. Lake looked at Sophia, and let her be the bearer of news for the both of them.

"We have something to say about Jasper." Jasper felt like he was about to throw up. "We had mentioned just in passing that it was a bit cold in the RV, and Jasper out of the kindness of his heart delivered some blankets from the house. We just wanted to thank him and deliver something." Jasper, frozen in shock, didn't flinch back as Lake strode up to him, leaned forward, and gave him a light kiss on the cheek.

"Thank you," she whispered, "and don't ever eavesdrop on us ever again. Or at least check that you're not in view of the mirrors."

Jasper, still in that motionless state, glanced over at the thoroughly confused boys. Emmett had a questioning smile on his face, and Cale had had a visibly sharp glare as Lake delivered her kiss.

"What's wrong, Jasper? Don't like being called out for your nobility?" Emmett joked. "Good man!" he complimented, smiling. He obviously knew there was more to the story and found it hard to pass off moments of embarrassment for Jasper. Jasper ignored Emmett and followed the women outside.

"Lake," he called softly. They were halfway across the driveway when he called to her, and Sophia continued toward the RV while Lake stepped back toward him. Jasper tried to work out what had just happened, but they met beside the concrete fountain before he could. So he offered a question.

"So you weren't serious about all that stuff?" he asked.

"Not all of it," she replied.

"So...does that mean that you don't want to end whatever this is?" Jasper asked, heart racing in anticipation of the answer.

She returned his gaze with a question. "What does my face tell you?" she asked.

He looked into her face. There were no definite micro-expressions for love, and guessing wrong now could be catastrophic. Her look was soft, relaxed. Her eyes dilated in the dwindling light, and her mouth twitched. ATTRACTION. HAPPINESS.

Instead of telling her, Jasper forced himself out of his comfort zone, wrapped his arms around her, pulled her close, and kissed her firmly. A single kiss, one that spoke his answer resoundingly. He let her go, but as he did, she opened her eyes with a withering smile.

"You're stuck with me, Jasper," she said and turned, leaving the awkward young man standing in the dark. "Sleep well."

Emmett desperately wanted an explanation and kept his face straight until he heard what the women said they would accuse Jasper of. That caused him to collapse into helpless gales of laughter. Jasper didn't know why he was laughing and wondered if he had misunderstood.

"What's so funny?" Jasper asked, more than a little frustrated with his older friend's amusement at his misfortune.

"You...doing something like that? That's hilarious. Number one. Those two women would beat you bloody if you tried any such thing. Number two, you're...Jasper. You barely can talk to a girl. But seduction?" His explanation trailed off into more laughter. When he was finished, he looked at Jasper, all traces of humor lost. "If you did do that, however, we would have to have a talk. Sleep tight," he said as he and Cale left to the basement.

FIFTEEN

THE DAYS PASSED QUICKLY as they prepared the lakeside sanctuary. Though the days went by in an instant, the nights were filled
with restless thoughts that kept Jasper from much sleep. When he did
manage to find it, he was greeted by the moody light that danced in
an infinity sign. Jasper often wondered if it was a message put into his
mind. Who put it there? The being Emmett called the Juggler had
influenced his mind before. How would he know if it was from him
or from God, the one he called his Father?

One night, he abandoned the idea of rest and returned to the fire
still burning low in the fireplace. He grabbed the tablet on the couch,
and since he'd gotten permission from Sophia to use it, he did. He
returned to his social media messages but refused to read the new
hateful messages that had piled up, likely from victims of the flood
who were told by their therapists to write these messages as coping
mechanisms. He scrolled until he saw the messages he had already
read and then found the chilling message from B.S. He clicked on the
profile to bring up its homepage.

B.S. was the name, but there was no profile picture, no back-
ground at all. The last post on the page was at least twenty years ago.

He scrolled through hundreds of reposted news articles about marriage, health, and social well-being. His hand became tired from scrolling, but every time he thought about quitting, his mind convinced him to scroll just one more page. That led to another, and soon enough, an anomaly popped into view—a message that was posted on the account. Another was after it. As Jasper flipped down through the feed, he found twenty or so messages of condolences for a significant loss. Now thoroughly confused, he kept scrolling until the end of the profile's history came in. With it was a solitary picture with writing on it.

The picture showed the bare stomach of a pregnant woman. On it was a man's hand placed protectively on its curve. On the lower third of the image was a bit of verse in an artistic font.

Blessed is the man who trusts in the Lord, whose trust is in the Lord. He is like a tree planted by water, that sends out its roots by the stream, and does not fear when heat comes, for its leaves remain green, and is not anxious in the year of drought, for it does not cease to bear fruit. Jeremiah 17:7-8

Emmett had never told him about this scripture, but he guessed that it was in the Bible. *Why is this picture here?* Jasper thought. Thoroughly confused, Jasper read the messages above that he had only glanced over.

I'm sorry, Bernie. You deserved much better. Faith will bring you through. Jenifer Ford

---

We're praying for you, Bernie. God's plan is greater than what we can know right now. Thomas Becker

Jasper sifted through the messages until he got to one near the end. It was left on his profile, not because someone had sent it, but because B.S. had commented on it.

So we say with confidence,

"The Lord is my helper; I will not fear;
What can man do to me?" Hebrews 13:6 ~ Pastor Stephen Walsh

Below the verse was one solitary comment.

Watch me. B.S.

Understanding rushed into Jasper's mind like a meteor out of space crashing into the earth. So many questions were answered, ones that he didn't even remember asking himself. He had to tell Emmett. Before leaving the room to go downstairs, he put Bernard Stockton's name into the search bar. The first article that arose was recent, just a few days prior. The title read, "*Rags to Riches: How Bernard Stockton grew to be security director of the whole western region of the United State.*"

He'd gotten promoted. *The man who wants us dead has become the second most powerful security officer in the country.* Jasper felt his body overcome with fear, and in response, he bowed his head and said a few words. Then he rushed down to wake Emmett to the disturbing realization.

Emmett took the realization better than Jasper had expected. He had a unique ability to look at the ordinary and remarkable and respond as if they were the same. Emmett's mood the next several days took on a shift, however. Where there had been a sense of calm in the man's demeanor since they had made the agreement with Sophia, the peace that had grown became singed by the truth Jasper had found. The jokes and smart remarks the group had grown used to became fewer, and the amount of time he spent alone increased.

SOPHIA MADE plans for the expansion of the basement. If anything had been compromised or searched by the State, she wanted to have hideouts around the property that could connect to the main house underground. This meant lots of digging.

Jasper had done everything he could during his education to avoid ever having to do manual labor. He soon found that it wasn't as bad as he had always thought; it was physically bearable and even satisfying. The young man was sore after the first few days, but the soreness paled in comparison to getting skewered by sharp wooden spears. Pain had taken on new meaning since the night he had met Emmett, and the soreness his body endured after long days of shoveling dirt and rock was minimal.

Sophia had given them an electric tool that assisted with tunneling into the mountains' rock, and he and Emmett took turns with the heavy machine. As they did, Cale would rake and haul the dirt and gravel away. He threw his smaller body at the task with ferocity. Emmett had told the youth that by the end of this project, he would be stronger than Jasper. Apparently that was something that Cale must have significantly desired. After a week of hard work, Jasper could feel his own body getting stronger. Although that wasn't a condition he had ever worked for or desired, he was strangely satisfied with the enhanced muscle power.

Toward the end of the week, Emmett proposed they take the last day of the week and rest the whole day. Lake and Jasper wondered at the reasoning but were glad for the break. While the boys had spent most of their time wrestling with the earth, Lake had begun learning from Sophia about the arts of design and structure. She had started sketching out plans for the expansion below, and to Sophia's delight, she had a well-tuned spatial mind and skills with math to assist it. Whether the work was physical or mental, the group welcomed the last day of the week with open arms.

That day, the one Emmett called Sabbath, quickly became the day that everyone looked forward to throughout the weeks. After a month had passed, they had created two tunnels that ran toward each other. One went from the basement of the house northeast toward the Cascade mountain faces, and another led back toward it that began under the cedar bridge that shone fiery red in the morning dew. They still had a distance to go but stopped for a week for Sophia to strengthen the tunnels to prevent cave-ins. She walked backward through both tunnels, spraying a solution that felt thick in the air. They required masks to protect their lungs as the liquid stuck to wall and ceiling alike, hardening it like termite mounds.

Once they had come back to the open air, and Sophia had given them the okay to take their masks off, Jasper ripped the device off backward. He shook his face and breathed in the air. Emmett, who had done the same, was stifling laughs.

"What? Is it something on my face?" Jasper asked self-consciously.

"You look like Ace Ventura!" he said, laughing.

"Who is that?" Jasper said, annoyed, as he touched the top of his head and found that the solution had gotten in his hair. When he had taken the mask off, it had styled his hair with a rhino horn that had been slicked back. Sophia instructed them to wash their hair with a solvent she gave them, and Jasper was eager to do it before Lake saw whatever had caused Emmett to snicker.

The group had developed schedules and patterns that resembled a family's routine—at least what Jasper thought constituted a family routine, given that his experience was with one that was minimally functional. He and Lake had taken on domestic duties with no hesitation. As long as they got to do it together, the job was no problem for them. This fact often left Cale alone with Emmett, who would prefer to do the job alone than to do it with only Sophia as company.

He obviously loved her, and it was evident that she reciprocated that. Jasper couldn't understand why Emmett would go out of his way to never speak to her alone. One, especially chilly morning, Jasper and Lake took a walk out to the fog-covered shore.

"Did you tell Emmett that we went for a walk?" Lake asked.

"Yes."

"Did he do it again?"

Jasper picked up a smooth cold rock and cast it skipping across the mirror-like face of the water. "He looked around for Cale," he said. "He couldn't find him, so he said he was going to check the bridge's tunnel entrance to see if the hardening had finished." He cast another stone. It skipped once but turned and burrowed itself in the frigid water. "I just don't get it. He will put himself outside for hours, just to not be alone with Sophia. It must make Sophia feel terrible."

"It does, but not how you probably think," she said as she threw a rock on the water.

"What do you mean?"

"Sophia and I talked a lot while you were all playing ground squirrel. Emmett doesn't let himself be around her when it's just the two of them because she is married to someone else. He believes that her marriage, though it is an unhappy one, is holy. Knowing that he and Sophia love each other, he thinks that if they are alone, they might be tempted to dishonor the marriage that she's in. She feels terrible, not because he is avoiding her, but because she made a decision a long time ago that means that she can't be with him the way both of them want to be."

"That's probably something he and I wouldn't have talked about. Thank you for the context." Jasper stood, looking out at the water. He felt his stomach turning at his friend's plight.

"There's a lot of things that we talk about that you probably wouldn't," Lake said with a hint of mischief in her voice. This made Jasper very uncomfortable.

"Like wha..." Jasper decided midquestion that he would probably rather not ask. Lake giggled in reply. "How is Cale doing about this?" Jasper asked, gesturing between himself and Lake.

"Better. I think he is at peak 'okayness' with us."

"That's not comforting. Especially because he tried to kill me twice before I even knew your name."

"He's grown a lot," she said, as if that explained it all.

"I just want to know if I have to sleep with one eye open just in case he relapses."

Lake put on her most nonchalant face and tossed her reply as if it was a wrapper into trash.

"He won't. He knows it would be an inconvenience to me. Cale would never do anything on purpose that would annoy me." Jasper looked at her, hurt in his eyes at her apathetic attitude toward her brother potentially murdering him. After she saw the effect she had wanted, Lake brightened her smile and hugged him, burrowing her cold nose into his neck, making Jasper flinch.

"I'm getting cold; let's go back." They did, and to Jasper's discomfort, she never reiterated whether or not he should be wary of Cale, something that Lake had intentionally omitted.

That night, Sophia informed the group that she would need to go home for a week to hold off any skepticism from her husband. She made preparations for their needs while she was gone, but things needed to be different around the lake house when she wasn't there to maintain the illusion that no one was there. They wouldn't be able to use the internet, and only some of the things powered by electricity to make sure there weren't spikes in their usage when "no one was there."

After covering all the bases that she felt necessary, she teared up, hugged them all, and expressed her gratitude that she had met them. It was more emotional than Jasper felt the situation required, and he wondered what weighed so heavily on Sophia's mind. One by one, the group left to go to bed. The last was Emmett, who remained adjacent to her in front of the fire.

Knowing the conversation that he had had with Lake and the insight into Emmett's sad plight, he felt a pang to remain in the room. It would have been evident and awkward for him to return, and as he went through the doorway, he glanced at his big friend's face. Emmett was intent, serious, and deep in thought as he sat near the fire. After Jasper went through the doorway and was out of view, he lingered before going down the stairs. He said a prayer of support for the two who were each other's first love before honor and dignity had collided, and then walked down the concrete steps. Jasper didn't remember hearing Emmett return to the basement apartment before he was caught by sleep.

The following day they arose and began life without Sophia. She had left early to be able to take Timber in for a vet checkup. There was a silence about the sanctuary. Sophia was by no means the loudest of the group. Still, without her there, the necessity for stealth became more important. On a routine hike with Lake, Jasper began to feel that it had even leached into their conversation, or lack thereof. After going to the lake's shore, they turned upstream. Jasper broke the silence, something that was typically Lake's specialty.

"Why was the mood so serious last night?" Jasper asked, hoping that it came out how he meant it.

"You don't know?"

"That would have been a pretty bad question if I did," Jasper replied.

"Sophia has risked so much to be able to provide a place for people who are persecuted for their faith."

"Persecuted. Never heard you use that one." Jasper said.

"I've been learning from Emmett and Sophia. Anyway, she didn't only give us a place to stay; she is distancing herself from every bit of security that she has to make this work and subjecting herself to emotional pain too."

Jasper nodded slowly, his eyebrows furrowed.

"Imagine us, if we weren't together—"

"I'd rather not," Jasper interjected.

"Oh, now you decide to be sweet. Anyway, imagine that we were apart and that you married someone else, and ten years later, you are convicted to attach yourself to something that would have you constantly interacting with me." Jasper acted as if he was understanding. "This won't be the first time she leaves. She's married to someone who treats her as if she's just an employee that he isn't allowed to fire. But she is bound to him either way. Then she spends most of her time with the man she wanted to marry, but there is a glass window between them they won't ever reach through."

"Why doesn't she divorce him and marry Emmett?"

"I asked her that last night. She told me that it would break the promise she made when they got married, but she also told me another reason, one that stood out more. She said that without her ties to her husband, they wouldn't have the freedom to do this. We wouldn't have the access to the files needed to rescue people from Soteria. She said that God had provided in His perfect plan a way for His followers to run from the State to worship Him. She is the only one who can do the job that will make it all work or not."

Jasper felt a lump grow in his throat as he envisioned the internal battle that was going on inside her. They continued on their walk, neither willing to break the mood. It had begun snowing, and by the time they arrived back at the workshop, the dusting of white contrasted with the fallen red and yellow leaves.

They came into the shed curious about the sound of metalwork. Lake was briefly showered with sparks by Cale, who was characteristically unapologetic. He was working with Emmett on a foot-and-a-half-long tube of some sort of metal. After Lake had convinced herself that her hair showed no signs of being lit on fire, she berated him on his lack of courtesy. He responded by continuing to grind the metal tube's end on the belt sander under Emmett's close supervision.

"Have a nice walk?" Emmett asked cheerfully.

"It was a bit cold, but fine. What are you making?" Jasper responded. Emmett beckoned them to follow him to a table with several sheets of plans. The first showed what looked like a Native American flute, something that he had seen in a museum at one point. The following page was more technical. It illustrated a metal strip with holes down its length. At its end was some contraption that housed a tube of some sort. The last piece of paper was transparent and had the shape of a wooden Native American flute with a stag standing proudly at its top. He began his explanation, then thought it better to wait.

"You'll see," he said.

His attention was snapped back by the resurgence of the unique sound of metal being sanded. He rushed back to Cale, who had resumed his work, but he flinched back, and the metal piece was torn from his hand by the belt sander, denting the piece. Emmett examined the warped metal tube, and Cale watched in quiet guilt. The big man shook his head sorrowfully and tossed the piece into a plastic bin, resulting in a loud clang of metal on metal. Jasper and Lake strode to the bin where Emmett had tossed the warped tube and found it half-filled with the same piece, with different imperfections. They looked at the two men in astonishment. Cale and Emmett shrugged their shoulders.

"We're excited for her to come back."

Lake and Jasper joined in their work for a time, and in several hours they had completed the metal inner piece and cut and sanded it to fit the cedar outing. The snow had layered its way to several inches when they finished for lunch. Per Sophia's orders, before the day was done, they began work on hats. The head coverings were designed with a blend of metals that would cause a distribution of the light around them when seen on a satellite camera, making whoever was wearing a hat look like a blur instead of a person. The material had already been purchased. It was an easy task for the day, as they spent almost their whole time in the workshop. If by any chance, a drone flew over, it wouldn't see them.

At the end of the day, Jasper sat relaxed on the couch playing cards with the other three when he noticed something that shouldn't be. It was hours past sundown, but the snow on the ground reflected the early moon's light that made the night less dark. Another light caught his eye. It began as a blur, then it was direct as it reflected off the RV parked on the other side of the fountain.

"There's a car coming!" Jasper almost yelled as he was thrown into panic. There was nowhere to run. The tunnels weren't done. Sophia wasn't supposed to be back for five or six more days. They all ran down into the basement and hurried into the ground entrance at the corner of the basement. It was dark, dirty, and cold in the glorified hole in the ground. After they all were in, Emmett slid the bed back into place to cover the entrance, and they waited in utter silence. Jasper had to remind himself to breathe on several occasions as they waited. After what felt like forever, though it was several minutes, they heard the door open. Footsteps accompanied them. Jasper strained to count them.

"Three pairs of steps. One heavy and slow, and two are quieter and faster," he whispered. He heard behind him in the hole the unnerving sound of a metal blade coming out of its sheath. The steps separated above them. Two pairs of feet picked up the pace and came down the stairs to the basement before Jasper could adjust his spatial mind. The lighter, quicker steps crept closer to the bed as they drew near. *Do they know where we were?* Jasper thought. As if the beings read his mind, there was a throaty and deep bellow.

"Aroo, Aroo!" bellowed an immense beast in triumph. They were found. The two heavier steps came down the stairs and approached the bed.

"You can come out now." It was Sophia. She sounded upset. *Maybe she is being held against her will to find us,* Jasper thought. "I know you're in there." Emmett began moving the covering, but Cale beat him to call out with his prepubescent voice.

"What's the password?" he shouted. Jasper felt a collective eye roll at Cale's ability to speak up whenever it wasn't convenient.

"Bad berries." they heard the women say, and Emmett moved the covering and the bed frame in a quick moment.

Sophia stood in front of them with Timber, who anticipated greeting the bunch with his long wet tongue. Sophia looked far less enthusiastic than her companion, and Jasper's confusion grew as he looked into her face. FATIGUE. She acknowledged what Jasper may have read on her face and turned away from him to head off immediate questioning.

"Cale, it's pretty late. How about you get to bed?" Sophia said in a tone that left no room for argument. He did as he was told, and Lake gave Sophia an affectionate hug before they all returned upstairs in nervous anticipation.

The living room had acted as a conference room for the group for weeks, and they instinctively sat in the couches near fireplace. Sophia was the last to sit down and chose to do so next to Lake. The two had grown close over the weeks of cohabiting. She filled a familial character that was in an odd space for Lake. Not a mother, potentially a big sister. But in any case, the two were evidently reliant on each other for support. Sophia took a deep breath and began.

"I guess you are wondering why I came back early. Well...I just pictured the sight of Emmett and Cale in my workshop without me and I couldn't stand it." There were a few nervous chuckles at the attempt at humor, but it didn't take a facial analyst to know that wasn't the truth, which was likely much darker. "You guys don't believe that, do you." Several compassionate head turns followed the assumption.

"I got back into town and ran some errands. Took Timber to the vet for a check, and bought some things that I'd rather not have on shipping transcripts. It took longer than I thought, but I got back to the house to surprise my husband with dinner. I had been excited to start showing him who Jesus was in my actions, hoping that would spark an open mind to our cause...but after I had prepared dinner, I waited to surprise him. After several hours he came home, but he wasn't alone. One of his interns, Lucia, was with him." She shuddered, obviously still raw from the situation. Lake enveloped Sophia's hand in hers and squeezed once, and the women continued.

"They came in, made some comments about past times where they have met. I didn't know what to do, so I just sat at the table, with the dinner I had already made for him between us. When they noticed I was there...they just looked at me. We were frozen, and after way longer than necessary, Lucia left. I prayed silently for guidance. I wanted to lash out; I wanted to hate. Devon sat across the table. I didn't know what else to do, so I just told him to eat. We ate, though not very much anticipating what we both knew would be a painful conversation.

"I was talking to God the whole time. Asking for help, trying not to hate him, trying to forgive to be able to save our marriage, whatever value there was in it." She paused, reliving emotions of shock. That switched to confusion with what was to come. "I was preparing a speech on loyalty and how I was going to forgive him. Before I could, he stopped me. He told me that this had been happening for some years, with different women. He said that, as long as I didn't release the affairs to the public or start an open relationship with someone else, he would support me with everything I want. His mind was made up, and I agreed to the terms as he wanted them. I left with Timber and a few other things, and I had way too much time to think on the way back here.

"I had listened to a song when I was a teenager, and the lyrics had me saying over and over again that I wanted my heart to want nothing but Jesus. I sang it on the drive several times. I had been making that call a hundred times before the interaction with my husband. During that horrendous dinner, I was hurt, but there was an overarching peace about it. On my drive here I pulled over several times because I wanted to cry. But I couldn't. I got angry at myself, yelling, hitting the wheel, because I wanted to feel the pain that comes with losing my marriage, all those years gone from betrayal. Every time I pulled off the road to have another fit, I got more angry. I screamed at God, asking why I wasn't feeling the pain that I should be." Still processing, she lifted her hands and face, looking around at all of them.

"That's when I realized what had happened. I had sung hundreds of times, "Jesus, I want to only want you. First and foremost, you." During that time my prayer was coming true; I wasn't feeling the pain that came with the loss because it paled in comparison to what I had my heart set on. I was angry because I was experiencing freedom from sorrow, and my body reacted by crying out wanting to return to the captivity of self-pity instead." Tears began falling from her eyes freely with her revelation. "I'm free. Even though I may not always want to be. I'm grateful for you guys, and I love you like family." She put her arm around Lake and squeezed her tight. "I've got all I need."

SIXTEEN

SEASONS PASSED that felt like weeks. The new-found convictions and opportunities brought on a sense of responsibility that Jasper hadn't felt. They spent several hours a day tunneling beneath the bridge or in the basement. They spent months working anew on the tunnels as Sophia's skilled hands worked feverishly in her workshop. During the winter, the snow had stuck, and whenever some melted away, more seemed to take its place, making Cale's wheelbarrowing of dirt sluggish. The boys underground, however, found it was warmer than the surface because there was no wind or snow, and in the spring and summer, they were able to flee the heat for the calm of the earth.

When not working with Sophia, Lake took personal charge of the garden. She spent much of the early spring months planning and planting, and was thrilled at the results when they came to fruition in time. It was short lived, however, as an unexpected heat wave in the late spring killed many of her plants, leaving her in a bad temper for several weeks.

By the end of the summer, Lake had redoubled her efforts in agriculture, Sophia had created several contraptions that none of them understood, and the boys had built a small labyrinth of tunnels around the property.

The routine became comforting to Jasper, who'd had little routine since he had been swept away from his former life. He hadn't realized how much he had depended on it. As they approached November, they were shocked to realize that it had been almost a year since this had begun.

One morning, as Jasper and Emmett worked in one of the new tunnels, Emmett wondered aloud where Cale was. Sophia had called Cale up from his duties earlier, and he hadn't returned. They came up to the top of the stairs and found Lake, Sophia, and Cale outside on the patio.

"What's for lunch?" Jasper asked. No one answered as they were all looking at Cale. In his hand was a foot-and-a-half-long Indian flute. It was carved from the red cedar, and Jasper recognized it from the plans he'd found in the workshop. At the top, just past the mouthpiece, was a carving of a deer. Cale blew into the flute and moved his fingers on the holes. He was awkward at first, but his fingers soon adjusted around the instrument. Emmett's and Jasper's breath was taken away by the sound that came from the flute, a sorrowful tune cloaked in a rich, warm tone. Cale played a song, one that Jasper had never heard before. It wasn't complex, but each note was played so skillfully that Jasper found it unbelievable that it came from such an odd, aggressive young boy.

Cale finished the song, leaving the hearts of all around him in awestruck melancholy. Jasper looked at his face, seeing a deep-seated sorrow written on it. For the briefest moment, that changed. A flicker of intense joy made an appearance too fast for the untrained eye to see. The boy slid the deer over the sound hole, and there was a faintly audible click. He kept the flute close to his mouth, though he didn't play it. He pointed the flute oddly between Emmett and Jasper, placed his index finger on the deer's antlers, and pulled backward.

There was the sound of compressed air, and a projectile flew between Jasper and Emmett's heads into the door between them.

Jasper looked behind him to find a target had been taped to it, and a four-inch-long dart lay embedded a few inches from the center.

"You got it to work!" Emmett said.

"Of course, I did." Sophia replied, sounding a bit hurt.

"What just happened?" Jasper said, his mind not making the connection.

"I told Sophia how Cale mastered our people's flute. You notice how he doesn't talk much; he was always better with communicating through the flute. He could play, and I could almost always understand what he wanted to say. Sophia had the brilliant idea to turn it into a sedative dart gun by housing the firing mechanism in the deer and having an extra piece below where his thumb goes to house the darts," Lake replied. Jasper glanced back at Cale, who had a wickedly gleeful look spread on his face.

"That was beautiful. Until you almost used our faces as targets," Jasper said, complimenting the boy.

"It's pretty accurate. I made the antlers align to be like a gun sight to help aim. The propellant cartridges are the best combination between power to increase range and accuracy, and quiet so that people won't hear a gunshot and come looking." Sophia explained proudly.

"That's great. Lake's sneezes are louder than this machine," Jasper said.

"Cale, can I have a try?" Lake asked mischievously. But Cale clutched the flute protectively.

"What would the dart do to someone?" Emmett asked.

"That's one of the things I wanted to buy with no record of shipment. I have a friend who works in a biochem distributor. She is a believer. I hadn't talked to her in years, but I convinced her to sell me a sedative they haven't brought into the hospitals yet. It is a sedative called Neshialam. Once in a muscle, it quickly paralyzes someone and puts them to sleep. When they wake, they'll be higher than heaven and likely won't remember what happened when they were struck. They were contracted to make the serum to bring people in for interrogations. But we're going to use it for something else. I do want to test it on one of us to make sure, though." She looked around for a volunteer, but all but Cale quickly retreated inside.

Sophia took a step to join them, but she heard a click and then a brief flicker of sound from that flute. It was strangely lyrical, and she knew clearly what Cale had said through the music. She didn't understand why she knew, but she turned to the boy anyway.

"You're welcome, Cale."

FEARING that her husband would remember his security system on the internet at the cabin and clear it, they downloaded all the information on Soteria, as well as the lists of people who had already been printed and were awaiting the completion of the complex to be transferred to begin their rehabilitation. They printed off hundreds of sheets containing all the names of people printed for the threat of religion-based insurrection. Jasper went through the databases one by one. After several hours of poring over names, his eyes latched on one in particular. Louis Antonio.

It's familiar, but why? he wondered. Jasper searched his mind for potential connections but decided to click on the man's file instead.

"Louis Antonio—Arrested under suspicion of alliance with domestic terrorists. Evidence is found on a social media post to one Jasper Wood. Citations include: Sympathetic pardon for acts of terrorism. Incitement of insurrection. A call for Theistic intervention. Rehabilitation Process: Printed, Confirmed, Prepped for transport to Soteria Rehabilitation Center."

It was that man. The one whose wife and daughter were killed in the dam explosion. *He wasn't a Christian, was he? Maybe. But the only thing he did was forgive me when everyone else condemned,* Jasper thought. He clicked on the link to the post. He found that since he last saw it, thousands had commented on Antonio's gracious response with equal or more malice than Jasper had received after the dam. People said horrible things. So much that Jasper had to close the page. Looking back at Louis's file, he saw at the bottom a date and time.

"Lake! What's today's date?" Jasper called.

"The twelfth, I think." Lake replied from across the room where she filed the pages as they came from the printer.

"We have a week."

JASPER EXPLAINED the situation to Emmett, Sophia, and Lake. They asked pointed questions and were hesitant. But Jasper's mind was made up. They had to get this guy out. He didn't deserve to be there with no chance of release just for acting with grace instead of rage and vengeance. Eventually, they were convinced. Even though they didn't know if he was a believer, they could see that he was someone who lived as if he was. That was good enough for them. When the decision had been made, and they broke, returning to what they had been doing, Jasper noticed a sidelong glance from Emmett.

"What?" Jasper asked the big man.

"One thing I have been asked the most is, What evidence is there in the here and now for the God of the Bible. I love when that question is answered over and over before my eyes. Radical positive change in people. Not in their situations. In themselves."

"I remember talking about that. But why are you thinking of that now?"

"Because the scared, young man who came into that room and met me wouldn't dream of doing anything noble that could put himself or his personal security at risk. But you...you just saw a name on a page and were convicted enough by the injustice done to him to put your life, and those of people you love, on the line for his freedom. Evidence. God is good?" Emmett asked in expectation of a reply.

"Yes, He is," Jasper replied.

"No. You're supposed to say, 'All the time.' Come on, we've tried this too many times for you to get it wrong," Emmett said, patting his friend on the back.

The group's preparations were expedited, and they began plans on how they would manage breaking these people free. The building of Soteria on the top of the reservation had gone faster than they thought and was essentially finished. Finished enough to warrant transfer of prisoner, who were conveniently called "patients."

Enough space had been dug from the basement that they began turning it into a livable space. They plastered the walls and fitted lights to the ceilings, creating a functional room that could almost convince people that they weren't underground. Sophia had come up with a genius ventilation system that would both condition and circulate fresh air in the otherwise musty space. Her energy seemed to be limitless as the days of hard work that required physical and mental stamina went on. Jasper had asked her about where her energy was coming from.

"Since I was married, I haven't really done anything. Not meaningful at least. Now that I get to use my brain and hands and have something meaningful to do, I seem to be able to keep going regardless of how tired I am."

As they finished preparing the basement for living, they began focusing on Antonio's rescue plan. Jasper realized more and more the reality that this plan was. It was his idea and, in spite of the support of the group, he felt an increasing weight of responsibility. One morning as he pored over possible routes the State police would use to transport Antonio to the new facility, he felt a little overwhelmed by so many variables. The one that was a needle in his mind was that there was a single main highway from the holding facility and the road that shot off from it to where Soteria was only a mile of space. So close to reinforcements if something went wrong. So far from any options for plan B. His mind searched feverishly for other options.

He felt Lake's hands fall on his shoulders and felt a wave of calm come over his mind. Her chin came down onto his head, and her wavy brown hair fell around his face. Her smell was soothing, almost bringing him out of his melancholic condition...almost. She had a gift for arriving when his mind approached the precipice of an anxiety overload and calming the storm before it met its climax.

They studied maps together, looking at charts they had downloaded and printed using IP addresses from other countries to confuse State investigators, who would likely trace signals that had anything to do with Antonio's disappearance. She pointed out several roads on the outside of the rocky amphitheater that would be options for a quiet exit. Still, the problem remained. Where would they get a hold of him in the first place?

They worked at it for several more hours before turning in for the night. The struggle was bearable when she was assisting him, even pleasant, regardless of the monumental implications.

In the past, Jasper had used his gift to try and understand what people were thinking—information that often he would've preferred to live without. The fear that came with every glance at a woman's face turned him into a social cripple by the time he was accepted into college. Then there was Lake. Someone who didn't know his gift, who looked at him with grace. Even after learning about his abilities, she leaned in more. Who in this time of mistrust could look unashamed at an emotional X-ray and survive its gaze? No one that Jasper had found. His attempts in search of such a one had become more infrequent, and his optimistic hope that one existed diminished.

But here in these crazy circumstances, he had found someone who was not afraid of him or his ability . The magnitude of it shocked him at times, causing him to take a step back, wondering if it was a dream. He knew, more and more, that he loved her. Not because she was the only girl who didn't run in fear or disgust at his gaze, but because as he learned more of the Father, His qualities in her became brighter. He was sure he loved her. The next step was evident, but it scared him, nonetheless.

Every night the group made a practice of joining together in the living room and listening to Emmett tell a story from the Bible. They had no genuine Bibles and only a copy of the "Revised New Testament," a piece of literature that had been cut and pasted to promote the State's values. This forced them to rely on the former teacher's memory. As he spoke, Sophia, who had heard most of the stories growing up, wrote down what he said for reference in case they never found an unaltered copy.

He had told the creation story. The story of a man named Abraham who had a covenant with the God of heaven. The flood and Joseph. Then came Jesus. He was the Messiah, the Son of God, who was prophesied, who lived, who died, and who rose from the dead all in line with what had been foretold over a thousand years before. Jasper was a natural skeptic, something that was drilled into him in his training. He felt this response fade throughout Emmett's nights of storytelling. He began thinking of questions, holes in the plot, and contradictions and pushing himself to not say them. Emmett caught that one night just by looking at him.

"Say it," Emmett said the previous night. "Say what your question is."

Jasper was taken aback and almost forgot what had aroused skepticism in his mind. He didn't lie and say that he didn't have questions, knowing that Emmett was aware that he did. Emmett had been telling the story of Joseph, who had been sold by his brothers and then became one of the most influential people in Egypt.

"You are talking about Joseph right. Well, his story seems like it had the same plot as when Jesus lived and died. Did the authors just run out of story lines, so they just started telling the same story with different people and changing minor things?" Jasper asked, hoping he didn't offend God. Emmett thought and a smile crept on his face.

"What is the Bible?" he asked to Jasper's dismay. The young man hated when Emmett asked these questions because they were often about nuances that he never answered correctly.

"It's one of God's ways of revealing Himself and His purpose for us. Records of His working in history to teach us about the now and prepare us for the future." Jasper was proud of himself for that one but braced for the follow-up question that was bound to come."

"Right. Do you think that the Bible is a record of every way that God has worked in the world?"

"I would think...no." Jasper replied. *Two for two,* he thought.

"Right. Would you say that you are someone who is flexible? Someone who takes on new ideas easily?" Jasper began to shake his head, and Emmett said what everyone knew. "No, right? You're not. You're kind of stubborn sometimes."

Jasper opened his mouth to object, but Emmett smiled and continued before he could. "It definitely bodes well for you to have the same thing be told to you in different ways. Sometimes it's the only way to get through. But in all seriousness, you find patterns in the Scripture because they are God's revelation about reality and reality has a pattern. You might have heard the phrase 'history repeats itself.' That is what you are noticing here. God has worked endlessly on earth, and He has worked a miracle in providing us with a record of a small bit of it. That small bit shows how God has patterns in what He is trying to tell us about Himself. The story of grace that is Joseph's is a great preamble to the climax of God's work here, where God comes down directly to redeem all mankind by His death. Joseph was betrayed by his own family. But Joseph shows us what happens in the end. The one who was betrayed shows a grace that is life changing!"

Each night, a new story was brought to the table, and the painting of God's character became clearer. As the new believers listened, not only did they take joy in learning more about their eternal Father, but they grew as well a need to share what they knew with others. They had news worth telling, and the inability to do that ate at them. Jasper began to understand why Emmett risked the life he had to share the news about God. Every night brought new comfort and conviction that started to conquer Jasper's fear about their mission to free the Printed.

THE DAY CAME when Antonio was to be transferred as one of a second wave of inductees to Soteria, which had begun admitting "patients" who would assist with the building process. The group had prayed for the transfer to happen at night, and that prayer was answered. Louis Antonio would be admitted at 7:30 p.m., a couple of hours after dark in the shortened days of winter in the northwest. All the confidence in the world couldn't have compressed the quiet nervousness that each of them emitted at the beginning of the day.

By the end of daylight, the anticipation was deafening. Before leaving, the group went over the plan once more, confirming that everyone knew their tasks. They prayed together, and as the sun dipped below the horizon, the group split between their two SUVs and set off.

Emmett and Jasper dropped their old gas cruiser a few miles from the first highway turnoff between the former reservation and Sophia's house. Sophia picked them up, and they lay under a blanket with Timber in the back for the rest of the trip. Bringing Timber was an attempt to cloud how many individuals were in the car while also hiding Jasper and Emmett's faces to cameras that could recognize them. Satellites could run heat scans, and the big dog would more than explain the heat in the back from the two men.

Sophia had disabled all navigation in her car, making her navigation skills critical to the whole endeavor. These skills, however, were not ones that Sophia had any claim to fame with, and they had soon taken several wrong turns.

"Why don't you stop at a burger place and ask directions to the nearest psych ward slash gulag?" Emmett asked from under the blanket. Before Sophia had a chance to reply, Timber lay back down, his solid front across Emmett's neck, cutting off any additional comments.

They reached the drop spot and crept to their places, their veins burning with adrenaline as the minutes passed. Jasper and Emmett lay face down behind the clump of bushes, covered with a black blanket to cloak their appearance. The night was quiet, but every time a bird fluttered or bug moved, it sounded like thunder against the silence of night.

Jasper, who never was one for romanticizing situations, reached out a hand to his friend's shoulder.

"What was that verse you told us last night?" he asked, hearing the crackle of tires on a gravel road ahead.

"Greater love has no one than this, that someone lay down his life for his friends. John 15:13" Emmett replied softly.

"If it makes you feel better...I think I'm ready," Jasper said, hoping that he meant it.

"Does it make you feel better?" Emmett asked with a smile. He never got an answer as the tires drew closer. They eventually came to a stop.

"Why is the cattle-guard gate up?" the pair heard, as a man came from the car to investigate what they thought was an accidental miscue by a guard.

"I don't know, but open it quick; you're letting the cold air in!" another voice said, confirming there was another in the car. The screech of the gate was piercing, something Lake had said would be the case. It was as she'd described and was the perfect cue for stage two of the plan. As the man finished pushing the gate wide, he hobbled back toward the vehicle.

LAKE AND CALE, positioned in the dark stillness of the tree limbs, heard the car door opening and muffled conversation. He lifted the flute to his mouth and began his song.

"What is that?" the guard said. "It sounds like...a flute?"

Lake could hear as whoever was speaking faced the trees. Then she heard a voice in the car. "Come on already! I'm freezing." It was a young woman's voice.

"I thought there weren't any survivors from the flood. You think any dregs made it?" A car door opened, and the second officer emerged. They both walked into the forest, and their voices became clearer.

"What are you doing? If this is...I told you last time was the end of it. I have a boyfriend."

The voices became clearer, and after a moment Lake could tell they were right under her.

Keeping to the plan, she took a deep breath and provided a soft voice harmonizing with the flute music.

"Whoa. What's that?" the first guard said. "Who is there. Show yourself!"

"This isn't funny, Jose. Is this your attempt to get me alone again?"

"No!" He whisper-screamed now. Lake and Cale angled their song like they had been taught, and the sounds whirled around the two guards on the ground.

"Maybe this is an old burial ground?"

"And maybe we stumbled into a pixie wonderland!" the young woman mocked, but by the tone of her voice she was less sure of herself. The pair were too close to engage, and they needed to separate them to do it safely. Lake angled her voice again.

"It's coming from over there," the woman said, brandishing a stun gun. She walked from the man, a few steps. Lake gave the vocal cue, and jumped from the trees. She landed on the ground, and before the guard could react, she jabbed a pen-like syringe into the exposed muscle on her arm. As she did, the flute music stopped, and the sharp sound of compressed air replaced it. A dart flew true to its target below, hitting the other guard between the shoulder and neck. He turned, but before he could finish a step, he collapsed to the ground.

A very long few minutes passed for Jasper and Emmett until they heard the music change. A wide grin formed on Emmett's face, one that Jasper could make out even in the black night. The music was no longer the lyrical tribal melody but had switched to something familiar.

"I know that song..." Jasper whispered.

"Yes?" Emmett said in anticipation.

"Was it in a movie?" Jasper asked. The smile on Emmett's face turned to a look of disbelief.

"You're hopeless... 'Was it in a movie?'" Emmett said in a childish voice. "The man doesn't recognize the theme of *Pirates of the Caribbean* when he hears it." Emmett muttered under his breath. "Let's go."

They strode into the trees where they found Lake and Cale sitting on the ground next to the two guards, who lay on the ground, eyes closed.

"Good on ya," Emmett commended the pair. They took their uniform coats off them and pulled them up for the trek back to the car. When they arrived, they found Antonio in the back seat, looking puzzled at the crew of four that approached his vehicle. The man was big. Bigger than Emmett, and he looked skeptical. Lake came to the car, checked for cameras that would give them away, and after finding none, she opened the door.

"Hi, are you Mr. Antonio?" she asked. The man waited before speaking, perhaps wondering if it was a trick from the State. Eventually he responded with a simple.

"Yes."

Wary of any microphones that could be hidden in the car, Lake unfolded a piece of paper and showed it to the cuffed man.

It read, "We know how much you have lost. We also know that the State printed you for no reason. We want to offer you a way out. If you want us to leave you alone, we will, but if you want a chance at freedom and a new start, please tell us now."

It was a nervous ten seconds of waiting for a reply. Jasper and Emmett looked down the road for any signs of traffic.

Antonio nodded in response, though it was clear he had doubts.

Lake motioned for them to bring the sleeping guards over. Jasper and Emmett placed them in the trunk and lay the blanket they had used to conceal themselves over them. Emmett took the wheel, and Jasper rode in the passenger seat. They drove along the south side of the crags that surrounded the reservation and found an open grassy area. Emmett began pitching the vehicle around, doing doughnuts, jumping over bumps, testing the SUVs limits.

When he was done, they unloaded the two guards. Jasper looked at Emmett, obviously nervous about how Antonio would take the unveiling of the identities. He was quite a big man, and Jasper wished that he had kept one of Sophia's darts around just in case. Emmett looked over at the man still sitting in the back, walked to him, and opened the door. Emmett and Jasper took off the jackets they had worn and replaced them on the guards.

Helping the big man from the back to a stump several feet away, they believed they could speak without fear of unseen microphones in the vehicle.

"So... I guess you're wondering who we are," Emmett asked the man, sure that his beard meant he wouldn't be recognized from the news footage.

"Emmett Walsh and Jasper Wood." he said flatly. "I've known since I first saw you two." Jasper was relieved in his shock that Antonio already knew and had yet to try to strangle them. He pulled out the tablet in his bag and opened a presentation that Sophia had made to prove their innocence. They showed each slide to him, and he showed little of any emotion, and only provided an occasional grunt of acknowledgment. By the end, he made no response. Emmett then asked his final question.

"We are believers in the God of heaven. I'm printed, you're printed, and he's probably worse off." He pointed at Jasper, who wondered what he meant by that. "I don't know if you are a believer, but we couldn't let anyone go to that place who had shown the kind of grace you did, given your circumstances, without giving you an invitation."

"Invitation to what?" he asked.

"We have a place that is hidden from the State's gaze, where we can live and worship freely without much threat. It's not much, but it's not a glorified prison. If you want us to return you, we can. If you want to be able to leave from here on your own, you are welcome to that. But you have a place for a fresh start if you want it."

The big man thought for a moment, knowing the weight of his decision. He took a deep breath before speaking, but when he did, his voice was filled with his heart.

"I hated you. That did nothing to bring my girls back. When I decided to forgive you, or at least say that I did, the wall of anger I had built turned to dust, and I began to see the way of healing. I knew my wife and daughter would want me to keep on going. When I saw the backlash I got for saying those simple things to you, it was like putting on glasses for the first time. I saw how the world was so set on its values, and forgiveness isn't one of them. It's even criminal, I've heard." He gestured to his hand restraints. "I don't know if I'm a 'believer' as you are, but I reject what the State has become, and if that's enough to go with you, then I would be grateful. If not, if you could send me on my way, I will be grateful for that too."

"Welcome to the family," Emmett replied. He jumped back in the car and took hold of the wheel again, this time power sliding into a tree, causing all of the airbags to go off. Emmett quickly checked for anything he may have left behind, and then the three men placed the guards back in their seats where they would wake up from their supposed joyride. They walked back to the dirt road where Sophia, Lake, and Cale waited for them. They piled in the back again as the stretch on the highway would be scrutinized by cameras scanning with facial recognition software for Antonio, once the State reported the newest patient had never arrived. Sophia got off the main highway, and they found the old SUV that had been waiting to take all but Sophia through the back way to the lake.

Emmett and Jasper had gotten used to the silence that accompanied Cale's presence, but as soon as he got accustomed to sitting next to the big man, questions abounded. After a quick bombardment, it seemed Louis knew only one way out of the onslaught.

"So, I heard the music while the guards came out. Do you have special magical instruments that can lull people to sleep?" he asked the pair in the back. Cale looked at Emmett for permission. When he got the nod from the driver, he turned to the man eager to reply.

"Yes. Definitely, magic instruments."

"Anything that could make Jasper dance must be magical," Emmett commented. Antonio, who obviously didn't buy the subterfuge, waited for a genuine answer, which Lake politely gave him.

"My brother is very good at the flute, and we made one that can also be used with tranquilizer darts. We lured them into the forest, and while we were in the trees, Cale shot one of them with one dart, and I got the other with a handheld dart."

They explained the rest of the encounter, with Emmett's support, as Antonio listened patiently.

"So it was you singing in the trees," Louis said. "You have a beautiful voice."

Jasper felt a pang of jealousy jab into his heart at the man's compliment. He recalled the first time he had offered that kindness. For his audacity, he received a kiss. Jasper looked back quickly in a mild panic. Lake noticed it, and he realized this gesture wouldn't be forgotten and would come up at another date. He looked at the man's face directly for the first time that he was sure of. This man's daughter had been close to Lake's age, making him in his mid-forties. The jealousy was replaced by a stab of guilt—the acknowledgment of what he had lost.

It took over an hour to reach the back road that they had initially taken by accident when finding the lake house. By that time, they had explained the rest of the ruse they had made to keep their anonymity ensured. The idea of driving the opposite way to the lake to plant the 'joyride' the drugged guards would have taken. The fact that they had a romantic history was the icing on the cake, as it wouldn't be hard to peg them for the type that would try out a new government drug and go on a joyride, leading to the disappearance of the detainee.

SEVENTEEN

ANTONIO ADJUSTED with relative ease to the new accommodations. After wrestling with ideas for names for weeks, the group had finally settled on "The Sanctuary." There was little time to rest as winter came in with a fury, with feet of snow as a gift from above. Louis, the oldest in the group by at least ten years, threw himself at the duties of the Sanctuary with abandon. It got to the point where Jasper and Emmett began to worry about the man as he constantly found things to do on the property.

The boys had been sent out to shovel the night's snow off the roundabout outside the house. Sophia had claimed the daily routine was for them to always have a clean paved way of quick escape via two ways.

"I think she just doesn't like walking in snow to the workshop. I don't think us doing this every day has anything to do with escape routes," Jasper complained as he tossed a shovel full of powder off the concrete. Emmett and Cale had always accompanied him in this duty, but even though he wasn't asked, Louis came freely to help.

"I wouldn't like walking in the snow if all I wore was slippers, either," Emmett said, being intentionally loud so that someone in the house might by chance hear. After no response, he tried another route. "What do you think, Mr. Antonio?"

"Please. Call me Louis. And no. I won't be taking jabs at the host a few days into my stay." The big man said, turning his shovel and letting the contents land in a bed with a soft thump.

"I think you've been replaced as the wisest in the land, Emmett." Jasper commented, shaking the snow out of his hair."

"I think we all knew that wasn't that case and who did have that title the whole time."

"Me!" Cale said with full confidence. The boy had scooped too large a load and struggled to lift it, but his assumption had drawn a full-throated laugh from their newest companion.

After they had finished, Sophia gave them the day off from other chores. Jasper and Emmett wanted to give Louis a tour of their normal walking path to the lake and bridge and back, but the girls insisted on going. It wasn't long before the questions rolled in for the man.

"So, Louis. What did you do, like as a job?" Lake asked, not sure if that was considered a personal question.

"I was an engineer," Louis began.

"Oh yeah? What kind?" Sophia asked excitedly.

"Electrical. I worked for the State in the Computer Science and Technology division," he said. Jasper glanced at Antonio's face and noticed a pang of guilt. Slipping that insight to the back of his mind, he continued listening.

"Very cool. I was mechanical, but I'm just now getting to apply it." Sophia said. They conversed freely, talking about the passions of engineers, a language the rest of the group had a hard time following. "I wanted to be a world class engineer, so much at the time that I was convinced I didn't want a family. When I met Devon, we seemed compatible because he didn't want one either, saying we would be drowning in work." Jasper and Emmett caught Louis's face before Sophia had noticed her misstep. When she did, her face looked mortified. "I'm so sorry. I didn't mean to bring up... I'm so stupid."

"No. It's okay," Louis sniffled. "I get emotional, but thinking about them makes me happy, which means talking about them does the same. Gina, my wife, and I met in high school. We got married soon after and had Suzy, our daughter, a couple of years after that." He looked at Lake. "She would be around your age. What are you... nineteen?" he asked. She nodded, even though it was a lie, she didn't want to stop the story by correcting technicalities. "Anyway, I was gone with work for most of her childhood, so after I finished the keystone project for my union, I retired to be with my family more. Gina was an artist, a painter. She loved to paint landscapes of mountains, rivers, and valleys, which meant being outside was always a priority. We needed money, though, so she started teaching at the local institution." He scratched his short salt and pepper beard and continued.

"Working at the institution was pretty eye-opening for Gina, and we realized it wasn't a place that we wanted Suzy to have to attend, but like everyone else, she was called in for her education." He turned back to Lake. "Did you end up going to one of the institutions?"

"No. I left home the night the transport came for me. It's the only reason I survived the flood that buried my home." Lake responded. Louis nodded in acknowledgment.

"I wish mine had done the same. I'm sorry about your home. Did any of your family survive?"

"Only Cale who was with me at the time."

"I'm sorry about that as well. Suzy was on break when it happened. We tried to spend as much time as we could with her when she was out of school. She had just started dating this boy, and he wanted to take her out to the mountains for the break. I was upset because I had to start worrying about boys chasing after her on top of all the other parental concerns. My concerns turned out to be unnecessary since she chose to visit us for break instead."

"She sounds like a beautiful soul," Lake said tenderly.

"She was. Both of them." They came to the shore of the lake.

Louis took a deep breath in and looked out over the lake. "I don't have much wisdom, but if I've learned anything in the past months, it's that you need to hold on tighter and tighter to those you love as time goes by, because the world doesn't discriminate on who it takes."

Jasper caught a glance at Lake as the widower spoke. Tighter and tighter. He had heard clichés about life and love before, but the advice that Louis spoke was real and came from an awful experience. Throughout the rest of the morning's snow-covered walk, Jasper's mind wrestled with applying the man's words.

Later that afternoon, he found himself alone for a moment with Emmett on the way back from checking on the animals. He knew what he was going to say and began constructing arguments and rebuttals to several different counterpoints Emmett could make to his proposition.

"Am I crazy?" This wasn't the first time that Jasper had asked a question that was three moves ahead of his original point.

"I don't know. Would a crazy person ask that question?" Emmett answered, confused.

"No, no. Let me try this again," Jasper said, glad Emmett restrained himself from joking about it. "You've taught me I shouldn't live in fear but to live in the identity that has been provided for me." Emmett nodded. "Louis got me thinking, too...about my life. I don't want to live in fear, because even people who do that can't fight floods, or the State, and truly escape them. Eventually it will come," Jasper said.

"Right. So what is on your mind that you want to step forward with?" Emmett smiled, and Jasper knew that Emmett already understood his plight. "Spit it out, man!" Emmett encouraged.

"I love Lake. It doesn't matter that she is the first woman to look at me that way...but I want her to be the only one who does...ever. So I want to marry her."

Emmett laughed at him, and Jasper didn't know whether to be angry with the man or not. Soon enough Emmett grabbed him in a rough embrace.

"You've done well, mate. That's a fine decision. I just want to remind you of the seriousness of that decision. It's a huge commitment." Jasper nodded in reply, and Emmett replied with a smile that bolstered his confidence in the decision.

Do you have a ring?"

Jasper hadn't thought of that or anything else that had to do with marriage besides the fact he wanted it.

"I had only focused my efforts on convincing you."

"Well, you did that, so I guess I can help you with what's next. Let's chat about it with Sophia. I'm sure she has a few rings lying around that you can use."

Everything about Jasper's childhood and development screamed at him internally in alarm at the monumental decision. He acknowledged the feeling and surprised himself at his willingness to move on. Jasper knew what he wanted, possibly for the first time. Emmett and Jasper spent several hours scheming quietly together throughout the day and found an opportunity to rope in Sophia as well. They found her in her workshop drafting something that neither of them could recognize.

When they informed her of the idea, she burst in excitement, and after Jasper and Emmett calmed her excited screams, they plotted some more.

"I actually don't have any extra rings! I'm sorry," Sophia said when Emmett asked. She looked at what she was drafting, then cleared the computer screen. "I'll make one!" She then kicked the two boys from her shop with instructions to keep Lake occupied and away from her to get it done. Emmett told Lake and Jasper they needed to check on the bridge entrance, and they obeyed without argument. Jasper walked especially slowly, hoping to make the task span as many minutes as possible.

As was their custom, they linked their hands only after they had made the turn from the house. Everyone knew about the two, but Jasper still felt uncomfortable with public displays of affection, something that Lake played with like a game. They'd had hundreds of conversations on their walks beyond the house, and the pair rarely had trouble finding topics. Jasper realized that the time they had spent together probably equaled the quality time of people who had been in relationships for years, and the insight solidifying his decision. He only hoped she was as convicted.

They arrived at the bridge and moved the plastic and resin rock that covered the opening to the tunnel that led back to the house.

"I think we may need to dig around the fake rock more. Once the snow melts the creek may expand and find its way in." Lake deduced.

"That would wake you up."

"It would be worse than that. This is the highest point of the tunnel system. If water comes in here, then it will eventually show up at all the other ends. I don't think Sophia would appreciate it if her basement turned into a pool."

"Then where would we sleep?" he asked, testing the ground around the covering. He said nothing until his eyes met Lake's gaze.

"Why do you sleep down there still? The rooms upstairs are available."

Jasper thought about it, noting her interest keenly.

"Emmett stayed down there. I wasn't going to leave him and take a room upstairs. It just doesn't feel right." He shook the snow from his hands and rubbed them together to regain their feeling. "I don't know. I don't feel like I deserve comfort more than him. It would feel weird." Lake came closer, and put her head between his shoulder and neck from behind. Something she had made a habit of doing.

"What do you deserve, Jasper?" The young man was staggered by the question. Though it was simple, he couldn't find a suitable answer.

"I don't know," he said, leaning his head on hers.

"Don't forget who you are in all of that sad nobility," she said in a mocking tone. He turned to find she had taken out the deer pendant from her shirt and was holding it. "Be confident in who you are. Humility isn't the willingness to tear yourself down. It's knowing how great your Father is." She smiled at him, satisfied with the opportunity to lecture the man.

"You've been reading old books with Sophia, haven't you?"

Lake said nothing in response, but stood up on her tiptoes and leaned in for a kiss. Jasper closed his eyes in anticipation. As his lips were about to meet hers, he felt an impact.

Jasper's back went stiff, and he felt it become covered with cold wet. He opened his eyes to the giddy eyes of the women he loved, who had just deviously dumped a handful of snow down his back. He shook out the snow and ran after Lake who squealed in delight. He eventually caught her, something he knew she had let him do, given how much faster she was, and they wrestled in the snow.

Jasper stalled on the way back, making the walk take much longer than anyone could assume it would. When they came into the house, they found Louis, Cale, and Emmett together playing an old board game that Cale had found. Jasper looked at Emmett's face, which showed a deep satisfaction indicating that everything was going to plan.

"Is Sophia done in her shop for the day?" Jasper asked, hoping to get an answer on what stage of the plan they were on.

"Yes, I am." Sophia answered, coming out of her old bedroom. "Did you need anything from it?" Jasper brushed off the question having gotten the signal she was finished.

"Nothing that can't wait."

⬥

THAT NIGHT, Jasper slipped from the house after Emmett led vespers. The moon was full, and its light reflected off the snow that surrounded him, making it easy to find his way to the workshop in the dark. The lights turned on as he entered and dusted the snow off his shoes, careful not to track snow close to anything that looked expensive or dangerous. He looked for the ring that Sophia had made, and after searching in all of the obvious places, he grew anxious about how long he had been gone. His internal time clock urged him to return to avoid suspicion. As he reached for the door, he saw an arrow pointing to the ceiling.

He reached up and put his hand on the doorframe and found a small leather pouch. He opened the bag to reveal a silver ring. The metal was bent and cut to resemble branches with leaves at their ends. The ring wasn't completely connected, something that he expected from Sophia not knowing the ring size. It was exquisite and brought a finality to the task ahead that caused his stomach to flutter.

A WEEK PASSED as Jasper waited for the right time. The excitement of his decision remained, but the work of the Sanctuary brought new challenges to their cause. Sophia began plans to create a network of believers in the region under a coded name. One that could link people of faith to support and worship as a family without overtly breaking the law. Louis, who had worked for the State in the realm of computer science, was extremely helpful with the mapping. He hadn't yet made any obvious professions of faith in the time he had been with them, but he listened carefully during vespers and occasionally said a prayer or two during meals.

The early-year fog had rolled in, and as the snow eventually melted, the fog had replaced its beauty with a gray melancholy. Jasper, however, was ready to make his move. He remembered again why Emmett had caught his attention in the first place. He was the man who showed no fear when everyone else had, guilty or not. Since then, he had seen a gradual walk in that regard with himself. He knew who he was and where his future lay. He began fiddling with the ring in his hands and considered the feeling in his stomach. *Am I afraid of asking her?* he wondered. He tried applying the same logic Emmett had taught him to this situation and found that it helped. He knew Lake would say yes. Therefore why not be excited rather than nervous.

He told Sophia and Emmett that he would ask Lake that night, sparking an excited response from them both. As sunset approached, Jasper invited Lake on a walk to the shore, hoping that the fog would have broken enough to witness the still waters reflecting the sun's dying light. She looked at him skeptically but followed.

The earth sank beneath their feet as they strode the familiar path. The sound of water dripping off the trees gave the impression of rain, even though there were no angry clouds in the sky. The air was fresh and new, almost like it was a symbol of what Jasper was going to do. He breathed deeply as they walked, taking in the moment.

"Jasper?" he heard Lake say. "Jasper?"

"What?"

"Were you ignoring me?" Lake asked, teasingly.

"No, I'm sorry. What did you say?" Jasper scrambled, waking up from his daze.

"I asked if Louis has talked to you about God yet? Do you think he believes?"

"I think he acts like he does. That's good enough for me right now. Maybe he will open up more when more people come."

"When do you think that will be?" she asked.

Jasper shrugged. "I don't know."

"Everything will change, won't it?"

Jasper didn't know if that was a rhetorical question or not.

"Probably," he said. "But for the better. I think we are better off with Louis here than before. I do have some lingering guilt for his family though. Everything was taken from him, with no chance to say goodbye."

They arrived at the shore, where the sunset had just begun. To their delight the clouds broke enough to let a warm, pinkish light shine over the mountains and glide over the top of the waters in an ever-changing painting. "That's one thing that I've been thinking about."

"What is?" Lake asked.

"I want to live without fear or regret." Turning to her he placed his shaking hands in hers and forced himself to look directly in her eyes. "I know that I love you and that I want to be with you forever. The assurance that that brings is wonderful, but not enough because forever here on earth isn't long. Forever could be today, next week, or a hundred years." He had more planned with the speech, but in his excitement he had already forgotten it. He couldn't turn back now, though. "I don't want to wait another day to state who you are to me, and who I want to be for you." The young man knelt on one knee as he took the small leather pouch from his pocket and opened it, revealing the polished silver ring. His voice caught in his throat, and he cleared it before saying the words he had seen in shows.

"Lake, would you be my wife?"

The girl looked back, a tear dropped down her cheek, and a smile registering on her face. Jasper forced himself not to read her face in case he saw something he'd rather not. After what felt like forever, she took the ring, slipped it on her finger, and brought his face close.

"Yes. But only on one condition," she answered. This didn't happen in movies. Jasper had done some research by watching proposals in films, and this was definitely off the beaten path.

"Yes?" he asked.

"Take care of yourself. You need to know you live for more than Jasper Wood. I don't want to lose another part of my family. Just promise you will remember that?" she asked. He nodded his agreement, still unsure of what he was agreeing to. Her face lit up, and she kissed him soundly in jubilation.

When they came back to the house, there was a celebration. Everyone knew what was happening while the pair were gone but wanted to give them the satisfaction of announcing it. Once they did that, they continued the ruse, exclaiming that they never saw this coming in their celebratory reaction. Sophia and Louis had made a banquet for the festivity. They feasted, knowing occasions like this were rare, and the group treated it as something special.

Afterward, the crew found their places around the fire for the nightly vespers. Emmett checked the Soteria transfer listing for any new members convicted under threat of religious insurrection. He flipped through the alphabetically listed names on the manifest for anything that stood out. Jasper and Lake sat on the floor together by the fire, Lake having teased Jasper into putting his arm around her.

Jasper had focused on enjoying the moment and didn't object to the simple PDA. Everyone seemed to be in good spirits, and he was keen on hearing the continuation of the Acts of the Apostles stories. The night before they had talked about a man named Stephen, who was one of the deacons of the early church. He glanced at the others around the room, noting the satisfied faces. In a moment, one changed. Once Emmett had reached the bottom of the page he was sifting through, Jasper noticed his emotions take a traumatic turn. SADNESS and DISGUST showed on Emmett's face. The man quickly readjusted his psyche, but it was too late. Emmett's eyes met Jaspers, and they knew a conversation that would change the tone of the night would be on the horizon.

EMMETT SPARED THE MOOD, and after glancing at the screen again, he set it aside, put on a smiling face, and prepared for the vespers. Jasper was distracted throughout the evening. Knowing Emmett knew something he didn't, and the emotions that accompanied the revelation, created an asterisk on the joyous occasion. Learning that the early Christian leader Stephen was stoned to death after a pointed speech he made didn't restore Jasper's psyche to a positive state.

After they had prayed together and said their goodnights, they all went to their rooms to sleep. All but three. Emmett remained with Louis and Jasper. Once they were sure that Cale had gone downstairs, Emmett met Jasper's accusatory gaze. Emmett had communicated with his micro expressions to Jasper on several occasions, and they had gotten quite good at nonverbal communication. Emmett shot over a look of caution, a flashed COMPASSION, both of which Jasper ignored.

"What is it?" Jasper said aloud.

"Jasper...enjoy the night. Just keep celebrating your new fiancée, and I'll tell you tomorrow night."

Jasper considered it. Not because it made sense, but because he knew that whatever was going to be revealed would poke a hole in the bliss he had found.

"Tell me." The young man said intently. Emmett sighed and stood to grab the tablet. He turned it on.

"I was checking new convictions. I always scroll down the list at least twice just in case it took me longer to remember believers I knew. When I went to the bottom, I found a name that was familiar, but not because I knew her." He turned the tablet and gave it to Jasper.

"Her?" Jasper asked, taking the screen. He looked down scanning the screen. The last name on the list was familiar. Jasper wanted to gasp, but his lungs were frozen, disallowing breath.

Ziva Wood - Arrested under suspicion of perjury, obstruction of justice, harboring fugitives. Printed - To undergo domestic terrorist rehab, sentencing to proceed after cleared.

Jasper felt Emmett take the screen away and replace it with his hands. The young man threw his hands away, burst the door open, and ran into the gray, fog-laced night.

Jasper ran like never before. Not from something specific, but out of a primal instinct to do anything. He heard calls from Emmett and Louis behind him, but he couldn't stop. He made it to the shore of the lake. Fog lingered again over its face though the night distorted most sight.

Not my sister, Jasper thought. If there was anyone to be hurt by this situation, it wasn't supposed to be her. He hadn't seen her or known anything about her since the parents split them up. *Why now? Printed!*

"Stockton," Jasper said. Knowing that the one man who had left a message that he knew of their existence didn't leave rocks unturned. He had seen many men printed, some women too. But never a girl, not one as young as her. She would be a teenager now. *Barely fifteen!* His mind struggled to find clarity. Guilt filled his heart, and with that he waded into the bone-chilling water, and stood.

The pain was keen, and it bit into his skin. His muscles cramped as he stood unmoving in the freezing water.

"Jasper!" Emmett said, catching up to the man. He ran into the water and pulled his friend out. He took off his shirt and jacket and began drying off the stubbornly motionless man.

"It's all my fault!" Jasper said softly. Louis, who had arrived and assisted Emmett, heard the statement. He looked Jasper in the eyes and hit him. Not a fist, but a loud slap across his face. Jasper's attention was gained, and his daze broken. He looked into the man's dark eyes.

"Who cares if it's your fault or not. Are you going to die here and make it worse? Or are we going to get her back? You can be a coward and satisfy whatever guilt you feel with self-flagellation, or you can stand up and make this right." Jasper, rife with emotions, knew the man was right and that his response was selfish and stupid. He took a deep breath. Emmett continued drying but gave Louis an appreciative look.

"We're going to get her back." Jasper responded.

"That's right," Emmett said. "Now let's get you back so that, when we do get her, she may have a brother to meet when she arrives."

They half-carried the freezing young man through the forest to the house. When they arrived, the women stood at the door waiting. Jasper was welcomed with a worried embrace from Lake, and Sophia went to prepare a place by the fire to warm his shivering body.

EIGHTEEN

"I'M SORRY," Jasper said as he stared into the fire in the living room. Lake, Sophia, and Emmett didn't know exactly who the words were for and consequently ignored the apology.

"It'll be okay," Emmett responded encouragingly. "Let's try and get this figured out. Can you think of any reasons the State would print your sister?"

"A couple, but I haven't seen her or talked to her since I was young. She couldn't have known anything about me. She's barely a teenager! How are they sadistic enough to print teenage girls!"

"What if she's a believer...and this has nothing to do with you?"

Jasper thought about the notion, a little of the guilt fading away. Emmett looked at him with sincerity. "Either way it doesn't change a thing. We are going to get her out." Emmett's words further calmed Jasper's anxiety.

"Why did you run?" Sophia asked. "Why sit in the frozen lake?"

Jasper didn't answer, his mind flooded by a jumble of emotions. They sat in silence until Louis came back into the room.

"I don't think I can talk about it right now." Jasper said.

Louis sat on the couch and gave a soft, reminiscent sigh. "The day before my girls died, I had put off my work on the canoe. Stupid things...got in my way of finishing it. She had come back the day before, skipping her last class to spend more time with us. She hoped to take it out on its maiden voyage...but I hadn't finished it. After the water took them, I looked for reasoning. I wouldn't have called myself a Christian since I was a boy, so I thought it may be God's way of punishing me for leaving the faith behind." The big man coughed a few times, emotion thickly embedded in his throat.

"That meaning for their deaths wasn't satisfying, so I kept coming back to my stalling of the project being the cause of their slumber. I did the same thing that you did in that river, only in more creative ways. I electrocuted myself. I ran my head into walls. I let my fire at home get so close to my face that I could see my beard hairs curl. Senseless things born from guilt. That if I punished myself enough, I would wake up from the nightmare to see them again."

Jasper looked into the man's face; a light filled his eyes.

"When I realized that, I was sick," Louis continued. "It led me to remember what I was taught when I was a kid." He paused and looked at Jasper and Emmett. "That's when I wrote that message... Does that sound familiar at all?"

Jasper nodded, and glanced over at his fiancée. She looked worried, and at the same time, she looked like she wanted to strangle him. Jasper knew this would be a conversation that would take more than he had at the moment. He turned to the group, and with tears filling his eyes, he sighed.

"Thank you."

THE NEXT DAY, they began making plans for breaking Jasper's sister from the State's grasp. Jasper had only escaped Lake's questioning looks for that night, and in the next few days, they engaged in multiple conversations on topics including loyalty, self-control, commitment, and most of all, boundaries. Jasper saw a different side of his new fiancée, one that changed his vision of the laid back, free spirit of a young woman. They talked it through, and eventually she was convinced she had gotten her point across.

According to the manifest, Ziva was being held in the Pasco white house in preparation for transport to Soteria. Emmett wondered why she hadn't immediately been transported. Assuming it was just because there wasn't a place prepared for younger "patients," they prepared for the worst and kept a vigilant eye at all times throughout the following days.

They hadn't seen or heard any chatter about Louis's disappearance, which led them to believe the ruse worked. They would no doubt use more competent and trustworthy officers to deliver patients, which required that they rely on the network of believers before they were apprehended.

Three days after the news, Jasper and Lake sat outside on the patio listening to Cale playing his flute. The instrument rarely left his side, and Jasper wondered if he slept with it at night. He had never heard a more pleasant sound than when Cale played. His skill wasn't the only thing that was surprising. Cale had the ability to make up marvelous melodies that rarely sounded like anything he had played previously. It was like listening to someone painting a piece of art by sight while flying around to a new subject every time they picked up a brush. Cale sat toward the house facing the young couple.

The sun was out that afternoon, and they were soaking up as much of the early spring warmth as they could before the fog and snow had a chance to return. Cale was playing a fluttering tune that danced happily. The sun's rays mingled with the tune to culminate in a feeling that almost made Jasper forget the anxiety for his sister. Jasper heard something behind him and knew what it must be without turning around. Cale's fluttery tune had finished with a note of dissonance, and the boy looked over Jasper and Lake's heads at someone in the doorway. They turned to find Sophia, the tablet in her hands.

"We need to go. They are transporting Ziva now," Sophia said.

LITTLE HAD CHANGED in the plan besides the precautionary backup plans in case the transport vehicle didn't stop or if there were more than two officers. They ran through each step anxiously on the tense drive there. If they did make it in time, it would be close. And any mistakes would be magnified terribly with the time constraints that they were under.

Jasper felt his heart beating rapidly as he and Emmett climbed under the dog blanket after dropping off the utility vehicle at the same spot. Adrenaline raced through Jasper's veins. He didn't even know what he would say to his sister once he found her.

They all carried darts with them so they could subdue the guards even if there were more than two. Jasper had still never been in a fight and still couldn't see many situations where he would come out on the winning end. His heart began to sink as he pictured what it would look like. *A fight scene from a movie?* he thought. Not a chance. It would be quick, and probably painful. As his melancholy grew, he felt a hand come from the rear seats to pat his covered shoulder. It was Lake.

What about her? he thought. *What about Ziva? What about Emmett and the rest?* His blood began to boil anew. The fear that stirred turned to exaltation, and his conviction was bolstered. If he was going to be captured or killed, he wouldn't go down without a fight.

They hurried to their spots and waited, hoping they weren't too late. Jasper and Emmett could hear Lake and Cale climbing into the trees, and finding their places in the canopy. After just fifteen minutes, they heard tires down the road. Jasper felt a tap on his shoulder.

"Ready to get your sister?" Emmett asked.

He needed no reply. Jasper had been ready for a long time. He was the cause of the separation of his parents and his sister as well. It was time he made right on his mistake.

They heard a sharp sound of air, audible evidence that plan A had begun. The vehicle continued but stopped in front of where Emmett and Jasper lay. Closer than they would have hoped. A door opened and the pair heard muffled swear words directed at the tire that audibly spewed air into the cold night. *Is there only one?* Jasper asked himself. Time was of the essence, and right on time they heard the lyrical flute music behind and to the left of them, leading into the forest.

"Who's there?" called the officer in a voice that betrayed his fear. The man was terrified. They heard steps going toward the woods, and the music continued. "Identify yourself!" the man said again. Jasper risked a glance and saw the officer, handgun drawn, frozen at the beginning of the canopy. He was a hefty individual, and he walked with an arrogant stride.

The flute music took on a new tone, attempting to create a different effect on the officer. It invited in a voice, an angelic voice that accompanied the sound as it pitched and moved.

Once the voice floated its way from the trees, the pair heard the officer swear. Jasper threw his head back flat against the ground as the pudgy man ran toward where they lay. They heard twigs snap and bushes crash as the man ran through all in panic.

"I didn't sign up for no ghosts!" he yelled. He came closer and closer. Jasper heard an impact beside him, and heard the slightest grunt from Emmett as the officer crashed over them and fell. The pair remained still, and the hysterical man quickly regained his feet and ran down the road, over the cattle gate, leaving the car behind.

"Are you okay?" Jasper said?

"He kicked me in the side!" Emmett responded in pain. The men got up, and scanned the surroundings for any other danger signs.

"It won't take him more than twenty minutes to get to the front entrance."

"You really think he can run the whole way?"

"If I thought I had just had an encounter with a ghost alone at night, I would." They walked to the car and studied the front seat for signs of a camera. Finding none, they opened the back door in expectation. Jasper's stomach turned at what he witnessed. Where his sister was supposed to be sitting, was nothing. He couldn't believe it. He wanted to cry. Emmett tapped him out of his paralysis, pointing to a small piece of paper left on the seat.

Jasper picked it up. It was a picture of a young girl in her midteens. She had flaxen hair that moved in long curls down her shoulders. Below the picture, were a date and a name.

Ziva Wood. Age 14. Printed. Admitted into Soteria rehab facility 2/04.

Jasper retched and turned to throw up into the bush nearby. Emmett closed the door, and returned to his friend.

"We need to go. Now!"

Jasper didn't argue. They gave a series of whistles indicating it was time to go, and the group raced back to the meeting point. Their return involved extra turns to avoid as many traffic cameras as possible. After several hours they finally returned to the house, all of them in a state of shocked confusion. They parked the cars and returned to the living room.

Jasper didn't speak the whole ride back, and Emmett provided little explanation. They sat in their normal spots.

"What happened?" Sophia asked.

Jasper still found it hard to find the words, but he knew he had to begin some way. He pulled the paper from his pocket and showed it to them as if it explained everything. It was his sister's picture; they could all be sure of that from the resemblance.

"That car was a diversion. The manifest was a diversion," Jasper said, his voice wavering. "She was admitted two days ago!"

"I don't understand. Why was that paper there in the back of the car?" Antonio asked.

Jasper began to answer, but he failed to find the air in his lungs to speak. He handed the paper to Emmett, who received it questioningly. His query was answered when he turned the paper around. Something had been written on the back of the admittance card.

Dear Jasper,

You should know better than most how good I am at my job. I will cleanse the minds young and old of the disease religion. This includes you, yes, you young Jasper. But before I get to you, I must assist young Ziva.

Sleep well, in the faith that your sister is in good hands ~ B.S.

Emmett instantly regretted reading the back out loud. A sickening feeling was aroused in everyone as the words fell on their ears, the presence of the sadistic man seeming to seep into the room itself.

"He knows," Jasper said. "I don't know how he knows, but he does. He is using her to find me."

"Why not just stage a whole team of operatives to arrest us in the delivery truck?" Emmett asked.

"I don't think his priority is arresting you two." The two men looked at Sophia quizzically. "He said in the message, he sees cleansing people of their religious allegiances as his purpose."

Emmett nodded in agreement. "That would make sense after what we found about his past. He was going to settle with killing us at the bridge. That was an opportunity the State couldn't pass up."

"So now he's putting Ziva in rehab, and waiting for Jasper to come and join her. That doesn't make sense still," Sophia replied.

Jasper had a thought that wouldn't leave. It hadn't made sense to him yet and did something uncharacteristic in response.

"It could be a test. A teaching opportunity... Maybe Stockton is making me decide between my faith and my family. If I run, then my faith is discredited. If I go directly there, I declare my relationship with God as unimportant. He wins either way." A weight lingered in the air after Jasper's explanation.

"Then go with the third option," Emmett said, gaining everyone's attention. "We go into Soteria and get her out."

THE NEXT MORNING the group at the Sanctuary began vigorously making preparations to do just that. There was an extra air of anxiety after the confirmation that director Stockton knew Jasper had been involved with Antonio's disappearance. The basement turned into a war room. Files layered tables and blueprints covered the walls as they looked for any weaknesses they could exploit in their mission to infiltrate the facility. It led to days of frustration, however, and Jasper became more ill-tempered as time went on.

"What if we take one of their trucks and dress up like the guards." Jasper suggested.

"They'll be checking cars. If Stockton knew we were going to be there, then he would be sure to do print checks on all the drivers coming in," Emmett answered. "We are still dealing with three problems. And we haven't been able to solve any of them yet." He erased the white board wall they had mounted and began to write.

"One. We have no undetectable entry. We could hijack a car and burst through the front door. But they'll have us down in seconds.

"Two. We have no way to move around when we get inside. There's no way Stockton lets her outside where we could get to her, which would mean we need a key. But security buildings don't use keys. Only prints.

"Three. Unique exit. We need an accessible way to leave that will not give them a starting point to track us back home," Emmett expounded.

Three days, and three questions left unanswered. The madness left the pair pacing while Lake and Sophia sat on the couch studying files.

"Maybe we're going about this wrong." Lake broke the silence and gained the attention of everyone in the room. "It's obvious God brought us together for a reason, so why are we acting like it's all on us to make this happen?" They knew she was right, and they took time to ask the One who had set this in motion to take control again. After another hour had passed, Jasper was back to nervously pacing.

Louis came down the stairs from checking the garden. Since he had come, he had stepped out for most of the time they worked on battle plans and preferred to tend to other matters. Cale came down the stairs with him, his hands covered in dark-brown mud. The boy walked up to the page covered area and gave it a quick study. Jasper, feeling his impatience take over, kicked a crumpled piece of paper across the room.

"What about the sea snake?" Cale asked. The rest of them looked quizzically at the boy.

"And we've lost him," Jasper said.

"No, he's right!" Lake sprang to his defense.

"Sea snake?" Emmett asked.

"Not an actual sea snake. We used to tell him it was one. We've been trying to find a way into Soteria using its blueprints. We have forgotten what this was built over!" She looked at Sophia, who had already begun searching something on the tablet, having guessed where Lake was going. "When we were kids, we used to play by the trees on the south side of the reservation. There was an opening there, a concrete tube that ran back home. I think it was some kind of storm drain. Some of the kids used to play a game where we would dare each other to see how far you could go into the 'sea snake' without running back out scared."

Sophia brought up an old schematic of sewage and storm-drain tunnels that ran from Umchin. Lake pointed at the one where she and her friends had played the game. She also noticed three other openings on different ends of the town.

"That one we played at is a couple hundred yards from where we have done the two stoppages." She referenced the end of the other, which appeared as if it ended in the mountain face itself. "That may be our best bet to get in."

"I think that might just work," Emmett said and put a line through the first problem. Problem number two lingered, and its expanse clouded the possible fulfillment of problem one. Louis had stood in the back since he and Cale came down the steps. The tall man didn't often speak out of turn, but when he did it often seemed ordained.

"I may be able to help you with that problem." With those words he gained the attention of all in the basement. "I don't know if it was out of courtesy or indifference that you haven't asked more of my past professional life, but either way I have a confession to make. I was chosen with ten other techs some time ago to develop a device that could open up opportunities for regulating the mismanagement of the State's social programs. We were told to create a device that could manipulate characteristics of a human that set them apart. The iris was too complicated. Facial plastic surgery wasn't cost effective. That left us with handprints."

"So you developed the original printer?" Sophia asked.

Louis nodded.

"How does that solve the problem?" Lake responded, but Jasper already knew. He looked at Emmett. A look of understanding passed between the two.

"If Louis can make another machine, then he can print me with a set that has clearance in Soteria." The absurdity of it seemed to have stunned everyone in the room...except Louis, who sat nodding his head solemnly.

"You can't print yourself!" Sophia exclaimed.

"Why not?" Jasper responded, looking at his hands. "If it means we can get in, I'll do it. And it's not like my handprints will do me much good in the world considering I'm a wanted man or dead in all the databases. My mind is made up."

THE SEVERITY of the situation weighed heavier on the group as each day went by. Sophia and Louis worked feverishly on the device that could wipe away Jasper's identifying marks to the State forever. Whenever he came into the workshop to check on its progress, Jasper's face took on a steely seriousness.

While Louis worked on the device, Jasper, Emmett, Lake, and Cale took a trip to the side of the mountain where they would find Cale's "sea snake." It was supposedly close to the end of the crag where they had lost sight of Umchin after finding its mortifying condition. They arrived at dusk, hoping that if they needed to get out, they knew the area well enough to escape arrest in the dark.

Soon enough they had passed the home of the old cruiser they drove, and the blessing of the old shed was magnified in the memories of the four. After an hour of searching, Emmett found a cement opening that stretched into the black mountain. Water ran smoothly out, creating a creek that moved away from the grate. The group made the effort to remember landmarks to find it again, and drove back to the house spirits, enlivened with progress.

The next morning, after a night of restless work, the improvised printer had been finished. The rest of the group stood outside the shop, anxiously waiting and watching as Louis searched through the State's database to find a suitable print configuration to use.

They had little access to information about which prints grant access to where, leaving them with name-guessing levels of clearance. This game became less and less fun, and Emmett joined in the search. Louis scoured the list of officials until Emmett stopped him. He didn't say anything but waited patiently for Louis to see what he had.

"What?" Jasper said, taking a look. Emmett and Louis didn't answer him. Jasper scanned the list for what had caught their attention. A name stuck out on the page, a name that's utility haunted him.

"Well, that would make the most sense," he said to the others.

"We can find another," Louis said. Emmett studied Jasper's face as he gave a response. The pride he felt for his young friend brought him to the brink of tears as Jasper spoke.

"Prints are prints. I know who I am...and I know who I was created. If it takes having Bernie's prints on my hands to have a chance at seeing Ziva,"—he put his hands on the machine, looking up in expectation—"then it's not even a question."

The printing procedure was never created to be painless, but there were certain measures taken to knock out the convicted during the most painful part. This was not a luxury that Louis was able to install. Jasper's hands sweated before it started. He had seen it before. Hundreds of times. He never could have dreamed that his hands would one day be voluntarily stripped and replaced with new identifications.

Once Louis pressed the button engaging the function, Jasper felt a slow warmth flow into his hands. The warmth crescendoed quickly into a roaring blaze. Like thousands of lightning bolts that raged across his hands. He managed to not scream; at least he couldn't remember if he did. He kept focused on the task of not moving his hands away.

After the last bit of reconstruction, Sophia applied ice to the hands to solidify the prints and ease the pain. Lake left before the end, not wanting to witness the event any longer. She came back eventually to check on him and to officially cross off problem two on their list. After bundling his hands and applying ointments they rested in wait for the date when the Printed would come for their family.

NINETEEN

KNOWING that Stockton was aware of Jasper's survival made the drive to the tunnel's end by the old shed tense for everyone in the group. There was anticipation, almost excitement, at the beginning of the previous excursions because they knew that they had the element of surprise to bolster their chances. This time Stockton and his people knew someone would be coming and Stockton knew what they were coming for. With that in mind keenly, the group couldn't help but realize that whatever attempt they made at retrieval was close to suicide. At the rehab facility, they likely kept Ziva in the most secure location, with a sea of guards, guns, and cameras surrounding her. At least that's what Jasper would do if he were them.

He wasn't them, however; he had grown into something different. Independent. Stockton was also anything but normal. It had taken a while for Jasper to understand him, but after cracking his moral code, he realized that Stockton's mind was straighter than most and definitely more ordered than his mannerisms portrayed.

Stockton was a victim of tragedy. His newfound faith was tested beyond measure, and he broke. He saw his life before him taken away by death and vowed to cleanse the world of what coaxed him to love in the first place. Faith was a virus. With his newfound ideology, he must have felt that a veil was taken from his eyes to reveal a pandemic that required drastic measures.

The cruiser jumped as it hit an unseen log in the darkness, jolting the few in the back.

"Sorry," Emmett said as he nearly ran into a massive oak tree.

"I thought you were going to find a replacement headlight before we did this," Louis said from the passenger seat.

"It's not as easy as it used to be to find a replacement headlight for a fifty-year-old car that has been illegal for five years, friend," Emmett said, gritting his teeth as he dodged another tree that came into view at the last moment.

"How long do you think it will take for the others to find the southern entrance?"

"Hopefully less time than it'll take for us to get out with Ziva."

"Obviously. Do we have a backup plan just in case we have soldiers chasing us out of the sea snake?" Silence. "That's a no. That's what that is."

They had rehearsed the plan for hours that day, knowing the consequences that would come if just one link went wrong. Sophia and Louis mapped out the storm-drain system to give a general sense of where they would come up in the compound. They had identified several places where they assumed the facility would keep her, but they couldn't know for sure.

Right before they all set off, the group prayed.

"No one dies. We do this for opportunities to open people's eyes to see who our God is, not to shut them permanently," Emmett said. They had all nodded at his proclamation. "This includes us. We go into this with faith that our Father can bring us through, not with fervor that leads to suicidal madness." Lake had been uncharacteristically cheery about the process. When they parted ways to their separate marks in the plan, her last words were spoken with such optimism that it almost unnerved the man she hoped to marry.

"See you in the morning, love."

Jasper pondered her words as they found the opening of the northwestern storm drain, just past the old shed. After finding out about Ziva, the plan of getting married had been completely set aside in his mind. It came back with a rush as the car stopped, and he was almost trembling as he got out and shut the door.

Emmett glanced at his watch, which was constantly updating GPS coordinates below. There was no smell in the tunnel, for which the three men were grateful as they crouched through the concrete mouth into the mountain above.

They moved slowly up the subtle grade for the good part of an hour. They all had flashlights and could see where they were going fine enough, but occasionally they came to debris that resembled barbed wire and sharp metal stakes that made them think twice before picking up their pace. Eventually, the concrete tunnel widened and met with two other openings.

Emmett checked his watch, confirming the coordinates with the ones Sophia had given him on their map.

"All right, we're about on time," Emmett said as he searched the top for a ladder and a grate that they assumed would accompany the congregation of drains.

"Found it," Louis said, pointing to a metal circle in the ceiling with his light.

They tried pushing it up, but it was predictably solid. Louis whipped out an excavation drill from the bag he had on his back, and they took turns drilling a hole in the concrete next to the grate. Once a suitable hole was created in the concrete, they found layers of sediment above it.

"Wow, the State was in a hurry to build this place. Lazy buggers," Emmett said digging with the bitt into the dirt above. After rotating digging, they finally broke through to a two-foot space between the sediment and the foundation of the structure above. Emmett peeked around, then, finding no cameras or lights beneath the foundation, he jumped back down to the bottom.

"We can get up. I think they have the whole facility rooted on structure poles like a bridge. Maybe it's because they heard that there is occasionally flooding in this part of the region." Emmett said with dark humor. He studied the map Sophia had given them.

"Is there a spot close by where a ton of cords go up into the same place?" Jasper asked.

"Yeah. It was a couple of feet from the hole," Emmett told him.

"Good, that should be the server room. Hopefully no one is in there. There should be an AC vein that opens up below to cool the computers."

"I saw that too."

"Thank you, Sophia" Jasper said, preparing to climb up with Emmett.

There was a fan in the AC intake. Instead of stopping it, the two cut out a panel just beyond it as it went up. Jasper was encouraged to go first after several skinny jokes from Emmett. He slid into the thin steel rectangle until his face was met by a vent that led directly into a dark room illuminated only by colored LED lights on racks of electronics. He checked if there was anyone in there, and after finding none, he looked down.

"We're good. It's the server room." Emmett handed him a drill, and he opened the vent carefully. The opening was a couple of feet wide and a foot and a half tall.

"Give me the sleepy sauce," Jasper whispered down, hearing snickers from the two men.

Emmett handed him a modified dart that Sophia had made for this very night, and Jasper, his heart beating out of his chest, said a quick prayer and climbed through the vent into the server room.

Jasper surveyed the rest of the room carefully as Emmett made his way up. The room consisted of racks of electronics. There weren't any cameras, something they had counted on, thinking the State was in too much of a hurry to finish the building to have time to provide them.

"Ready?" Emmett asked.

"Sure." Jasper responded unconvincingly. He pulled one of the cords from an antenna on one of the farthest racks from the door.

"How long do you think it'll take for them to send people to fix it?"

"We'll, considering the cord I pulled was labeled, 'Staff Wireless,' pretty fast," Jasper said, smiling mischievously.

Jasper stood quietly behind the door, and Emmet took his place behind one of the racks, waiting.

As Jasper had predicted, two men didn't hesitate to rush down to investigate the dropped network access. Two men came through the door.

"Quick. Turn it back on," a high-pitched male voice said, tapping his phone furiously. "It's going to forfeit my turn soon!"

"Calm yourself," the other returned. Jasper couldn't dream of a better circumstance. He crept behind the squeaky man who remained engrossed in his phone and jabbed the pen into the side of the man's neck. In his excitement, he may have jabbed too hard. Regardless, the sleepy sauce did its job, and he let the man down to the ground. He heard a similar reaction from Emmett.

"Got 'em?"

"Yeah." Jasper replaced the cord that he had unplugged, giving the indication that the problem was fixed, and dragged his subdued captive to the end by the vent.

"Maybe we should've waited for guys to come with uniforms that actually fit us."

"Too late now," Jasper responded, and they began putting on the uniforms. Once they were done, they slid the two men down the steel unit where Louis was waiting.

"Gosh, man! You couldn't have waited till after you handed them down to me to take their clothes?" Louis said, lowering the men to the ground.

"EMMETT, you may want to take a look at this." The big man dropped the second man to Louis, and strode over to Jasper who was looking at the phone the squeaky voiced man was using when they came in. Emmett looked at a stream of messages regarding a stay-at-home order given by the State. The man's phone was peppered with concerning messages from family regarding threats made by the Far East Coalition.

"This guy got called in on an off day because they needed more people here. Why?" Jasper asked.

"I don't know, but anything that helps keep the State occupied on other things but us, I'm pretty happy with," he said, putting encouragement in his voice. "How are your hands doing?"

Jasper looked at his hands; the redness had dissipated. "Fine. A little gritty, but fine."

They replaced the vent, said a quick goodbye to Louis through the duct, and went from the server room.

Their eyes weren't used to the bright light that was in the halls. They had to cover their eyes to get readjusted. The walls of the facility were white like the place Jasper had worked at. Several people passed them as they walked in their poorly fitting uniforms down the hall, looking for any signage that could help them find Ziva.

Several men and women passed them in different colored uniforms that indicated their job within the compound. They all had similar expressions on their faces. Jasper didn't chance making eye contact with any of them for fear that they could recognize him, but he caught glimpses of their faces. Each showed a combination of fear and anxiety as they moved throughout the halls.

"They're afraid about something," Jasper whispered to Emmett as they walked.

"They must have heard big bad Jasper was coming to town. They've probably heard the stories of your military conquests and skill. Jasper Wood, slayer of thousands of men. Ruthless, tyrannical, and above all...cuddly."

"Probably not the time to be making jokes."

"I disagree. It's times like these that we need to make jokes the most."

They walked on through another corridor to a separate wing of the building. Emmett checked his watch and showed it to Jasper.

"It's official. I don't know where we are," the big man admitted. "But let's keep walking as if we did."

They turned into an area that was dominated by white uninformed individuals who were obviously not military or law enforcement. Jasper noticed a tablet that resided beside one of the doctors that passed by. Emmett had noticed, as well, and they gave each other a look, indicating the decision to follow.

The doctor left the area littered with white-coated personnel and walked down the hall to an office space. When Jasper and Emmett turned the corner with him, they were confronted with the last voice they wanted to hear.

"General, I have the security of this facility as my number one priority. There are other threats to consider besides the FEC. We still haven't apprehended the analyst who blew up Evergreen dam!" It was Bernie. They heard a second voice reply to him.

"I'm not going to put your vendetta against a dead man over the security of the State. Surveillance staff will be ordered to scan for airborne targets, and analysts will be prioritizing getting as much information from our captured FEC's as possible. Is that clear?"

Emmett and Jasper didn't hear a reply. The general came from the office and walked briskly into the hall the two were in and turned away from the two blue uniformed men.

They turned away from the door in case Bernie came through as well, but after a moment, they saw no sign. The two walked into the hallway where the conversation had taken place to find a control room flooded with bustling people. Jasper chanced a quick look at one of the screens to find a girl, sitting in a chair looking at a screen.

Jasper almost jumped with excitement. It was her. He looked at the room number on the screen. 1260. Right after he nudged Emmett with his revelation, a sound came from on the intercom.

"All surveillance staff switch from internal to arial scanning. Analysts report to section Bravo for job assignments."

"Thank you, Jesus," Emmet muttered after Jasper had told him the number. Their uniforms were blue, indicating their roles as analysts, and they joined a flood of blue that went down the halls to adjoining sections of the compound. They counted door numbers until they reached a hall labeled 1200–1300. Jasper took a deep breath, and before Emmett could stop him, he placed his hand on the scanner in front of the door. It took longer than usual, but after a few seconds the screen lit green, a name showing at the top. "Bernard Stockton."

The rooms were the typical rooms of a psych ward—white walls, white doors, and little plexiglass windows. There was hardly anyone in the wing. Emmett walked down the halls looking as if he was on official business. The secretary at the desk paid no attention to them, likely assuming if they had clearance to get in, there was no cause for concern.

Emmett walked in front of Jasper and eventually stopped at the room labeled 1260. The girl still sat watching the television, but now they could see that she was magnetically confined to the chair pointed at the screen. Jasper placed his hand on the scanner to the room, and as he did, Emmett gave him a squeeze on the arm and flashed a look of encouragement. Jasper opened the door and entered.

His sister looked like the picture that he had found. Maybe slightly thinner and she had a paleness to her skin that was unlike what he remembered her complexion to be. He looked at her, and she didn't turn from the screen. Wondering why, Jasper looked around and found a control panel to his right. Once he found the button releasing the magnetic cuffs on her arms and legs on the tablet, he tapped it.. He walked slowly to her, and she looked up at his face.

Jasper trembled, seeing the teenager's eyes locked on him; words escaped him with his trembling.

He crouched down to get on the sitting girl's level, leaving a comfortable amount of space between him and the girl. After a few seconds of silent eye contact, he forced himself to speak.

"I don't know how to tell you this, but—"

The girl flung herself at the young man so fast that he flinched back at the possible attack. He straightened. *I'm not hurting*, he thought. He opened his eyes to find the young girl hugging him tightly.

"Jasper," she said embracing him as if he had just returned from a long journey. He hugged her back for a moment. He then heard a tap on the glass, and saw Emmett's face through it. CONCERN blanketed his face, and Jasper knew they needed to hurry.

"We need to go. I can explain everything later, but you need to come with me, okay?" Jasper said urgently, looking as Emmett's face became more demanding. Ziva looked unsure but did as her brother asked.

They opened the door to find Emmett in the hallway between them and the door into the hallway. Jasper looked at the man's face, which now bore a look of SADNESS. He and Ziva started walking quickly to him. Then he heard something behind him down the hall —a voice, cynical and chilling. One that resembled a python that would sing to its prey as it suffocated it.

"Jasper, I'm glad you two joined us."

Jasper turned his head to find Bernard Stockton twenty paces down the hall. His face was calm and showed a subdued deep pain that flowed through his wrinkles. In his hand was a pistol. One that definitely wasn't standard issue for the State. Jasper walked backward slowly.

"It's okay," Stockton continued. "Me and Mr. Walsh were just having a little chat while you were in there getting reacquainted."

They continued backing up until Jasper got close enough to the door to place his hand on the scanner. The light flashed red, and the door remained sealed. He looked back at the man down the hall, who had a grin on his face.

"After I found that you had used my signature to get in here, I just made a quick call to take my clearance away. So that leaves all of us stuck here together. Don't worry, I asked the secretary to take her break, so we won't be disturbed." He opened his arms in a hospitable fashion to them, the weapon in his hand gleaming in the ceiling lights.

Jasper began frantically looking around for other opportunities. He saw Emmett mumbling, his eyes closed like they had been at the dam and several times since then.

"I recognize that, Mr. Walsh. That's something your father taught me when I was young." Stockton slowly stepped forward toward them. "Of course, all it did was lead me into the pit of hell. It didn't save the woman I loved, it didn't save the baby, and it didn't save me."

The scrawny man continued forward. Emmett stopped his whispering.

"I've never been shot by a wax bullet before, but I've heard it doesn't feel too good." Emmett said, nudging the two toward the other side of the door to the hall. Jasper saw something on Stockton's face. Not annoyance, but a deep flash of SATISFACTION. Something wasn't right. Stockton had a pattern of showing all his cards so plainly to you that you would miss the one under the table. He glanced at Emmett and realized the man knew something he didn't. In his hand, concealed in his sleeve, Jasper saw the remaining tranquilizer pen they had brought.

"Stay where you are, and we can begin your rehabilitation here. You won't even need to pack anything, will you! How convenient. If you give yourself up now, I may even give you a room adjoining your sister's," Stockton said in his childish voice.

Jasper planted his feet to launch himself at the man. But the director pointed the gun at his feet and shot, causing Jasper to freeze. He looked at the ground a foot in front of his feet to find a bullet hole in the hard flooring. His heart jumped. Bernard would be arrested and stripped of his position if he was caught with lead bullets in a weapon. Jasper realized that he didn't care about his position or status. He looked up at the man's face and found a RESENTMENT that raged deeper than any fear of consequence. He didn't want to arrest the Printed; he wanted only to cleanse their beliefs from the world.

"You have nowhere to go. Come and sit in the chairs, and we can talk this out," Stockton sneered.

Emmett, whose normal joking demeanor had left him, showed his hand to the man. He then turned, and placed it on the scanner.

"It's not going to work, we printed you a year ago."

Emmett kept his hand on the scanner.

The scanner turned green, and the door clicked open. Everyone stood in shock. The name at the top of the scanner read "Prince Emmett." Stockton was only fifteen feet away from them, and could read the name on the scanner.

"Impossible," he stammered and began to shake. Emmett looked in SADNESS at the man, confident in himself.

"No. It's not. You took my fingerprints away. But you can never erase the imprint of the One who made me."

Jasper, in amazed shock, opened the door further and pushed his sister out into the hall. Stockton, recovering from his shock, took a step in chase. Gun leveled. Jasper slipped through the door expecting the big man to join him. But he hesitated. Jasper looked through the door's window. Emmett looked at him, and closed the door. In his eyes was a clear expression of LOVE as he looked at his friend through that window.

The man turned, dart in hand, and stepped toward Stockton. He closed on him quickly. Stockton's face had regained its edge, and he pointed the weapon at the man and fired. Twice Jasper saw rounds impacting his friend, but they didn't stop his momentum. Emmett leaped and stuck the dart into the director's shoulder as the gun fired again, this time into the ground. Both men fell to the floor unmoving.

Jasper saw bright red blood spill from his friend's leg just above the knee and from his side.

Emmett turned around, his heart in his eyes. Jasper forced his hand on the scanner. Red. He did it again. Red. Tears filling his eyes he began to beat on the door, throwing his shoulder into it. After a moment he knew it was impossible. He looked at his friend who lay on his side. Emmett said nothing, he didn't need to. He looked at Jasper, allowing him to read his expression, and Jasper knew he needed to go. Breaking that gaze shattered Jasper's heart. He moved quickly from the door, taking his sister toward the room they had entered through.

When they were in sight of the door, a siren began sounding.

"Alert. Escaped convicts in section 120." Two guards burst into the hall behind them Recognizing the rehab clothes Ziva wore, they began to chase. Jasper and Ziva ran into the server room.

"Crawl down the vent," Jasper said. He pushed over two heavy server racks to block the door. As he was crawling down the vent, the two guards burst the door open and seeing the vent open, ran in pursuit.

Louis had been waiting for them when they dropped down. He asked where Emmett was, but after seeing Jasper's tear worn face in the light, he didn't push further. They began down the eastern tunnel, running as fast as they could in the little light they had. After a short while of running, they heard voices behind them.

"How many?" Louis said, easily keeping pace with the two youths.

"Two, I think. I don't think they waited to call for more," Jasper said as they continued down the concrete dome. This side was shorter, though not by much. They had kept a steady pace for almost twenty minutes, but every time they slowed to a walk, they were driven forward by racing feet behind them. They began to feel fresh air as they continued and soon ran down the concrete ramp into the free night air. Jasper led Ziva into the forest and gave the signal whistle. He heard the flute's response, and they continued farther into the forest. They slowed to a walking pace as they heard Cale's familiar flute playing.

Jasper found a group of bushes and crouched in them with his sister, waiting for the signal to come out. After several minutes he heard voices, then the arrival of the flute and Lake's voice mingled together. Jasper's heart still beat heavily, and his throat was still aching with emotion. The sound of Lake's voice dampened the pain, if only for a moment.

It was a quick moment, as it was interrupted by a shrill scream that pierced the sound of the music. He heard another sound of compressed air in the trees and soon recognized the signal sound that Emmett had introduced to them. They came out of their hiding place and walked back toward the tunnel.

"Jasper?" Lake asked.

"We're here!" They found two limp guards on the ground. Louis took a dart from the neck of one, but then hesitated with the other. Jasper looked accusingly at Cale, who had shown a rare expression of guilt on his young face.

The second guard was a young woman. While one dart had found its way into her shoulder, there was another embedded through the young woman's nose.

"She moved at the last second, didn't she?" Louis assumed. Cale nodded, ashamed. They cut the dart and pulled the barbed side out the other end of the young woman's nose.

"Where is Emmett?" Lake asked, coming down from her tree and embracing the young man. He trembled in her embrace, and when she looked at his face, she knew.

"No." Was the only thing that escaped her lips. He embraced her again and stepped aside by way of introduction.

"This is Ziva." The girl stepped forward. "Ziva, this is Lake."

Lake's eyes had welled, but she smiled at the girl, who returned her smile with an embrace of her own.

"We need to get to Sophia."

"Are you sure Emmett is...?" Jasper turned to answer Louis, but as he did, there came several flashes of light from above. Contrasted in the midnight sky, four missiles sped from a drone that flew directly over their heads above the mountain crags and exploded into the compound, filling the night sky with light enough to illuminate the snowy peak of the great mountain above.

They moved toward the south side of the forest and found Sophia sitting in her car waiting.

"What's going on?" she called as they hurried to the car.

"Can't talk! I'll explain later," Jasper said as he led Ziva to the trunk where he joined her.

"Where's Emmett?" she asked, but once again Jasper's face answered the question. Pain struck her face, but Sophia quickly controlled it and drove north.

"Who was that?" Lake asked.

"When we were in there, they had gotten threats from the FEC. That's why security inside was more lax than usual."

"Seems like they were more than just threats," Louis said, looking at the orange glow that sprang from the sky above.

They made it to the second vehicle, where they split the cars again to trek back to the Sanctuary.

Jasper drove the way back, as he had made the trip more than anyone else. Neither of them asked questions, but regardless of how it happened, the fact remained. They were returning without Emmett.

UPON SEEING Sophia come out of her garage, Jasper knew that the stoicism that she had shown had faded on the ride back. Her face was tear streaked, but her complexion hid the redness about the face from recent bouts of crying. The mood was heavy. Though many aspects of the plan went flawlessly, in essence it felt like a failure. Emmett hadn't returned.

Jasper, hoping to take potential feelings of guilt off of his newly reunited sister, held back his emotion as much as he could until he could be alone. They all wanted an explanation, something Jasper granted as they sat by the fire in the living room. Without thinking, Jasper left the seat Emmett often took vacant, and no one else chose that seat. If anyone thought it out of the ordinary, no one made note of it.

"He closed the door after I had left. I think he knew that if he got through then nothing would stop Stockton from tracking us. He had the dart ready." Jasper stopped, racking his tired mind for answers. "I tried to open the door...but my print didn't have clearance. I kept hitting it, but it wouldn't open." He said, struggling with the words. "He looked at me..."

"So he didn't die from the shots?" Sophia said, a soft hope touching her eyes.

"No. He looked at me...and told me to go." It wasn't true, at least not how they would interpret his words. Jasper was an expert at knowing what strangers said with their face, but with Emmett, his connection dismissed what little room for error there was.

After his explanation, they prayed and then broke for the night. Jasper remained in the fire-lit room, knowing sleep would be impossible to find. The silence of the night was such a contrast to the night's events that he felt unsettled by its peace.

Only a few hours passed until the soft color of morning began to illuminate the trees. Sophia came to the patio where Jasper sat in quiet melancholy. At first neither of them spoke. Jasper was rarely one to open conversation without invitation, and Sophia rarely engaged in small talk, wanting rather to skip to the important bits of conversation. Emmett had been the one to supplement both temperaments in ways they knew could never be replaced. Sophia beat Jasper after several moments to speak.

"Emmett loved mornings. I don't think I remember a sunrise that he didn't wake up for. There was something about it that made him get out of bed every day to see it." Jasper nodded his agreement.

"He told me it was because he didn't like things sneaking up on him. Even the sun." Sophia smiled at what she hoped was a joke.

Jasper paused. "If someone was to hear the story of how all this started, I think they would say that I saved Emmett by breaking him out of Pasco. It's not the truth, but that's what people would think."

"Are you saying that Emmett saved you instead?"

Jasper paused at the question. "No...I mean yes, but not directly. Emmett saved me, by showing me that someone else already had. He introduced me to the One who had saved me before I was born." He paused for a moment, taking in another breath. Hoping his words came out as clearly as his thoughts. "There were times where he prevented my life from being taken, but that wasn't what saved me. He saved me by being the greatest evidence of God that I ever found."

"So what now?" she asked.

"I guess we keep going. Live like the way he died. Living in the truth that we don't have to live in fear, regardless of what we face. Live like we are saved, nobles of heaven. Living in truth."

Sophia smiled at his answer. "Do you know what his name means?" she asked the young man.

"No?"

"It's Hebrew for truth."

Jasper smiled, his face casting away the sternness that dominated his features when deep in thought. As he did, the RV door opened, and Ziva came out and walked toward the pair.

"Looks like our new family member has a little bit of Emmett in her," Sophia said, rising from her seat. "And Jasper." He tipped his head up. "You want to honor what Emmett did for you? Continue the work he started."

TWENTY

MARRIAGE AS AN IDEA didn't scare him. Jasper had no problems with commitment, and the fact that he would be with Lake for as long as they lived produced no adverse effects. A wedding however, scared him out of his skull.

The weeks since the event of Ziva's rescue had been busy as the group prepared for different events—each requiring more grace than stealth. They had a funeral for Emmett, one with a tone of finality even though Jasper didn't see his last breath. The group felt with certainty that his injuries were severe enough that his escaping before the compound's destruction would be a hope better let go than held. The second event was the wedding between Jasper and Lake, a happy distraction from their grief at the loss of Emmett.

Since Jasper had decided to ask Lake to marry him, he had never imagined anyone else officiating the ceremony besides Emmett. Since he had grown up, marriage had become somewhat of an old-fashioned practice. Fewer than half of all adults got married, but as he did with many things, Emmett explained its utility to the point that Jasper became amazed at the culture shift his generation had arrived at. Their choices of a replacement officiant were slim, but in the end, there was only one answer.

Sophia agreed to officiate, as well as plan and mentor and do basically everything that could have been done at the time regarding the event. She threw herself at the tasks with enthusiasm, almost to the point of causing Jasper and Lake to worry.

There was one issue that Jasper had been concerned about. Cale.

The boy had gone through a significant transformation since their first meeting, though the primary encounter was no hard thing to improve on. The boy was naturally protective of his sister, and Jasper understood that. After the beaver dam event, Cale had developed a side to him that Jasper identified as different than before. He had to talk to him, to make sure that they were on the same page and he wouldn't find a boulder above his head because he had married his sister.

Jasper found the boy playing with Timber on the road beside the other animals. He had devoted much thought to coming up with ways Cale would respond, to prepare for any backlash he may encounter. As Jasper walked closer, the ball that the boy threw for the dog bounced toward him. Jasper stopped the ball before Timber could reach it and threw it in the other direction for Timber to chase, giving him an opportunity to chat with his future brother-in-law. He knew it was silly, but for a brief moment he kicked himself for sending away the only possible witness if Cale decided to use the moment to kill him. He shook it off and prepared his speech.

"Hey, Cale! Can we talk for a bit?"

The boy glanced at the dog, who had gotten lost finding the ball, then looked up at Jasper as he approached. He shrugged his assent.

"I know we haven't talked about this, Cale...but I want to make sure that before we go any further with the...um....wedding, that you're okay with this."

The boy looked almost bored by the speech, and Jasper wondered what Cale knew that he didn't. "I know you love your sister, and I'm sorry for not asking before I proposed, but I didn't really know that was something you were supposed to do." Cale's face remained flat.

This was one of the ways Jasper thought it may turn out, sadly his rehearsed plan for it fled from his mind, leaving him with a simple question.

"All right. I'm just going to say it like this. I love your sister, and—believe it or not—you too. I would be proud to be your brother, and I want to ask you if that is something you would consider being okay with." Jasper realized after his short speech that it was one of the weakest possible ways of asking for a blessing.

The boy didn't answer immediately. Instead, he reached one of his hands around Jasper's back. The boy put his hand underneath the loose shirt Jasper had on, placing his hand on each one of the scars Jasper had from the wooden spikes. The boy withdrew his hand, confident that his point was made, and Jasper heard something he never imagined the boy would say.

"You're already my brother. You almost died to save me." The boy did something even more uncharacteristic. He hugged Jasper, and the weight of weeks of stressing about this moment melted away in that brotherly embrace.

THE WEDDING WAS SIMPLE, as there was very little potential for intricate festivities when the attendance, other than the bride and groom, numbered five: the officiant, a girl, a boy, a man, and a dog. It was, however, a tasteful event. Jasper had been convinced by Lake and Sophia that the bride would wear a simple spring dress for the occasion, but his mind wasn't prepared for what he saw coming by the lakeside from the house.

Lake wore a perfectly tailored wedding dress of white with the slightest tint of green in its coloring. She looked tall in the dress, and she moved with impeccable grace toward her dumbstruck fiancé. Her long wavy dark hair had been done half up, and it moved about her shoulders as she walked.

By the time she arrived in front of Jasper, his heart beat like a drum. They linked their hands, and Sophia began the ceremony There was an ode to Emmett, at the expressed request of both Jasper and Lake, as everyone knew that it was by his courage that this was possible. As Sophia spoke, Jasper became lost in his bride's eyes. Women's faces had been a source of pain for him for years, but as he looked into her features, he saw a look that bolstered his resolve.

When it was time for the kiss, Lake had believed Jasper, not being one for public displays of affection, would try to brush it off. In the past she had been the one to have a semblance of enthusiasm for the topic and fully expected to have to do the same here. Jasper had a different idea. After getting the go ahead from Sophia, he promptly picked her up and kissed her with the confidence of a prince and the joy of a young man who found what he never thought was possible.

THE ARRANGEMENTS at the house changed only marginally after the wedding. Jasper and Lake were given the RV as a wedding present from Sophia, leaving her to finish work on repairing her old room in her house.

As life went on at the Sanctuary, nobody could have noticed that the world had been thrown into war if they didn't look at the media. The drone strike on Soteria was only one of hundreds in a mass undertaking by the Far East Coalition. The State retaliated, but sizable damage had been done. There were reports that surviving patients from the compound had escaped, but the State had little interest in hunting them down in comparison with what could be the Third World War.

The family of believers at the Sanctuary worked together to

develop spaces for refugees to stay. If the evacuees were willing, the body of believers would be ready. The Printed would always have a place to worship at Truth's Sanctuary.

CPSIA information can be obtained
at www.ICGtesting.com
Printed in the USA
BVHW070340060821
613737BV00006B/1025